WALLFLOWERS OF WEST LANE
BOOK FOUR

A.S. FENICHEL

CONTENTS

NOT EVEN FOR A DUKE

Finishing school brought four young wallflowers together. The perils of London's marriage market inspired a pact to protect each other for a lifetime...

Survivor of a hellish marriage, Aurora Sherbourn, Dowager Countess of Radcliff, is determined to never be taken in by love. With the other Wallflowers married and starting families, her West Lane residence is empty and lonely. What's missing is a child of her own, to raise and make her house a home. Intent on marrying only to have children, Aurora wants nothing to do with romantic attachments.

The newly minted Duke of Corwin, Garrett Winslow, has known Aurora all her life, and loved her nearly as long. Recently returned from his travels abroad, he was certain the infatuation was left in the past, but upon seeing the now-widowed Aurora, those feelings come rushing back.

Maddeningly, Aurora regards him as nothing more than her brother's best friend. Determined to make her his, Garrett will use every tender weapon to seduce her—and prove she's worthy of true love.

ACKNOWLEDGMENTS

As always, I must thank my sweet husband Dave for always believing in me, and being my personal hero as well as a hero to many. This is my twenty-fifth published book and he has stood by me through each and every one.

Special thanks to my dearest friend, Karla who has also spanned the long years with me and never wavered in her belief in me. It is rare to find a kindred spirit, and our friendship will survive everything, including living a country apart.

This book is dedicated to the women and men who survive and thrive after suffering abuse.

CHAPTER ONE

Helmsbury Manor country seat of the Earl of Marsden

$\mathcal{H}$elmsbury Manor was just as it had always been, and that offered no comfort. Aurora had avoided the home of her birth even after her brother Rhys had become earl and married one of her best friends, Poppy. Of course, she'd returned for her father's funeral, but not since.

The death of their neighbor, the Duke of Corwin, had brought her back home. The duke had always been kind, and

Aurora appreciated kindness above all things as it was something her own parents tended to neglect. Garrett, the new duke, was a close friend of both Rhys' and her. They had played together as children. It had been more the boys running off and trying to avoid the nagging little sister, but she held many lovely memories of Garrett.

She picked up the figurine of a milkmaid from the parlor table and ran her thumb across the tiny crack at the base. When she was a girl, she'd knocked it to the floor while chasing a kitten. In fact, it had been in the same spot all those years ago. She took another look around the familiar room. Every chair and table were in precisely the same spot they had been when Mother ran the house.

She looked at her closest friend and asked, "Why have you changed nothing, Poppy?"

Poppy flopped on the deep pine green sofa. It was not the most ladylike pose, but only Rhys and Aurora were present, and they were more than family. They were the Wallflowers of West Lane. Of course, Rhys was only an honorary member, but Aurora and Poppy along with Mercy and Faith were committed to a lifelong friendship. They never stood on ceremony.

Despite the rather easy afternoon they'd had riding in the carriage, bits of Poppy's dark hair had escaped her chignon. Her blue eyes flashed, she kicked off her slippers and curled her feet under her. "Altering Helmsbury Manor to suit our tastes is not worth the fight with your mother."

"Poppy, I thought you had more grit than that. You mustn't let Mother boss you. You are the Countess of Marsden, and this is your home." Aurora sat opposite Poppy in a stiff-backed chair with a drab brown cushion.

Rhys shook his head and sat next to his wife. "I have told

her the same thing, but after the incident with the flowers on the foyer table, I rather see Poppy's point."

"What happened?" Aurora sat forward.

Poppy let out another despondent breath. "I had picked some lovely wildflowers one morning while walking the lane. They really were charming. I had them placed in a vase on the table in the foyer. The dowager paid a call that very afternoon for tea. You'd have thought I'd taken an ax to the banisters the way she carried on about my base tastes and the way I'm ruining the whole of Helmsbury Manor."

"Gracious." Aurora hid her amusement behind her hand.

"Go ahead and laugh." Poppy smiled. "Rhys and I had a good guffaw after she'd gone."

Despite her giggle, Aurora sympathized. She had dealt with her mother's antics since birth revealed her female and duty bound to marry any rich sod with a title who came along. As it turned out, her father had married her off to a complete monster. Though, now that he was dead, she supposed she should be more kind in her thoughts of the late Earl of Radcliff. "Mother will just have to live with the fact that the new Countess of Marsden likes wildflowers better than hothouse or cultivated. And you should stand up to her, remind her that this is your home, not hers. She has two dower houses and should be pleased as punch with that. Not many dowagers can boast a home in London and one in the country. You have been more than generous with her."

Rhys shrugged. "She's impossible, but she's still our mother." He drew a long breath. "And at the heart of her, she means well for us. Though, sometimes its damned hard to tell."

They all laughed as the parlor door opened.

Wimple, the butler, stood at attention. "The Duke of Corwin to see you."

A quiver of butterflies, which she couldn't account for, started in Aurora's stomach and heat flushed her cheeks. She'd seen Garrett hundreds of times. There were very few men in the world whom she trusted completely, and Garrett was one.

They all stood.

Rhys crossed the room and shook Garrett's hand. "Good lord, man, we'd not expected you this evening. We thought we'd not see you until the funeral tomorrow. Is there something you need?"

"F-forgive me. I'm intruding." Usually so assured, Garrett's sad eyes and stutter was out of character.

Poppy joined them. "Never, Your Grace. Come and sit with us. We were just having a laugh at my mother-in-law's expense."

He bowed over Poppy's hand before turning to Aurora. "Hello, Rora. You look well." Garrett took the seat beside her and smiled.

"I'm pleased to see you, Your Grace. I hope you will accept my condolences on the loss of your dear father. I'm sure you know I was quite fond of him." Tightness gripped Aurora's throat. Hearing of Garrett's father's death had hit her harder than the death of her own five years earlier. The Duke of Corwin had been a brilliant and kind man with friends far and wide. He'd offered her cheer whenever she'd run from home to get away from her own less than loving, parents.

"I do know and thank you. He was very fond of you and Rhys as well. May I ask a favor?" Garrett shifted his gaze from her to Poppy.

"Of course, anything." Aurora couldn't imagine a thing she wouldn't do for Garrett Winslow.

"Do not call me your grace. At least in private, it would be nice to know my title is not important."

Joy pulled at Aurora's lips. "As you wish, Garrett."

Poppy said, "One never knows how one's friends will wish to be addressed after they have elevated. I'm happy to know a grand title will not change you."

"What brings you out this evening?" Rhys smoothed his blond hair and brushed a wayward strand from his eye. "I'd have thought you would be mired in all sorts of business for weeks to come."

The sorrow bled back into Garrett's usually mirthful eyes. His shoulders slumped. "The house is filled to capacity with friends and family come to pay their respects. It's been a steady stream for three days. I could take no more and thought to just go for a ride to clear my head. The solicitor and estate manager have things in hand. Father left everything in good order and the entailments are quite clear. I rode to the ridge with full intentions of returning home, but once I saw Helmsbury, I thought a bit of true friendship couldn't hurt."

"I'm glad you came," Poppy said. "We took the carriage over to pay our own respects yesterday, but there were people and vehicles on the lane clear out to the road. We thought we'd wait and see you at the funeral and then have a visit when things had settled a bit."

Garrett nodded. "As I said, it's been a bit mad with sympathizers. My father had a lot of friends."

"He was beloved." Aurora's chest ached when she thought of all Garrett had lost.

Rhys stood. "I'll get some brandy and we'll toast the Duke of Corwin both past and present. Ladies, will you join us?"

A wide grin brightened Poppy's face and lit up the entire room. "Of course."

"I'm not much of a brandy drinker, but I shall make a new habit of it tonight." Aurora reached out and took Garrett's hand. A warm shock ran up her arm and settled in her chest.

He gave her hand a squeeze, smiled and released her. "I'm honored. Thank you."

"You never need to thank us for our friendship, Garrett. You shall have it no matter what." Aurora tamped down the effects of a simple touch of his hand to hers. She was being an imbecile. This was Garrett, and she was no green girl out for her first season.

Wimple, who had remained, presumably in case the duke's stay was cut short or they required refreshment sprang into action. His black livery and white waistcoat gleamed. His dark hair was slicked back and thinning, but even with his portly shape there was an elegance about the butler who had known Aurora and Rhys since they were children. Once he'd poured four snifters, he brought them over on a silver tray, serving the ladies first.

"Thank you, Wimple." Aurora smiled with the memory of all the sweets the butler had sneaked to her throughout her childhood.

"My lady," was his dour reply.

Rhys lifted his glass. "To the Duke of Corwin. Never have I known a finer man and his son shall do well to follow in his footsteps."

They all lifted their glasses land said, "The Duke of Corwin."

Garrett put his glass aside and leaned toward her. "You

were very kind to have come all the way from London, Rora. I wasn't expecting you. But perhaps you're here on some other business. I'm being presumptive." He shook his head as if dispelling the silly notion.

"I came for your father's funeral, of course. We have been friends all our lives, Garrett. I wouldn't want to be absent when you might have need of my support." There was that tightness again. For the life of her, she couldn't imagine why she roiled with so much untamed emotion.

Those admirable eyes, a lighter brown than one would expect locked with hers a long moment. "I'm very grateful."

Aurora drew a long breath and suppressed any sign of sentiment. "It is the least we can do. We have been friends and neighbors for many years. You would do, and have done the same for us."

"I would do anything for you." He paused and cleared his throat. "And of course, for Rhys. He and I have been friends since birth."

Rhys and Poppy drifted away from them and slid into the love seat where they whispered to each other.

"Before my father died, I had plans to come and pay you a call in London to see how you get on, but I never managed to make my way there and now this week has been busy." He rubbed the back of his neck and kept his gaze on the floor.

"You never need an appointment, Garrett. I will tell you, I am well. I miss having the other Wallflowers living at the West Lane house, but I have some plans to fill my time in the coming months." She'd not told anyone of her plans and had no idea why she hinted at it now. Maybe she wanted to distract her friend from his own problems.

His head snapped up and his eyes lit with interest. "What are you plotting, Rora?"

Of course, he was going to think her a complete fool, but at least he would not be sad for a few moments. She took a deep breath. "You know, Rhys gave me the land and house in Cheshire, which was part of my marriage contract?"

"I had heard as much." Garrett cocked his head, and the candlelight caught the red streaks in his hair. It had been curly when he was a boy, but now he combed the wavy locks into submission. "Do you plan to retire to the country?"

"No. Well not exactly. Though, I expect I shall have to spend a good amount of time at Whickette Park over the coming months." Excitement bubbled inside Aurora. She was very schooled at keeping her outward appearance calm regardless of what happened within.

Interest mixed with amusement in Garrett's eyes. "You have me intrigued. What are you up to?"

"Mercy suggested the enormous house might make a fine school. At first, I thought it a strange idea, but the more I considered it, and our own schooling, the more the idea appeals to me. If I could create a school for young ladies to learn the same things as men do if they wish. If they could also have the opportunity to pursue their passions for art or music or figures and literature, that would be something worth doing." Realizing her excitement had begun to show, she folded her hands in her lap and waited to be laughed at.

Garrett's smile had faded, but she saw no censure in his look, only thoughtfulness. "It is a bold plan, Rora, but if you go about it the right way, I think it could be interesting."

"Interesting? It's brilliant!" Poppy shouted as she jumped from the sofa she shared with Rhys.

"Do you really think so?" Aurora looked from one to the other.

Rhys sat forward staring intently. "Who would run the school?"

Aurora had let the cat out of the bag, and there was no getting her back in, so she swallowed her fear. "I would have to hire a suitable headmistress for the day to day, but I would handle the business and perhaps enrollment."

Eyes wide, Poppy cringed. "Mrs. Agatha Wormbattle comes to Cheshire." She made reference to the headmistress from the Swiss school they had been sent away to as punishment for bad behavior.

Aurora laughed. "I'd like to find someone a bit kinder but just as disciplined, if such a woman exists. I don't want the girls to be terrified of school the way we were when we arrived."

"I was more afraid of my parents than school. However, I see your point. The only good thing about the Wormbattle School for Young Ladies was meeting you, Mercy, and Faith. The rest was a waste of time." Poppy began pacing the room. "I want to help you, Aurora. I'm sure that Mercy and Faith will want too as well."

Knowing her friends were on her side eased the fear that had been building inside Aurora since she began nurturing her mad idea. "I will take all the help I can get. Since Whickette Park is connected with Wesley's family, I will discuss my entire plan with him when I return to London."

Poppy sank back into the love seat. "I can't imagine Wesley will object, but of course, you're right to give him ample notice. I don't know how you will find a proper headmistress. It's a big job and you'll need someone brilliant to do it right."

"I think I can help." Garrett announced.

Aurora had been so caught up in Poppy's reaction, she'd almost forgotten they were not alone. "How so?"

"I know a woman..."

Rhys laughed too loud. "Many a terrible tale have started with those four words. What on earth can this have to do with anything? I'm sure with all the nonsensical travel you've done, you met a myriad of women, but how does that help?"

Standing, Garrett shook his head. "You have very low ideas of what I did during my years of travel, old friend. The lady I'm thinking of is extremely proper and well educated. I don't know her current situation, but if you wish, Rora, I will write to her."

"What is her name?" Why it should matter, Aurora didn't know, but she asked anyway.

"Mrs. Helen Hazlett-Barrow."

Poppy's eyes narrowed. "How did she come by her education?"

"Rumor has it, she impersonated a man and gained entrance to Oxford. Of course, she had to have lied about a great many things to accomplish this, so if you feel her tactics disqualify her from your school, I shall refrain from contacting her." Garrett ran his hand over his neck in the way he did when he was deep in thought.

"That's Brilliant!" Poppy laughed and clapped her hands.

Aurora had to agree. "I think I would like to meet Mrs. Hazlett-Barrow."

Garrett's smile sent a bolt of something strange and unfamiliar to the center of Aurora. "I will write to her at my first opportunity." He sighed low and long. "I suppose, I must go home."

Poppy went to him. "You are welcome to stay the night

here, Garrett. We shall have a room made up, and you can ride home early in the morning."

"As tempting as that sounds, dear Poppy, I cannot run away from my problems or hide from them. Besides, I'll hardly be finding rest tonight."

His pain settled in Aurora's chest as she rose. "I'll walk you out."

Once he'd said his goodbyes to Poppy and Rhys, Aurora slid her arm through his elbow, and they walked to the foyer.

"I'm very happy to see you, Rora." His voice barely above a whisper, she wondered if she'd misheard him.

"That is kind. I'm very sorry for your loss, Garrett. I hope you will rely on our friendship should you need a shoulder to lean on." They stopped at the front door. The foyer was empty. She'd never know what came over her at that moment. Turning toward him, she wrapped her arms around his waist and pressed her cheek to his chest.

The world seemed to stop for a long beat, and then Garrett's fierce hug enveloped her. His lips pressed to the crown of her head. "Oh, Rora," he breathed.

From the shadows, Wimple cleared his throat. "Forgive me, my lady."

She dropped her hands and they stepped away from each other. Looking up into Garrett's eyes she saw frustration or passion, but which she couldn't guess. Their friendship or his lost father, perhaps. Whatever it was, she didn't have the nerve to ask. "Forgive me. I don't know what came over me."

The corner of his mouth turned up and hinted at a smile. "Whatever it was, I thank you."

Heat flushed up Aurora's neck and face, and she thought her ears might burst into flames.

Garrett leaned in and whispered, "If Wimple was not

standing in the shadows, I would have been quite unable to stop myself from kissing you, Rora. I don't think I've ever seen you blush before."

Stepping back, she lightly slapped his chest. "Don't be ridiculous."

A quick frown tugged at his full lips before he schooled his features and bowed. "I shall see you tomorrow then."

"Yes, of course."

Wimple strode into the foyer with Garrett's hat and overcoat. He opened the door. The cool spring breeze gave Aurora gooseflesh. Even so, she stayed by the door until Garrett climbed into the saddle and Wimple closed the door.

CHAPTER TWO

A week had passed since his father's funeral. In London it was already common knowledge that he was now the Duke of Corwin. People stopped him on the street to congratulate him on his new title. Garrett thought the practice rather graceless. After all, his father had died. It was not as if the king had bestowed a new title on his family. He had become the sixth Duke of Corwin because his very good father had dropped dead on the parlor floor.

He longed to say as much to Lord Darble when he'd given him a hearty punch in the arm for his good fortune, but he just nodded and thanked the imbecile. It was hardly worth the scandal to try to educate someone that ridiculous.

In the future, he would travel in his carriage with the blinds drawn and avoid speaking to the thoughtless masses. Still, he refused to be sullen since he was going to West Lane and would see Aurora. His foolish heart would not let go of the notion that she was perfection. Even when it was obvious the lady had no interest in him. Yet the impulsive hug she'd given him and her blush told a slightly different story. It was wishful thinking on his part, but he couldn't help himself.

Her unexpected marriage to Radcliff had sent Garrett to the Continent for more than three years of wandering. He refused to watch her squired around town by a man not worthy of her.

Ignoring the wave and smile from Sir John Metcalf, he pretended he'd not seen the portly gentleman. He had only two blocks to go, and refusing to be further delayed, he turned down West Lane, away from the crowds.

She had hugged him.

The memory had gotten him through a terrible week. Of her own volition, Aurora had thrown her arms around him and pressed her soft cheek to his chest. Like a boy in short pants, he'd been too stunned to react at first. Then he'd have given every penny he owned to have the moment again without Wimple's interruption. He'd never been so perfectly content than when they'd shared that embrace, even if it was just for a moment.

At Aurora's townhouse, he tied off his horse and took the steps two at a time.

The butler, Tipton, opened the door before he reached the top. "Your Grace, my lady told me to expect you."

"Hello, Tipton. I gather you are well?" Garrett handed the fiercely protective butler his hat and gloves.

"Tolerably well, Your Grace. They are waiting for you in the ladies' parlor. If you will follow me?" Without waiting for an answer, Tipton walked to the short hall leading to the informal parlor that the Wallflowers of West Lane preferred for their private sanctuary.

The house was far different from the first time Garrett had visited. It was less formal. Light streamed into the foyer from the great parlor, and it shone with new furniture and softer draperies.

Aurora had made the place her own after her husband's notorious murder at a gaming hell. The man was a fool, but he had been an earl, and his death had made the papers in Italy, where Garrett had been enjoying the sunshine for several months. The news had set him in motion to return to England.

At the door to the ladies' parlor, Tipton announced, "The Duke of Corwin."

Garrett was aware that several people stood as he entered, but his gaze locked on Aurora. She was in a blue day dress with white lace around the collar and sleeves.

Her smile was bright, and her eyes clear as she curtsied. "Garrett, you're here at last."

He bowed before crossing the room and taking her hands. "Have you been waiting on me?"

"We are all desperate to know more about Mrs. Hazlett-Barrow." Mercedes Heath, the Countess of Castlewick said from his right. Mercy was the last of the Wallflowers to marry. Her rise to countess had been the talk of the ton only last season.

Looking about, he found himself surrounded by

Wallflowers and their spouses. Wesley Renshaw, the Earl of Castlewick smiled warmly at his wife.

The Duke and Duchess of Breckenridge watched the proceedings. Faith and Nick had married after some very strange circumstances, but Garrett hadn't yet heard all of those details. He'd visited Aurora once when she was at school in Lucerne. Her three friends had quickly adopted him as a brother and he was glad of it.

Poppy and Rhys rounded out the group. Garrett's heart yearned to belong among them in a more permanent way, but his mind flashed back to the way Aurora had dismissed their intimate moment as quickly as she had hugged him. She thought of him like she thought of her brother, and dash it, he would have to live with that.

"I can invite her to meet you all whenever it is convenient. I assumed that was the reason I have been summoned."

Faith stepped forward. "We thought you might need some company, Your Grace. I'm dreadfully sorry to hear about your father."

No congratulations. Relief flooded him. "That is very kind of you."

He said his felicitations to each of them before waiting for the ladies to sit. He was oddly out of place and comfortable at the same time. "When would you like to meet Helen Hazlett-Barrow? Shall I invite her round for an interview?"

Aurora pulled a face of distaste. "That sounds dreadful. I hardly think one can get to know a person with an hour chat where they are required to behave perfectly."

"Tea then?" Mercy suggested.

Tapping her finger on her lush lips, Aurora cocked her

head. "That would be better, but still might seem daunting. Why don't I host a dinner party? We would all be there, and I shall invite Mr. Arafa to make the numbers even. Would that not be more comfortable for everyone?"

Rhys shook his head. "You are hoping to hire this woman, Rora. I hardly think you need to entertain a person who might be in your employ."

"I like the idea." Wesley's voice was serious. I think a headmistress should have a higher place in our estimation. If you want to put my name on this school, Aurora, I would wish it to be something special and not a run of the mill establishment."

No doubt his wife agreed. She looked at him so besotted that Garrett felt a bit embarrassed to bear witness.

"I think you will find Mrs. Hazlett-Barrow up to any task, including dinner with the ton. What day did you have in mind?" Garrett would carry a note around the world for Aurora. An invitation to an old friend was a simple task.

Aurora's eyes were round as saucers. "You're a duke, Garrett. I hardly expect you to deliver my mail."

"She will have little notion of why a stranger would invite her if I don't intervene. It's nothing, Rora. I'm happy to make the introductions."

Something unpleasant flashed in Aurora's clear blue eyes. It left just as quickly. "You are too kind. Do you think Friday will be too soon?"

He shrugged. "I'll have to ask the lady."

"Are you available?" She stared at him and waited.

Did she mean the question for the entire room? No one else answered. Garrett had no notion of what was on his agenda, but he knew he would cancel an audience with the king to spend an evening with Aurora. "I will see that I am free."

The silence continued.

Poppy stood and pulled the cord for the butler. "We are also free, Aurora. In case you plan to invite us."

The slightest blushed filled her cheeks. She rolled her eyes to cover it. "Of course I know you're free, Poppy."

Tipton entered. "My lady?"

"Can you ask Cook to please make some tea, Tipton? I'm famished. And if she would include a few of those lovely biscuits?" Poppy made it sound as if she were desperate.

If he noticed, Tipton gave no indication. He made a smart bow. "I shall see to it, my lady."

Once Tipton closed the door, Mercy said, "Poppy, you don't live here anymore. You should allow Aurora to call for tea."

A sweet, bell-like laugh tinkled from Aurora. "I don't mind if any of you wish to play lady of this house. I'm just happy to have you here every Tuesday."

Rhys said, "I'd have thought you would have had enough of us after a week with Poppy and me in the country."

"Not yet," Aurora said with narrowed eyes, as if it were a warning.

The banter continued, and Garrett was more than pleased to be part of it all. Once the tea arrived, Nicholas Ellsworth, Duke of Breckenridge pulled Aurora to the side.

Garrett knew it was ungentlemanly, but he strained to hear.

"You seem much better, Aurora." Nicholas said.

"I am feeling more myself. You have been a great help to me." It was hardly above a whisper, but Aurora sounded genuinely grateful to the duke for some service he'd rendered her.

Nicholas nodded. "You have done me just as great a turn, Aurora. I don't think I could have recovered so well this last year without you."

The urge to run over and demand to know what they could be speaking of was so great that Garrett had to close his eyes until it passed. Whatever it was, it was none of his business. He had no right to jealousy. Besides, Faith was only across the room, and she didn't seem the least bit bothered by her husband and close friend stealing away for a private chat.

To keep himself from total embarrassment and never being invited back to West Lane, Garrett rose and joined Rhys, Wesley, Poppy and Mercy where they sat talking of subjects they might like to see taught at the Castlewick School for Young Ladies.

Whickette Park, the site of this planned school, was the ancestral home of the Earl of Castlewick. It had been lost to him through an arrangement between his grandfather and the king to keep out of debtors' prison. Garrett was surprised Wesley, the current Earl, was so keen on this project.

Mercy said, "I wonder what we shall do when we need other talented instructors."

"What do you mean?" Wesley asked.

"What if a student comes in with a passion for art or music rather than figures or literature?"

Wesley rubbed his chin. "I'm not planning on moving our household to Cheshire so you can teach pianoforte. Besides, you have your own school here in London to keep you very busy."

"I wouldn't mind going to Cheshire to help, but I prefer town." Mercy grinned at her husband. "Well, I suppose we shall figure this all out as our students' needs arise."

Garrett picked up on the word our. "Are you joining Aurora in the running of this new school?"

Wesley drew back his shoulders. "We have decided to not only add funding to the new school, but also lend the Castlewick name to give it more credence. We shall attract fine students."

"From all walks of life," Mercy added.

Taking his wife's hand, Wesley kissed her knuckles. "Of course."

"I am intrigued," Garrett admitted. "I think this shall be quite an interesting project."

Aurora would have quite a job ahead of her if this school was to be all she hoped. He was even more confident that Helen would be perfect for the job.

The days between tea on Tuesday and dinner on Friday seemed to drag on for months. Garrett could have called to see Aurora, but he could think of no reason to give for an impromptu visit. At least none that would prevent him from looking like a fool.

Of course, he was a fool and always had been when it came to his best friend's sister. As hard as he'd tried to forget her, and as far as he'd run from England, her clear blue eyes, measured smile and wicked, often-hidden sense of humor had followed him.

He'd barely recognized that his carriage had pulled to a stop until Reggie, his driver, opened the door. "We've arrived, Your Grace. Several other carriages are arriving at the same time. Do you wish to wait here until they have pulled away?"

Shaking himself out of his musings, Garrett looked into the street. Mrs. Helen Hazlett-Barrow was stepping from the carriage ahead of his. "This is fine, Reggie."

Exiting, he put his hat on and then went to greet his friend. "Hello, Helen. I'm glad you decided to attend."

She curtsied, her bright green eyes alight with mischief. "How could I resist being summoned to a dowager's house under such a veil of mystery? And having the invitation delivered by a duke was too delicious to decline."

"You have not changed one bit, Helen." He offered her his arm.

"Would you have me different, Garrett? I am what I am, and that rarely fits into any kind of society." She was only a few inches shorter than him, and while shapely, she cut a strong figure. Still, he had a hard time imagining how anyone could have mistaken her for a man when she'd lied her way into Oxford. He said as much.

She shrugged. "People see what they want to see. I created Helmet Barrow, and no one questioned him. My grades were better than all my mates, and you men could never believe a woman was smarter than you. It was easy."

"I can't imagine that is true. You would have had little privacy for..." He was at a loss for what to say. "For whatever it is women do when they need privacy."

Helen's laugh was full and round, lacking any of the normal guile of a debutante. "I managed."

Halfway up the steps, the door to the West Lane house opened, and Tipton stood sentinel. "Your Grace, welcome."

"This is Mrs. Hazlett-Barrow, Tipton. We are both expected for dinner."

For the briefest moment, Tipton's eyes widened, but then his normal state of dour returned, and Garrett thought he might have imagined the surprise. Helen was formidable even in an evening gown, and despite her decisions to follow a different path than most women, she was extremely pretty. "Please come in. The rest of the guests are gathered in the great parlor."

Once they were announced, Garrett escorted Helen into the formal and grand room. Aurora had managed to make the room far more welcoming with lighter rugs and curtains. If he wasn't mistaken, she had replaced some rather grim wallpaper with a pale cream damask.

Aurora rushed over, her light green gown hugging her curves and cut low enough to reveal the swell of her breasts. Garrett's mouth watered.

"Your Grace, I'm so pleased you have arrived." She made a quick curtsy before turning her attention to Helen. "You must be Mrs. Hazlett-Barrow. Welcome. I'm so happy you could join us."

Helen curtsied and accepted Aurora's hand. "I have to admit I was more than a little surprised to receive your invitation, Countess."

"Were you? Has Garrett not informed you of the plot behind my desire to meet you?" Her eyes widened, but her smile remained.

"I thought it better to leave that task to you, Rora."

"Indeed." She gave him a reproving look. "Do you prefer to be addressed as Mrs. Hazlett-Barrow? I would be honored if you would call me Aurora. We are all quite informal in this group." She waved her hand toward the Wallflowers and their spouses milling around the parlor, sipping wine and chatting in intimate groups.

"Thank you, my lady. Helen will do nicely, if you like." Helen's smile remained steady, but her shoulders relaxed. She stood a head taller than Aurora, but neither woman seemed to feel intimidated. Not Helen by the titles in the room, nor Aurora by Helen's stature or past.

"Let me introduce you to my friends, Helen."

"Perhaps you might tell me why I'm here first, Aurora." Head cocked, Helen asked directly.

"Of course, you're right. I don't want you to think we have some dark secret. You see His Grace tells me you are quite brilliant and also strong minded."

"Does he?" Helen's cheeks pinkened ever so slightly. "How flattering."

Garrett might have blushed himself with the two women staring at him. "I told her only the truth, Helen. Please go on, Rora, before I'm felled under such scrutiny."

They both had the grace to giggle at him. He'd rarely heard either one giggle, and it was quite beguiling.

Aurora shook her head. "As amusing as it is to see Garrett squirm, I won't torture either of you any longer. I'm planning to open a school in Cheshire and hoped you might be a good fit for the headmistress. I wanted to get to know you in some situation that was not an interview to determine if we might suit as benefactor and headmistress of a school for girls. I have certain ideas about how I would want things done."

As she spoke, she clasped her hands under her chin and her eye lit with each word.

The way her passion poured from her description of the school made Garrett wish he were at liberty to bring other kinds of passions out of her.

Helen blinked several times. "As flattering as this is, my lady, I doubt I am the person for the position. I don't believe a girls' finishing school is where I would excel."

With a clap, Aurora grinned then whispered, "That's just it, Helen, I want a real school for girls. I want them to learn philosophy, literature, economics, geography, Latin, and every other subject that might fill an inquisitive mind. Of course, if they have some great talent for art or music, we would wish that encouraged as well."

Again, Helen seemed not sure how to continue, and she stood blinking. "I know of no such schools for girls to rival Eton."

Rather than spew more ideas at poor rattled Helen, Aurora offered her arm. "Let me introduce you to my friends. There is plenty of time to talk of the school as the evening progresses."

Dutifully, Garrett followed behind as Aurora made the introductions. He slipped away for a glass of wine when they reached Rhys. "It seems to be going well enough."

Rhys shrugged. "It's so hard to tell with ladies. They are trained from birth to hide their true feelings."

Aurora, Poppy, Mercy, and Faith had gathered around Helen and laughed at something Helen said. "You don't think they are genuine?"

"I think it is in their nature to make your friend feel welcome, and they are brilliant enough in their own rights to recognize her assets. I don't know if that means they will like her or not." Rhys drained his glass and took another from the tray Tipton carried while leaving the empty for the butler to take away. "Thank you, Tipton."

"Should I be worried for Mrs. Hazlett-Barrow?" Garrett asked, watching the ladies' banter with greater interest.

Rhys slapped him on the back. "She's safe enough, and dinner will be served before they do any real damage."

"You are not assuaging my concerns." Though, Helen looked happy enough and was likely in no imminent danger.

"She's lovely. I hadn't expected that. You described a woman who fooled all of Oxford. I expected a less feminine adversary for those great minds." Rhys leaned back, watching the ladies.

Garrett didn't bother to hide his laughter. "You, of all people, should know that a beautiful woman can be formidable. Helen could outwit any one of us if that were her game."

Rhys leaned against the mantel. The fireplace was dark, as the evening was comfortably warm for April. "You make an excellent point. My wife outwits me daily." Grinning, he turned away from the others and looked at Garrett. "I supposed your title will keep you in England more."

"For the time being have no plans to travel." Garrett kept Aurora in his sight. Would she remarry? The idea of standing around while another man escorted her about soured his stomach.

Nick joined them. He was grinning and sat on the sofa facing the door. "Will you be taking your seat at the House of Lords then?"

Wesley had joined the ladies and stood very close to Mercy. Probably too close for being in company. Garrett felt a pang of jealousy for what these couples had found. He pushed down the feelings. "Not just yet. I have so much to familiarize myself with to run the estates, I'll be busy with that for some time."

"You could sell one or two if it's too much. They can't all be entailed, and it's absurd to think the acquiring of land as important as our fathers did." Nick put down his wine and leaned back.

Garrett gave the door a glance as Nick seemed to be studying the entry. "I may sell off some of the less profitable bits if I can get a decent price. It will depend on the tenants, of course."

"It's a pity you haven't any siblings you can give some land to. Look at how nicely that Cheshire property has worked out. Wesley's grandfather lost the place to some ancestor of Rora's deceased husband, Radcliff gave it to my father in exchange for Rora, and Wesley wanted it back and wound up falling in love with Mercy, and now Rora and Wesley will turn it into a school for girls and it will bear Wesley's name. It's a crazy world." Rhys raised his glass as if in toast.

"It is that," Garrett agreed.

The door opened, and Tipton barely had time to announce, "Mr. Arafa."

"I am so sorry to be late." Geb smiled brightly and rounded the butler. His dark eyes sparkled with glee as Aurora rushed over to greet him.

"I was beginning to worry for you, Mr. Arafa." She made a pretty curtsy.

Garrett had met Geb a time or two. He was a close friend of Nick's and often attended parties with his circle of friends. Of Egyptian background, he was a collector of artifacts. Garrett suspected he and Nick had been spies, but it was none of his business.

Garrett had heard his name mentioned in such circles long before he'd met the man in person. During his travels, he'd chanced to dine with an English diplomat on an assignment in Spain for Francis Drake. He'd said he had a package delivered from Mr. Arafa that would entice his Spanish counterpart to give him the information he needed to return to England. When Garrett had questioned the man about who Mr. Arafa was, he'd become silent and soon changed the subject.

Garrett bowed. "Mr. Arafa, it is nice to see you again."

"The pleasure is mine, Your Grace. I was very sorry to hear of the loss of your father. It is a difficult thing to lose a parent," Geb said regretfully.

"Thank you. It is nice to be among people who understand that gaining a title means losing something far more dear." Garrett had no idea why he'd said such a thing to a man who was little more than a stranger. Perhaps it was the sincerity in his condolences, or maybe spies know how to get people to speak the truth.

Geb nodded. "I have always found it an odd habit of the English to celebrate a man's rising to a title. But I suppose not every man has deep affection for his father."

"I suppose that's true. Mine was a good man. He didn't approve of my wanderlust, but he was always on my side of an argument." Garrett's chest tightened as he thought of his father.

"It is good then that you have a family of sorts here with the Wallflowers. Though, I suppose, they can hardly be called that now." Geb laughed, and they looked at the ladies who were in deep conversation with Helen.

"I'm not family here," Garrett corrected.

"No?" Geb studied him. "I think you are mistaken, Your Grace, but I will leave it for you to work out. Who is the tall lady with rosy curls?"

Garrett followed Geb's gaze to Helen, whose red hair did take on a rosy color in the candlelight.

"That is Mrs. Helen Hazlett-Barrow. Shall I introduce you?"

Geb searched the room. "Is her husband not with her?"

"She is not married, sir."

"I see."

Garrett didn't know how Geb could see, since he had no idea how Helen had obtained the missus before her name. Still, Garrett liked that Geb always seemed open minded to the quirks and habits of others.

"An introduction before we sit for dinner would be helpful," Geb's attention remained on Helen.

CHAPTER THREE

Aurora didn't know what to make of Helen Hazlett-Barrow. She was smart and witty to be sure, but more than that was hard to assess. For some reason, she hadn't expected the lady to be so lovely. Tall enough to be a man, perhaps, but Helen had beautiful red hair, fine skin, and a narrow jaw. She had sharp blue-green eyes and long lashes. Her nose was straight and proportionate. How had anyone at Oxford thought this was a man?

It was her duty to enter the dining room first and Garrett escorted her, but had he wanted to take Mrs. Hazlett-

Barrow's arm instead? A knot formed low in Aurora's stomach. She pushed aside all negativity. If her dear friend was in love with Helen Hazlett-Barrow, Aurora would do all in her power to help them through the opposition they would face. For surely a woman of no title and a duke was not the best match on paper. Still, all would be well if they truly loved each other.

As soon as the first course of white soup was before them, Poppy said, "Mrs. Hazlett-Barrow, I don't wish to be rude."

Rhys covered a laugh, as did Mercy.

Poppy gave them both a scathing look before returning her attention to their newest acquaintance. "I was wondering how you came to be called Mrs and why you maintain two surnames?"

"Poppy, that is none of your business." Faith reprimanded, but looked over at Helen with equal parts curiosity and apology.

Helen took a sip of the soup, then put her spoon down. She looked across the table and locked gazes with Poppy. "It is quite uncommon for people to be so direct. Are you always thus?"

It was impossible to know where this would go and Aurora feared her dinner party designed to evaluate Helen's character was about to come crashing to an end.

With a long sigh, Poppy nodded. "I'm afraid so. We are none of us four very good at dissembling, and I am the worst of the group. I assure you, I don't mean to be rude, and my question derives from an honest curiosity and nothing malicious."

Helen smiled making her even lovelier than before. "What an odd assortment of dukes, duchesses, earls, and countesses you are."

Wesley barked out a laugh. "That much is certain."

"And we shall take it as a compliment," Nick added raising his wine glass in toast.

No one made an attempt to release Helen from the question. Aurora thought to ease the situation, however her own curiosity kept her silent but attentive.

"I see I shall get no piece this night until I have told you, but you may wish me out of the house when you learn the truth." Helen took another sip of soup. Perhaps she thought to gain some nourishment before being thrust back into the street.

Aurora found herself leaning forward in anticipation of whatever tale Helen might tell. "I doubt that very much."

"As do I," Mr. Arafa said in a low rumble.

It was possible that Aurora detected a blush from Helen when Mr. Arafa spoke. She filed that away and waited for whatever was to come.

Putting down her spoon yet again, Helen took a long breath and let it out. "Several years ago, I was Miss Helen Hazlett. My father is a country gentleman with a small estate and enough funds to live, but not enough to live very well. However, my family has always been happy. My mother runs a very amusing household. My two younger sisters and I were well educated by Mother, who is quite brilliant.

"When I was one and twenty, it became clear that marriage to the simpletons in my purview was not an option. I decided rather than marry I would get a proper education. I felt myself as bright as any man and so I invented an identity, Helmet Barrow. Barrow was my mother's maiden name."

"I hardly believed it could be true." Faith sounded quite rapturous with a wide eyed and grinning expression.

Helen gasped. "You knew?"

Aurora said, "The Duke of Corwin did mention you had attended Oxford, but nothing more."

"And still you invited me?" She shook her head mystified.

A low laugh sounded from Poppy. "My dear Mrs. Hazlett-Barrow, it is the very reason we wished to meet you."

"And the school, of course." Mercy sipped her soup as if she'd barely been listening.

"Do continue with your story, madam. How did you gain entrance to Oxford as Helmet Barrow?" It was the first time they had seen Geb appear anxious to have more information. He was generally so calm and relaxed though they all knew information was his specialty.

Another pinkening of Helen's cheek and she continued. "I sent my application and letter. When they asked me to meet with them, I cut my hair, dressed as a man, and put on a pair of spectacles. They never questioned me. I claimed to have been educated at home by my father. I passed all their tests and had the education of my dreams."

"Amazing." Aurora wished she were half so brave as Helen.

"Indeed," Geb said grinning from ear to ear.

"It is fascinating," Faith said. "But it does not answer the question."

All heads turned back toward Helen. "No. I suppose not." She grinned. "I found that after I had matriculated, I wished to write papers on several pieces of research I'd been delving into. Philosophy is my greatest passion, but I also find chemistry intriguing. As Miss Hazlett, no one would even agree to speak with me. I didn't wish to go on as a man indefinitely, so I thought I would try as a respectable married woman. I began putting Mrs. Hazlett-Barrow on the pages and immediately was read and published. I think of it much as a cook or the housekeeper in a fine house would be called Mrs. regardless of her marital status. If those ladies can be made legitimate why not a scholar?"

"Indeed, why not?" Aurora couldn't have agreed more. "Though it is a shame such legitimacy is needed."

Helen shrugged as the squab was placed before her. "Such are the times we live in."

Stabbing the poor bird on her plate, Poppy said, "Exactly the reason we need the Castlewick School to be something really special."

With a quick glance at Wesley, Helen cut into her squab far more gently. "Are you not the Earl of Castlewick, my lord?"

Nodding, Wesley finished the bite in his mouth. "I am. The house Aurora plans to convert once belonged to my family."

A tight crease formed between Helen's brows.

Mercy said, "It is rather a long story."

"I'm certain it is, my lady." Helen cut a bite of the succulent roasted squab.

Aurora was certain that Helen had dozens of questions, but she refrained from asking. They finished the remainder of the meal with talk of weather, art, and music. Mercy offered to play after dinner and Helen confessed to knowing little on the subject of good music.

By the middle of the second song Helen dabbed moisture from her eyes.

Aurora leaned across the space between them on the settee. "I thought you knew nothing of music."

A wry smile played on Helen's lips. "It seems when someone is that magnificent it makes little difference if one knows much of the subject."

Mercy touched each key on the pianoforte as if it were a lover and from those notes formed a phrase and a story followed. Tears streamed down Mercy's face even more than her audience who were enraptured. When the song of Mozart's lost love was at an end, Mercy let her hands slide to her lap.

At the ready, Wesley handed his wife a handkerchief so she could dab her wet cheeks before turning toward the room.

Applause followed, but Mercy shrugged off the accolades and sat in the chair to Helen's right. "Do you play, Mrs. Hazlett-Barrow?"

"I would be delighted if you would call me Helen, my lady. No. I never learned." Her eyes shifted away as if the lack in her female education was an embarrassment.

A wide smile filled Mercy's face. "Helen, it is not a crime to spend one's days on loftier pursuits than the pianoforte. And please call me Mercy."

The men busied themselves with turning and moving chairs so that they formed a large circle for conversation. The warm butter and blue tones of her lady's parlor had always soothed Aurora, but since their numbers had grown to include men, the movement of furniture had become a regular event. She'd come to love the lively conversation of her family of friends.

Helen cocked her head and a ruby curl escaped to slide down and rest alone her elegant neck. "I think it would have been a very large crime had you not learned, Mercy. Your gift is a gift to us all."

A rare blush colored Mercy's cheeks and she muttered her thanks.

To spare Mercy any more embarrassment, Aurora asked,

"Would you like to hear more about my thoughts about the Castlewick School?"

"I thought you'd never ask." Helen put her glass of sherry aside and gave Aurora her full attention, which was a bit daunting when those blue-green eyes focused so intently.

For over an hour they chatted and threw out ideas about how young girls should be educated. By the time everyone had left, Aurora felt confident she'd found her headmistress. She stepped into the garden and took a deep breath of cool spring air.

Steps sounded on the path behind her. She swiveled around to find Garrett rushing down toward her with her shawl in hand. "I hope you don't mind, I stayed behind to gain your thoughts about Helen."

He settled the shawl on her shoulders. Did his hands remain a moment longer than was necessary as his fingers brushed the exposed flesh at her throat? It must have been her imagination. She'd seen the way he spoke to Helen and how attentive he'd been to her. Yet her skin warmed and her breath caught.

"I think Helen is perfect. I'm surprised you didn't marry her when the two of you were abroad. You are a charming couple." Aurora hated the hint of jealousy that wound its way into her voice.

Clasping his hands behind his back, he looked out over the moonlit garden. It was a bright night and she saw the crisp cut of his shoulders against the dark background. His shoulders lifted and fell in a deep breath, worrying the fine material of his coat.

His voice was low and far away. "I never had any romantic interest in Helen. We met in Italy and again in Spain by chance. We are friends. She is a fascinating woman, and I enjoyed having someone from home to chat with. It may sound strange, but it is nice to joke with someone who can grasp the humor. I think it is difficult to translate humor in a second language."

"She is very beautiful." Aurora couldn't imagine why she was poking a sleeping bear, but she couldn't seem to help herself.

Turning, the intensity of his gaze made Aurora take a step back. He nodded. "She is lovely. Just because I am not interested does not mean I am blind."

"Were you not lovers?" Everything inside her clenched at the idea of Garrett and Helen wrapped in each other's arms. She tried to push the vision away, but it wouldn't leave her.

"No." He stepped closer.

"Really?" Aurora bit her lip. Two healthy adults living abroad with nothing to keep them apart seemed the perfect scenario for a tryst. "I assumed with all your traveling you flitted from one bed to the next and that is why you didn't come home."

An instant later, he stood inches from her and ran his knuckles down her jaw. "Rora, is it possible you do not know why I left England and didn't return for so many years?"

Heart lodged in her throat, Aurora swallowed several times so she could speak. Had he always been so tall and broad? Had intensity always shone so brightly in his eyes? "Rhys said you wanted to see the world. I once asked your father and he said, you had to sow your wild oats. I hadn't any notion at the time of what that meant, but I assumed it was to do with women you would make conquests of."

"Rora." His whisper drilled down to the pit of her soul.

"Garrett, have I said something wrong?" Part of her urged to run away and not pursue whatever was happening in the garden. Another part wanted her friend to know that nothing he could say would change their friendship.

He stepped back and dropped his hand. His expression was sad, far away for a long moment before he grinned. "Not at all. I did my fair share of oat sowing while on the continent. It was a great deal amusing though left one rather unfulfilled. However, Helen is a lady and never offered herself in such a way. Since I had no intention of marrying her, I would not insult her by attempting to seduce her. She is good company and we share a mutual friendship that has been fulfilling. I would never do anything to harm that relationship."

"Why shouldn't you have wished to marry a beautiful and brilliant woman?" Aurora couldn't imagine a man better suited to a woman of great mind and beauty. Some men might not like to have a wife with a fine mind, but Garrett loved a good debate regardless of the sex of his companion and opponent.

"I am not in love with Helen, though I like her very much." His smile was part amusement and part wicked. "I am happy to hear that you missed me enough to make inquiries as to why I had gone away."

A small cloud passed over the moon and the garden dimmed before brightening again. Garrett offered his arm. "Do you think it would be too scandalous if we walked in the garden for a while longer?"

Slipping her arm through his, she laughed. "I can't imagine anyone caring that a widow and an old family friend walked in a garden on a fine night."

He leaned in. "With the house empty of anyone to keep things proper? All our friends have gone home, Rora. Do you not think someone might consider me a suitor?"

What an odd thing to say. "I don't think anyone on West Lane gives a fig about what I do, and no one would believe you would court me."

An oak tree blocked the light of the moon. Garrett stopped and turned so they were too close. "Why wouldn't they believe it?"

It was too intimate. He was too close and not at all behaving like himself. She hadn't noticed him drinking overmuch, but the hair on the back of her neck stood up as if he were a threat. Dropping his arm, she stepped back. "Anyone who knows me would be aware that I shall not court anyone. I'm not in the market for a husband, nor shall I ever be."

The muscle on the side of Garrett's jaw ticked. "What did Radcliff do to make you so determined to never court again?"

Panic rushed blood to her head. Another few steps backward put a distance between them. "I don't know what you mean. Radcliff is long dead."

He looked as if he might leap to close the space, but he held his ground. "I think there is more to it than that. I wonder why you would keep secrets from me, Rora. I'm your friend. I would never harm you or speak about you out of turn. Might not telling me relieve some of your burden?"

"I have no need of such relief from you, Garrett. I'm fine. I don't know what it is you want to know, but I think it is time you went home." Her heart thrummed so loudly that she didn't know if she could bear the sound much longer. It was like a cacophony in her head. The notion of Garrett ever knowing what her marriage had been like, made her stomach turn. He would never look upon her the same way should he know the truth. To have him look at her with pity, would be unbearable.

Sorrow burned in his eyes. "I see my time away has put more than distance between us. I shall endeavor to earn back our friendship. Good night, Rora."

Before she could tell him how wrong he was, he was gone. She wanted to scream that she was fine. Radcliff had not ruined her, but she knew it was a lie. In three years of marriage to Bertram Sherbourn, the Earl of Radcliff, she had endured abuse that made her damaged beyond repair. A tear rolled down her cheek and then another.

Running for the house, Aurora bounded up the steps to her room and bolted the door. Her private cry couldn't last. Soon Gillian, her maid would come to help her undress. It was actually surprising to find the room empty so long after the guests had left.

Did her maid think she would have an affair with Garrett and that was why she was not already waiting to help her lady to bed? The thought sobered her.

Wiping her face, she sat on the edge of her bed and drew several long breaths. She went to the basin of water and washed her face before pulling the cord to call for Gillian.

CHAPTER FOUR

Entering the Breckenridge townhouse with more trepidation than was normal, Garrett chided himself. He was a duke in his own right now and had no reason to feel awkward. It had been more than two weeks since the dinner party and walk in the garden, yet he could think of little else besides the way Aurora had laughed off any possible notion of him being a suitor.

He'd been more disappointed than he could remember in recent history, perhaps ever. It was well she'd asked him to leave before he'd said anything he might regret. Aurora was a puzzle, to be sure. Despite what she had said, she was one of his oldest friends, and regardless of his feeling beyond friendship, he would never abandon her. With a sigh, he entered the ballroom.

Large chandeliers were fully lighted, there crystals casting a glow to every corner of the large, elegant room. Frescoes spanned the ornate arched ceilings and the light and shadow played upon the scenes of angels, cherubs, and the lower humans who frolicked in fields.

A rather sour note from the orchestra made Garrett cringe. Surely Nick and Faith could do better than these musicians. He imagined Mercy was grinding her teeth at the sound.

It was the first ball thrown by the new Duchess of Breckenridge and it seemed all of good society had come to see how she would fare. Garrett couldn't care less beyond that he liked Faith and hoped she wouldn't let the wagging tongues of bored society ladies and gentlemen ruin her pleasure. For his part, he'd only come to see and speak to Aurora.

After their last talk, he'd been haunted with how to make her see how perfect they could be with each other. Maybe that was too much too soon. He would settle for knowing she didn't detest him.

"You look like a man on a mission, Corwin." Rhys slapped him on the back. "It still feels odd to call you Corwin."

It sounded far stranger. "Then call me Garrett as you always have, Rhys. This is such a crush no one will hear you. Besides we've been friends long enough to survive the scandal of someone overhearing. We need only bow a greeting, and everyone will be satisfied."

They both bowed and then chuckled at the ridiculous

need for formality even between childhood friends when in public.

"I've learned from my disruptive and beautiful wife that caring what the ton thinks is a waste of time. Give them a moment and they will be on to the next scandal." Warmth shone in his blue eyes when he spoke of Poppy.

Being jealous of his friend's situation was becoming a bad habit. "She is a wise woman."

Rhys laughed. "Lord! Don't let her hear you say such a thing. I'll never hear the end of it."

"What won't you hear the end of?" Poppy arrived with Mercy and each carried a small crystal goblet of some kind of punch.

Without regard for his own warning, Rhys indulged her. "His Grace thinks you wise, my love."

Beaming, Poppy blushed. "Zeus's beard! He is a very brilliant man, and I for one shall not argue the point."

Mercy sipped her punch. "You would not, I dare say."

Poppy laughed. "You are my friend and your sarcasm is unkind."

"I shall remember that the next time you employ the same, which shall likely be in the next ten minutes." Mercy cocked her head and grinned.

Laughing harder, Poppy nodded. "Probably so."

"Have any of you seen our hosts?" Garrett thought he should make a formal salutation and since he'd arrived late, Nick and Faith had no longer been in the foyer receiving guests.

"They are dancing." Mercy raised one strawberry blond brow. "Together. It will be the talk of London tomorrow."

"Shall we always be plagued with what the ton think of us?" Poppy heaved a great breath.

"I'm afraid so, my love." Rhys took her punch and put it on the mantel then clasped her hand and gently pulled her onto the dance floor where they joined a rousing waltz.

Garrett watched with another pang of jealousy. "Lady Castlewick, since I don't see your husband, would you care to dance with me. I am a poor substitute, but it would be my honor."

A wide grin made Mercy from a pretty woman into a beauty. She discarded her punch to sit beside Poppy's. "He has gone off to talk to someone about some piece of land he's intent on regaining for the Castlewick title. I would very much like to dance, as I have several questions I've been wanting to ask you, Your Grace."

They joined the dancers and Mercy danced lithely and with grace.

Garrett wished only that the musicians were better. "You must be horrified by the pitiful orchestra."

She turned her green eyes toward the corner where the music drifted from then returned her attention to him. "They are pitiful, but most of the listeners will not notice. I had no idea you were musically inclined, Your Grace. Do you play?"

Shrugging, his neck heated. "Compared to you, I do not play. However, I can manage the pianoforte and a bit of violin when forced. I do have a great love of music and certainly can decipher good from bad. Perhaps that's why I never endeavored to practice as I should. I was bad and couldn't bear the sound of my own performance.

"I'm certain you play very well." Mercy's eyes wandered before she returned her attention to him. "Are you planning to court Aurora?"

The blunt question took him by surprise, and he had to

swallow twice before he could find his voice. "Why on earth would you ask such a thing?"

She shrugged. "You seemed well suited. You like each other very much. I suspect there may be more than that. You are a duke and also kind as far as I can tell. You have decided to remain in England these last several months."

With no apparent conclusion forthcoming, Garrett inferred he must add all of those speculations up for himself. "I have had no indication from the lady to lead me to believe she has any interest in being courted."

As if what he said made no difference, Mercy went on. "Did you know my husband attempted to court Aurora? That's how he and I were thrown together so frequently. It is why we fell in love and married. Had Aurora been the least bit interested in Wesley, I would have stepped back, or never stepped forward..." She looked confused for a moment. "I don't suppose I ever did step forward. I had to be pushed and dragged a bit. You see, we Wallflowers have seen a darker side of marriage and we are very cautious."

"What does that mean?" The hair on the back of Garrett's neck prickled with dread.

A myriad of emotions flitted through Mercy's eyes. He didn't know her well enough to be sure, but he thought anxiety and worry were among them. She allowed those emotions to move through her then gave him a sad smile. "I'm not at liberty to tell that story, Your Grace."

"I see." Frustration warred with his need to be a gentleman. "Then perhaps you might at least call me Garrett and dispense with the formalities."

Her smile returned. "And you will call me Mercy. What a relief. All that Your Gracing would soon become tiring. I never expected to be more than Miss Heath, so you can imagine my discomfort with my current title."

"I thought all women wanted to marry men with titles." Didn't they?

"Not all women are created equal, Garrett. Some women just want to play music to their heart's content while other women want to be scholars. There are even those of us who want to be loved unconditionally and tenderly even if she may not know it herself." The music ended and Mercy gave him a sly smile before making a pretty curtsy and walking into the thick crowd.

The moment Aurora entered the room, Garrett knew it. His entire body came alive with hope and his heart pounded out an army march. She scanned the room as if she had little care who she found. Never had he met anyone who hid their emotions as well as Aurora. Yet when her gaze found his, something lit those cool blue eyes. It might not have been joy, but it certainly wasn't indifference.

He gave her a slight bow, and she returned a hint of a smile.

She didn't hate him. After weeks of worry, his tension eased.

She left the room and turned down the hall.

Hastily, Garrett wound his way through the crowd. When he reached the ballroom exit, he nearly collided with Mr. Arafa. "I beg your pardon, sir."

With a slow and formal bow, Mr. Arafa said, "My fault entirely, Your Grace."

Aurora was nowhere in sight. Disappointment shot through Garrett's heart, but that was no excuse for nearly toppling a very good man. "No. I was in a hurry and didn't watch where I was walking. You are kind to take the blame, but it is not necessary. How have you been these last weeks, Mr. Arafa?

"I am well. My business will take me out of London for several months. I was pleased to gain the invitation to attend tonight as I won't see these fine friends for some time." Mr. Arafa frowned as if he questioned the wisdom of leaving for his business.

"We shall all be here when you return, friend. What troubles you?"

A forced smile didn't reach Geb's eyes. "I worry that I shall miss being accepted as I have been by these Wallflowers of West Lane and the men they have married. It's silly really. After all, I lived years in England with only one good friend in Nicholas. It seems I have become spoiled by friendship and dare I say, family."

Garrett would never doubt the kindness of Aurora and her friends. "I think the ladies would be delighted to hear that you think of them so fondly. I am sure they regard you the same way. Furthermore, I am confident they will miss you as much as you miss them, but if your journey is necessary and cannot be delayed, then write to us here in London and we shall keep you up to date on how we all get on."

Wide-eyed, Geb stepped back enough to look at Garrett fully. "That is most kind of you, Your Grace. Do you think the others would mind a letter or two from me as well?"

"I think they would be very put out if they didn't hear from you."

He offered Garrett his hand, which was accepted immediately. "You have given me much comfort, Your Grace. Thank you."

"Nonsense. I have only told you where you stand. It's

more than I know myself to be honest. You would do me a great favor if you would call me Garrett and not by some title I'm hardly worthy of." A twinge tugged at Garrett's heart as he remembered how perfectly the Duke of Corwin fit his father and how lacking he was in most of the qualities needed for the roll.

Geb lowered his voice and leaned in. "Garrett, you will fill the shoes of your father in due time. A good man always feels he is lacking. It gives him something to strive for."

Not knowing what to say to such a compliment, Garrett nodded and looked back at the ballroom as another round of dancing began.

A wide smile lit Geb's face. "I think I will see if Lady Marsden will honor me with a dance."

"A fine idea." Garrett wished he'd been quicker and seen where Aurora ran off to.

Geb whispered. "I think you might check the door at the end of the hall to the right. What you are looking for may be in there." With a wink, Geb rushed into the crush of people in search of Poppy.

A bit stunned by the information and the conspiratorial way it was delivered, Garrett stared down the hall for a long moment. Lit candles led toward the back of the house. It seemed there were stones in his shoes as he forced them one after the other down the hall. The further he moved from the party goers and the music, the more rapid his heart throbbed against his ribs. What an idiot he'd become.

He stood at the door a moment his hand on the knob and listened. If Aurora was in there and she'd gone to meet a lover, the last thing he wanted was to find her in some romantic state. A flush of anger rose up his neck and cheeks. This would be a hell of a place to have an assignation. She should know better. He pushed the door open.

The distinctly feminine yet comfortable sitting room was well lit with two large candelabras each holding seven candles and the moon shining in the large French doors. In a ruby gown Aurora stood looking out onto a private terrace and garden beyond. The moonlight caught her golden hair in all its perfect curls and braids.

Garrett struggled to draw breath even as he thanked God she was alone. "Are you hiding from me or someone else?"

Looking back at him, she gave a wan smile. "Neither. I was warm and a bit overwhelmed by the crush. This room is Faith's private parlor. I went out on the terrace, but I could hear several lovers through the shrubbery, so I came back inside."

He closed the distance between them. "Why should what lovers say bother you, Rora?"

"Perhaps it's jealousy or perhaps I was embarrassed." She looked back to the terrace.

He took her soft hand and kissed her knuckles. Even there she smelled of flowers and fresh rains in the spring. He had to quash his feelings. "I doubt either of those emotions forced you back inside."

She sighed and turned toward him. "No. I just thought it best not to know too many people's secrets. It is especially difficult to hold such notions when one would have been eavesdropping. Besides, I thought you might come and find me."

"Did you wish me to seek you out?" His pulse raced.

She closed the space between them and pressed her cheek to his chest. "I did not like the way we last parted."

Breathing her in, he leaned his chin on her hair and

wrapped her in his arms. Perfection and torture. "Nor I. I should not have pressed you for information you are not willing to divulge."

"One day I will tell you, Garrett. But, I..." She put her arms around his waist and gripped him tightly. "I do not wish for our friendship to change. You must understand that I value your regard above most."

His regard? Good gracious. "My regard has not, and will not, ever change, Rora."

Pushing back from his embrace, she blinked back tears.

Garrett offered his handkerchief.

"I remember when you first had your initials placed on these." She ran her fingers over the stitching that formed GW on the soft cloth.

"There have been many new ones over the years, I'm afraid. Those originals are long gone." It was wonderful to have people in his life who remembered such trivia and he warmed at the memories.

"Will you have new ones made with the Corwin crest?" She dabbed her eyes and offered the cloth back to him.

He gently pushed her hands away meaning for her to keep the handkerchief. "I think my valet, Bronson, has already placed an order. Though, I imagine I shall always be more accustomed to a simple GW than my new title."

"You will get used to it with time and a wife to remind you of who you are. I can't fathom that your mother has not made a long list of appropriate ladies to fill the role." She joked and brushed away the last of her tears.

He nodded. "I have instructed Mother to be patient for a year or so."

A musical giggle filled the room and he wished he could bottle the sound and listen to it every day for the rest of his life. "You will do fine." She frowned. "I'm sorry I upset you after the dinner party."

She thought his reaction was because she kept her secrets about her marriage. His mind reeled with what to say. Too soon. His good sense told him it was too soon to enlighten her with feeling she would not return. He pulled her into a hug and kissed her forehead. "We all have our secrets, Rora. I hope you know that I shall always be here for you as your friend, or whatever you need."

Tightening her hug, she sighed. "I am so lucky in my friends. Thank you, Garrett."

He didn't know how long he could stand holding her without it becoming obvious how he felt or at least how much he wanted her. Another kiss on her forehead, and he let her go. "You had better get back to the ball before the other Wallflowers come looking for you."

She looked at the clock on the mantel and gasped at the late hour. "You're right."

Once she had brushed out her skirts and fixed imaginary flaws in her coif, she turned to him. "How do I look?"

She was a vision with her golden hair soft and smooth. Curls dangled around her heart shaped face. Her skin was like the finest silk with just the hint of a flush. The gown hugged her waist and her breasts pushed the limit of the low neckline. The flair of her hips mesmerized him for an instant before he looked into those deep blue eyes. "To me you shall always be the most beautiful woman in the room." His heart lodged in his throat.

She giggled. "I'm the only woman in the room. You wicked."

He bowed and forced a smile.

With another giggle, she headed for the door. With her

hand on the knob, she turned back to him. "I had more I wanted to tell you. About the school."

Delighted to be in her confidence, he held his joy at bay. "Perhaps you will honor me with the next waltz and regale me with all the details then?"

A wide, fully-joyful smile from her pierced his soul. "That would be most agreeable."

Once she'd gone, he settled into a soft overstuffed chair. How had she laid him so low? She rarely showed the slightest bit of emotion, but those glimpses of her sorrow, her affection for him or joy in her school plans, were a shot to his heart that couldn't be denied.

The first strains of a waltz roused him from his thoughts and shot him out of the lady's parlor, down the hall and into the ballroom. Aurora shone as the brightest star in the sky or the ballroom, as the case may be.

CHAPTER FIVE

As soon as the first strains of the waltz began, Aurora scanned the room for her partner. The dancers were still taking the floor, colorful gowns swaying like flowers in the breeze, when she excused herself from a group of dowagers and made her way toward Garrett, who was already striding toward her. Her stomach fluttered at the sight of his broad shoulders stretching the cut of his black coat. His eyes sparked with intensity.

He offered his arm to Aurora. "You seem a bit young for that circle."

The ladies smiled and nodded approval as Aurora took his arm. Indeed, the group of ladies were in their fifties and sixties, more than twice her age. Most were half in their cups and the conversation had been bawdier than one might imagine. "They feel compelled to befriend me as I too am a dowager."

"I think your Wallflowers are a better fit." He swept her into his arms and joined the other dancers in the dance.

She shrugged off her incompatibility with the ladies of similar title even as the strength in his arms had her holding her breath. It took all her will to relax into the music and the simple steps. "My dear friends are all married and will probably have children soon. As their families grow, they will have less time for their widowed friend who they now have little in common with. They will talk of first steps and whose son is taller. I shall have nothing to add to such conversation."

Pangs of regret rifled through her, but she knew how to hide any signs from her expression and the tone of her voice. Years of being a disappointing child to her parents and then a punching bag to her husband had taught Aurora how to hide her feelings. She'd become a master at it.

"You are still a young woman of three and twenty, Rora. You may yet have a large brood of children." His eyes filled with warmth and kindness.

Aurora's chest ached. The damage done by the Earl of Radcliff was permanent. No amount of time could renew her hope of being the girl who returned from Switzerland with her friends. Then they had been so excited about her coming marriage, but all happiness had died by her wedding night. Her father had married her to a monster who had ruined her for all time. "You are kind, Garrett, but no man would want what I have become, and there will be no children in my future."

For a moment he looked as if he might have more to say on the subject. She was thankful when he moved on to safer topics. "Tell me about your new school. Have you decided Mrs. Hazlett-Barrow will do for a headmistress?"

"Oh, yes. She and I have spent hours together plotting how we will manage, but decided she would need to see the house before we go any further." She'd tried to describe the enormous house and grounds to Helen, but she herself had only been there once and found the task impossible.

"So, you are going to Cheshire?" Something in his expression dimmed.

Putting aside the possibility that he might be troubled by her leaving, she continued. "That is what I wished to discuss with you. I will go the day after tomorrow. Mercy and Wesley will travel with me. Unfortunately, Mrs. Hazlett-Barrow is unable to join us until next week. Faith and Nick cannot come for another month at least, but Poppy will travel with Mrs. Hazlett-Barrow."

"Just the two of them for that distance?" A crease formed between Garrett's eyes as it always did when he was thoughtful or concerned.

"The ladies think I am overly protective, but I was hoping you might be able to travel with them. If not, I shall insist they wait until Rhys can get away in a few weeks."

He spun them around a clumsy couple who, while enjoying the dance, did not do it justice. "I shall speak to my steward and clean up a few things so that I might escort the ladies next week."

"Thank you, Garrett. I knew I could count on you."

Nothing was so comforting as a friend one could always go to when needed. That gave her a sobering thought. "Do I take advantage of you, Garrett?"

His step faltered the slightest bit. Warmth from where his gloved hands cradled her back and captured her hand seeped through her clothes. She pushed the sentiment aside, thinking perhaps she should take a lover, but then disregarded that notion as well.

Garrett asked, "In what way, Rora?"

"It seems I am always asking favors of you, but perhaps do not give you anything in return." A knot formed in her throat at the idea that he might feel used by her.

The music ended and he brought them to a halt in the center of the dance floor. "You and I have been the best of friends for most of my life. I am happy to do what I can to help you, and you most definitely have returned the favor on many occasions. If I could not help next week, I would tell you so. As it is, I am little occupied with anything that cannot be handled via post." He bowed.

"You are my oldest and most precious friend, Garrett." She curtsied.

Something flashed in his eyes that made her at once excited and cautious. He offered his arm then escorted her to the edge of the dance floor where their hosts were waiting.

Whatever put the wicked smile on Faith's lips, Aurora didn't like it. Her friend might be a duchess now, but that didn't excuse smugness. Her friends all thought there was something more than friendship between her and Garrett, but they were all wrong. She would never marry again, and nothing short of a miracle would change her mind on that score. Besides, Garrett had always been like a brother to her.

The men shook hands and chatted about politics while Faith gripped Aurora's arm and pulled her aside. "Well?"

"Well, what?"

"Has the new Duke of Corwin declared his intentions yet?" Faith waved an elaborate peacock fan in front of her face.

If Aurora hadn't admired the pretty fan so much, she might have snatched it away. "Garrett is my friend and nothing more. We have been good friends since we were children. His intentions toward me at this moment are to carry Mrs. Hazlett-Barrow and Poppy to Cheshire next week. That is all. I'm sorry to disappoint you."

Faith frowned. "I *am* disappointed. Well, at least he's helpful if not a prospect."

"I need no prospects, as you well know, my dearest. If you are going to act like my mother, we are going to have a long talk, Faith." Aurora watched the dancing begin again and cringed as she had promised this dance to Douglass Mulroony. The enormous oaf was crossing the ballroom to collect her.

"My lady?" Mulroony bowed and offered his hand.

Hiding all her dread, and terribly worried about her poor toes, she took his hand and followed him to the dance floor.

Something niggled at the back of her neck. Just as they joined a group, she turned back. Garrett's eyes flashed before he noticed her gaze, and his intensity turned to amusement.

On the very first movement, Mulroony stepped on her toes. It took all her concentration to keep her own steps and watch out for his, lest he cripple her.

Near dawn, she was waiting for her carriage in the foyer of Faith and Nick's home. For twenty minutes, she'd been staring at the marble floor and elaborate chandelier. It was a grand house, and in time, Faith would make her own mark on it. Most of the guests had already left so footsteps echoed loudly in the silence.

She couldn't imagine what was keeping John, her driver.

"Are you stranded, Rora?" Garrett stepped beside her, accepting his hat from the butler.

"To be honest, I don't know. John has not arrived. He must have some trouble." She walked to the open door. The moon was setting leaving the street mostly in darkness.

"I shall go and check on him. Remain here." Garrett was out the door in a moment.

Faith entered from the ballroom. "You're still here? Is something amiss?"

"There must be some issue. John has not come to collect me."

"Oh? That's odd. Shall I send someone to check on him?" Faith frowned in concern.

"Garrett has gone to check." She admitted, knowing it would create speculation within Faith's imagination.

Before Faith could say anything, Garrett trotted up the steps. "Your carriage has a broken wheel. John had hoped to fix it before you needed him, but the repairs have proved difficult. I can take you home. John will bring the horses home and return to have the carriage fixed in the morning."

"Is John alright?" Her driver had been with her a long time and had suffered much for the sake of the Wallflowers of West Lane. He'd nearly been killed by a madman who'd taken all the Wallflowers hostage in an attempt to get some documents from Nick.

"I'm fine, my lady." John and the two horses clomped down the street. "I'll be in West Lane in no time." With a crooked toothed smile, he tipped his cap and headed toward home.

"Thank you, Garrett. I'm grateful for your kindness." Before she could say more, Garrett's carriage rolled up to the front of the Breckenridge townhouse.

Nick joined them, and Faith kissed her cheek.

"The evening was a singular event, Faith. You will be the talk of London tomorrow, and for all the right reasons," Aurora said.

"And the day after, it shall all be forgotten and someone else will be the center of attention." Faith grinned and shrugged.

Aurora couldn't help her giggle. "True enough, but such is the world we live in. I will see you in a month or so when you come to the Castlewick School. I've already written to have servants air out the house and do some cleaning. I shall hire more once I get there, and we will have rooms ready for you when you arrive."

"We are looking forward to it." Nick bowed then shook Garrett's hand.

After another hug from Faith, Aurora took Garrett's arm and let him help her into his carriage.

Once inside, Garrett was quiet. He looked out the window with his chin leaning on his hand.

"Are you troubled, Garrett?" He didn't look sick, but she rarely saw him without laughter in his eyes. He had always been full of life and humor.

She'd almost decided he would not answer when he turned his head and those expressive eyes locked with hers. "I am torn, Rora. You and I have been friends a long time, and I don't know what to tell you."

"I don't understand." She leaned forward and took his

hand. With no gloves, the warmth of him seeped into her, enfolding her like a blanket. She'd always found comfort in being near Garrett. When they were children, she'd even harbored a crush, but that had ended long ago. Still, she noted how strong his hand was as it wrapped around hers and yet how gentle at the same time.

Gently rubbing her fingers, he smiled sadly. "No. I know you don't. I have kept something from you because you do not wish to hear it. Yet, if I continue to withhold these thoughts and feelings, is it not the same as lying to you?"

The skin on her forehead prickled with perspiration and the hair on the back of her neck stood up. "Whatever it is, we shall deal with it together. I will never abandon you in your hour of need."

"I wonder if that is true." His gaze was so intense she wanted to look away but couldn't.

Shocked by his doubt, stared mouth agape. "Of course it is."

The carriage rolled to a stop in front of her West Lane townhouse.

Garrett moved to get out as his driver opened the door and put down the step.

Touching his arm, she stopped him. "Wait. Will you not tell me?"

His smile was kind and warm and full of trust. "We ran out of road, Rora. If I come in, the neighbors will see, and we cannot stay here in the carriage with my crest blazing on the side."

"But..." She chewed her lip. "You do know you can trust in my friendship?"

He stepped out and handed her down. They walked up the steps where Tipton was already opening the door.

Garrett faced her. "We will have plenty of time to talk and for me to make my confessions in Cheshire. Goodnight, Rora." He bowed and left her to watch his retreat

"My lady?" Tipton said, unsure what to do with the door wide open.

Confused and worried, Aurora stepped inside. "Thank you, Tipton. I'm going up to bed."

"Gillian is already above to wait on you, my lady."

Two days later, the Castlewick carriage bumped down the road out of London toward Cheshire. Aurora hadn't been able to get Garrett out of her mind. The way he'd seemed so out of sorts and concerned and worried over their friendship. What could he be concealing that was so dire?

Mercy reached across the carriage and touched her hand. "What is troubling you, Aurora?"

Always the voice of reason, Mercy was the Wallflower who would always take care of whatever needed doing, though Poppy and Faith were always available as well. Mercy was perhaps the quietest of the four. She had been orphaned at a young age and taken in by her Aunt Phyllis who was more parent to them all than their own mothers and fathers had ever been. Mercy's gentle ways and determined character always bolstered Aurora's courage.

Aurora even had a notion that her monstrous husband's death may have been orchestrated by Mercy, but the idea was so ridiculous she brushed it aside each time the thought occurred to her.

Looking at her friend, Aurora shrugged. "It's nothing. Garrett said something when he drove me home from the ball the other night, and it's been niggling at my mind. I should forget it. I'm sure it's nothing."

Those clear green eyes of Mercy's took in every nuance before she asked, "What did he say, or was it in confidence?"

"Since it was more what he did not say than what he did, I cannot imagine I'm to conceal what I don't know." Aurora's heart ached at the worry she'd seen in Garrett's eyes. Eyes that for her had always held joy and laughter.

"Now you have me intrigued as well," Wesley said and put down the book he'd been reading.

"I don't know why it has me so out of sorts." Aurora had examined it since stepping into her home after the ball. Whatever secrets Garrett kept could not be terrible as he was the best man she knew. He was kind and thoughtful in every way. But why did he look so full of guilt?

"Gracious, Aurora, you look very bad. What did he say?" Mercy squeezed her hand.

"That he was keeping something from me and whatever it was made him feel dishonest." It sounded so simple when she said it aloud, but the way he'd looked nagged at her.

"But he didn't tell you what he'd been holding back?" Mercy asked.

Aurora shook her head. "We arrived at West Lane, and we couldn't create a scandal by remaining in the carriage or both going inside the house." She shrugged. "He said he would see me in Cheshire, and we said goodnight."

"How frustrating." Mercy sat back and pursed her lips.

Wesley smiled and gripped his book. "I'm sure it is

nothing of such consequence as to have you so wrought up, Aurora. You don't know what he has to say, and he had no time to report it. Let it go. The Duke of Corwin is a good man. I'm sure you've nothing to concern yourself about."

"You're right, of course. Still, something in his manner was out of character." With a sigh, Aurora tried to let go of any negative notions she might have conjured.

"Did you not speak to him during the ball? I saw the two of you dancing." Mercy took the book from Wesley, read the spine, frowned, and gave it back.

"We talked in private and also danced a waltz. He said nothing about a secret to tell. We made our apologies for the unpleasantness after the dinner party and spoke of plans regarding this journey." Aurora had already told the Wallflowers about the small disagreement over her unwillingness to speak of Radcliff or her marriage.

"Maybe he has learned the truth and gathered the information in a way he is not proud of." Mercy nodded, seeming content with that explanation.

It had merit. "Perhaps. I suppose it is possible."

"Of course it is." Mercy folded her hands in her lap. "However he learned it, he must be ashamed of himself. He will admit his error, you will forgive him, and that will be all."

Shame settled inside Aurora. She hated the notion of Garrett knowing how she had been a victim in her marriage. It was stupid, but she was weak in her own eyes for not being more clever than Radcliff. Well, if Garrett knew, there was nothing to be done about it. She would let him tell her and, Mercy was right, it would be over. She'd never remain angry with him. It was a bit of a relief to not have to conceal the truth anymore.

Wesley picked his book back up and began reading again. Mercy leaned on his shoulder and closed her eyes.

Staring out the window, Aurora considered how she would handle Garrett's knowing her terrible secret. Brushing aside a tear, she steeled herself. It could not be harder to speak to her friend about her suffering than it was to endure marriage to a monster.

CHAPTER SIX

Garrett watched from the carriage as Whickette Park came into view. The open iron gates were a friendly welcome after the three-day journey to Aurora's new school. Two large stone pillars held the gates in place. Vines grew around the door of the sand-colored house. An oblong yard had a garden in the middle, and a path for carriages wrapped around the small wilderness. The manor and outbuildings followed the arched drive of the enormous home. It was manicured and lovely, making it difficult for Garrett to picture the shambles that Aurora had originally found the estate in.

While Garrett's traveling companions were delightful, his own worries had made the travel torture. He wanted to be strong enough to put his impending admission of romantic feelings for Aurora out of his mind, but he was not a magician and that's what the task would have taken.

Even with his growing trepidation, seeing her as they drove up the lane was like coming home. His heart beat faster and excitement churned in his belly. It didn't matter that he knew he was ridiculous, he couldn't help that the sight of her shot joy through him like a lightning bolt.

Aurora and the small staff met them at the front door along with a large gray cat with tufted ears. The stone lions and stately columns led to a grand entrance.

Garrett tried to take it all in because it meant so much to Aurora, but he couldn't help noticing how lovely she looked even with the smudge of exhaustion under her eyes.

After the initial hellos, they were taken on a short tour of the house's main rooms. He longed to drag Aurora away and declare his intentions or at least his feelings.

"I was thinking that most of the parlors might be turned into classrooms without too much trouble. I'm uncertain about the ballroom as you may wish to hold a ball at some point, Helen." Aurora walked them into the enormous room with sun streaming through the tall windows and French doors highlighting the parquet floors.

Another cat, this one orange, purred and curled around Poppy's skirts. She bent down and scratched the happy beast behind his ear. "I cannot believe the size of this house. I think the school is the only good use for such a castle. I can't imagine you would ever live here, so far from town, Aurora."

Brushing the dust away from her nose, Aurora led them out of the uncleaned parts of the house down a gallery with the most ornate fireplace Garrett had ever seen. They stepped through a music room with an elegant white pianoforte. They passed the grand entry again and stepped into a parlor, which gleamed with a fresh cleaning compared to the rest of the house. "I'm afraid, I've only had time to have the new maids clean this room, the dining room and the bed chambers. They are doing their best, but the house stood empty for so long, we've had to have men in to make repairs as they go."

Helen had quietly watched and studied all they had seen so far. "I'm impressed, my lady."

"Aurora. Please. There are only friends here. We don't stand on formality." She pulled the cord as it was approaching the hour for tea.

Garrett waited for the ladies before he, too, sat. "It is very large."

With a cry of delight, Mercy and Wesley rushed into the room.

Garrett rose again while the Wallflowers hugged in greeting.

Helen looked at him in surprise. "I have never had such comradery with female friends or anyone besides my sisters."

The warmth in Aurora's face shot a bolt to Garrett's heart. She sat and looked with sympathy at Helen. "Has it been a long time since you have seen your sisters?"

"Several years. I should go to Sussex more. It's not as if it's far, but somehow time has created a great distance." Helen shook off her thoughtfulness and smiled.

Wesley sat next to Mercy on the royal blue settee. "Time has a way of doing that, but I'm sure your family will be pleased to see you, and the distance will fall away in a moment."

"Perhaps it is the fear of that not being the case that keeps me from returning," Helen admitted.

The tea arrived and relieved Helen of having to say more on the subject. Aurora poured, and they chatted of travel and learned that the early arrivals had spent three nights in the town of Plumbly while repairs were completed and rooms were cleaned.

After tea, Poppy and Helen went to their rooms to rest. Mercy and Wesley retired to the music room, and strains from the pianoforte wafted through the house.

Garrett and Aurora sat in silence for an uncomfortable minute before he broke the spell. "Are the grounds too wild to view or can you give me a tour?"

Relief bloomed on her lovely face, and laughter sparkled in her eyes. "I thought we would be estranged for a moment."

"Never." Rising, he walked to the high-back blue and cream floral chair she made into a throne just by sitting there.

She took his arm.

They took the main hall toward the back of the house. Large supports and a grand staircase gave the hall elegance. "It's a very striking house, Rora. Are you sure you wish to give it over to a school?"

With a nod, she said, "It is far too big and far away from town for my liking. I shall come once or twice a year as the school needs me, but I would never retire here. Besides, this way, Wesley's family name is again connected with the estate."

"It is very pretty country." Garrett held open the door at the back of the house and waited while Aurora went through. He offered his arm again and his heart pounded as she took it easily.

The grounds were a bit of a wilderness, but a stone path had been cleared for walking.

"I hired a gardener and three men to help him. They have a long cleanup ahead of them, but this path was not passable a week ago, nor was the front of the house so appealing. Then there are the cats. I've had most of them removed from the house to the barn and convinced several townspeople to take some as pets or mouse hunters. They're friendly, but we have an abundance. No rats or mice though." Aurora laughed and turned her face up toward the afternoon sun. "It is lovely, but I could never live here. Let it be useful in some way."

Confused by her distaste for what was a fine house, he stopped at a high point where they could look out over the sprawling land. "I don't think I understand. I agree it is far from town, but the roads are good, and this is a beautiful place."

She colored and looked away from him. "I imagine the secret you keep...the information you've gathered... I cannot live here."

It was so rare to see Aurora's composure slip, he nearly missed the oddity of what she'd said. Touching her shoulder, he left little room between them. If she needed someone to lean on, no matter her stress, he wanted to be that person. "My secret?"

"When last we met, in the carriage the night of the ball, you said you had kept information from me. It doesn't matter how you found out, Garrett. I should have told you myself long ago." When she turned her face up to his, her cheeks were splotched with red, and those beautiful blue eyes swam with tears.

Garrett looked back at the house to see if anyone might see them. As they were still in sight of the large windows, he gently wrapped his fingers around her arm and led her around an overgrown stand of rosebushes. When they were blocked from the house, he pulled her into his arms and kissed the top of her head. "Rora, I have no idea what you are talking about, but if there is something you should have told me, you may tell me now. My secret was nothing I might have surreptitiously discovered. It's really no secret, just something I have hesitated to share. I think it important we speak plainly so that whatever has gone amiss in our communication might be cleared up."

She pushed away, wiped her tears, and narrowed her gaze. "Then you did not discover the truth about my marriage to Radcliff?"

"I am aware that it was an unhappy match." The snap of her voice and her stern expression warned him that there was much more to know.

Ferocity flashed in her eyes, but then sorrow and resignation returned. He preferred the anger but waited for her to speak without his interruption or by voicing the torrent of questions building inside him.

Glancing around, she shivered despite the warm weather. "Might we walk a bit farther away from the house?"

"Is this something Poppy and Faith do not know?" He couldn't fathom that to be the case with his knowledge of how close the Wallflowers were.

She took to the path and hurried away. On a breath, she said, "They know."

Following her, he kept his distance. She was spooked.

While he might not know why, he knew tears and outward emotion were out of character for Aurora. Whether it was the information she would impart or that she planned to tell him, he didn't know, but the idea that it might be him hurt. He pushed it aside. This was not about him, and he had pledged long ago to be whatever Aurora needed him to be.

She finally paused under a grove of walnut trees. The full green leaves formed a canopy over them. She leaned on one trunk, tilted her head back and closed her eyes.

At a distance of only a few feet, Garrett stood in front of her. "May I ask, what is your hesitation in telling me?"

Those bright blue eyes popped open and a crease formed between them. "You will never look at me the same. You will see me as I am instead of as the girl who you played with as a child."

"Rora, I have not seen you as a little girl in a very long time." His gut tightened on the admission. "You are a bright, brilliant, and beautiful woman and have been for several years. Any man would be a fool to not see that."

"You are not just any man." She stared at her feet, her voice low.

Stepping close, he tipped her chin up. "I hope not, but there is nothing you could tell me that would change my feelings for, or about, you."

The urge to kiss the sorrow out of her and soften her full lips, was too great. Fighting with all his will, he dropped his hand, and stepped away but didn't look away from her pleading eyes.

She swallowed several times and sat on the sparse grass under the trees. Once Garrett joined her on the ground, she began. "You may already know that Whickette Park, this magnificent house and the property was part of a marriage agreement between my father and Radcliff. I'm not exactly certain why the deal was struck. Perhaps Radcliff owed my father money, but Father got this property and unloaded an unwanted daughter while Radcliff received thirty thousand pounds. That was the agreement as I know it.

"Father was completely delighted on my wedding day. It might have been the kindest he ever was to me. Radcliff was titled and handsome. I was young and idealistic. I assumed all would be well, and he would love me as a wife should be loved."

For several minutes, she tugged on bits of grass next to her lavender skirt.

When it seemed she was in the past so deeply that she might not continue, Garrett said, "I had some notion of this from Rhys, though not with so much detail."

Lifting her head, she met his gaze. She chewed her bottom lip for a moment before her eyes filled with strength. "It began on our wedding night when my new husband beat and raped me."

And just like that, bile rose in Garrett's throat. "What?" More words were building inside him. It was ridiculous to want to dig up a dead man so that he could kill him, but there it was. He held his tongue and his temper and waited for her to tell the rest of her story.

"I thought perhaps he was just drunk and that it might have even been my fault. I was only eighteen and inexperienced. I must have disappointed him in some way." Her voice became flat and dispassionate even as sorrow filled her crystal eyes.

"Not possible." His voice grated even to his own ears.

A hint of a smile pulled at her lips. "I learned over the three years that followed, Radcliff was a monster and nothing I could have done would have made him happy. He certainly made no attempt to assure my contentment. The notion of him loving me became a cruel joke. My dear friends did what they could. They came and took care of me after each beating. They called the surgeon on a few occasions when my injuries were more severe, and they made my excuses when bruises kept me from attending the theater or a ball."

"You didn't tell your father or Rhys?" Garrett hated himself for leaving the country. He'd been selfish in his desire to put distance between himself and the potential of love between Aurora and her new husband. *What an ass he'd been.*

"I told my father during the first year of the marriage. He often told me a wife was the property of her husband, and I would do my duty to my family. Mother seemed less informed. Rhys didn't know. If I had told him, he would have killed Radcliff and been hanged for the deed. I couldn't risk my brother's life."

Air wooshed back into Garrett's lungs. "Rora, you could have written to me. I would have found a way to help you."

She huffed a laugh. "Do you think I would risk your life any faster than I would risk my brother's. No. I couldn't let you be harmed on my account."

Trying to clear his head, he remembered something she'd said. "Did Mercy have something to do with how Radcliff died?"

With a shrug, Aurora smiled. "I don't know, but I suspect she may have somehow informed the gaming hell of his cheating ways. I can't quite figure out how she managed it or even if it was really her. I'll never ask. If Mercy did have a hand in it, she saved my life, and I'll not put her in a position where she has to either lie or admit responsibility for the death of a man. Even if the man deserved to die."

"I would applaud her." He said it through gritted teeth. His hands were fisted so tightly they ached, and he had to force them open.

"So, you see why I cannot, or rather, will not, live here. Even though Rhys gave it to me as some kind of compensation for my troubles, it is not a home for me. I want it transformed into something good, something special." Her expression turned back to the familiar serenity he associated with Aurora.

He rose, moved closer and sat beside her. "I'm so angry. I don't know what to do with those feelings, Rora. But I am also a bit hurt that you felt you could not tell me of your troubles. I suppose I shouldn't tell you that, but we've had too much hidden between us for too long."

Taking up her hand, he kissed her knuckles. Her warmth filled him with hope and fear. Everything about her called to him.

With her other hand, she cupped his cheek. "This is you angry?"

"Not all men rage and lash out when they are angry. And no man should take out his anger on those he has sworn before God to protect. If Radcliff were alive, you would have no doubt about my aggression." Meanwhile it took all his strength to keep his anger tightly coiled.

A hint of a smile tugged at those alluring lips of hers. "So, whenever you are angry, you are gentle?"

"No. Later, I shall go for a ride or challenge one of the men to a fencing match. I will let my anger out in a sensible way that does not endanger the people I care about."

A breeze blew through the trees, and several birds flew

up. She lifted her chin to watch them go. "I feel lighter having told you. Isn't that silly? It is not as if I have not had confidants. The Duke of Breckenridge has been very helpful to speak with."

"Has he?" Garrett thought the duke an odd confidant, but perhaps there was more to that story.

"Yes. Of course, his experiences differ from mine, but the damage…" She touched the side of her head and took a long breath. "…the damage is the same."

Garrett would have to get to know Nick better, but he understood enough. "Then I suppose you have been of value to His Grace as well."

She tugged a bit of grass and rolled it in her fingers. "I hope I have."

"How could you not be?" As the question was rhetorical and meant as a compliment, Garrett was rewarded with a rare, sweet blush.

They sat looking over the vista to the west. It was strange to sit quietly with anyone, but especially with a woman, and feel comfortable. But this was Aurora, and she wasn't just any woman. Garrett kept her fingers lightly held in his. She didn't pull away, and he needed to feel her skin, her essence, and know she was safe.

He could rage later. He *would* rage later. For now, he was content to watch the afternoon sky as the sun slipped below the trees on the next hill.

Leaning forward, she smiled then kissed his cheek. "Thank you, Garrett. You are a very good friend to me. I'm sorry I hurt your feelings by keeping silent, but do understand, I was ashamed of what had happened to me. Even now, something aches inside me that you might see me differently. You have said you could not, and I believe you, but the notion of being a victim in your eyes is painful."

"Not a victim, my dear, sweet Rora. A survivor." He stood and helped her rise. "It is getting late, and I assume you must dress for dinner?"

With a nod, she took one step before turning back to him. "But you had something to tell me as well."

Garrett's gut knotted. "I think one revelation is all I can endure for today. We can discuss the rest another day. There is no rush."

The sunset left them in shadows as they walked back to the house. The back side of the enormous Whickette Park displayed many windows inset in the tall golden stone. Light filtered out from the rooms that were in use, and he kept his distance in case someone was watching from above. "I think this will make a fine school. You and Wesley will create something really special here, Rora."

"Thank you. I just want a place where girls will learn more than how to be subservient and manage a great house. We should have the same opportunity to learn as a man if we are bright enough." Her voice was full of fire.

Lord how he loved to see her full of life and passion. "I can tell you that I have met many a man who should never have succeeded at Eton, but his money and his sex were enough to get him through."

"Imagine if women could attend a school like Eton." A dreamy quality infused her voice.

"That is your goal then. The Castlewick School will offer to girls and young women what Eton offers to boys and young men." He'd met many women, not all as bold as Helen, who should have had the opportunities reserved for men. He sobered. "I think there are many parents who will be reluctant to vary from the norm. You may struggle to gain students."

She shrugged as they stepped onto the veranda. "Perhaps, but a handful of students to begin will satisfy me. I intend to offer scholarships as well. I think education should be available to anyone, not just those born to privilege."

This woman was a miracle. "I think that's brilliant."

Stopping, she turned and stared at him. "You know most people think I've lost my senses. My mother particularly thinks me mad."

Taking a moment to decide how to respond, he longed to wrap a stray strand of golden hair around his finger and find out how soft it was. "As much as I respect your mother and her position in the world and in your life, I have never taken much stock in her opinions."

Her burst of laughter filled the evening air and warmed him to the bone. His body responded in other ways as well. Ways that he struggled to control lest he embarrass himself.

She said, "You are the perfect diplomat, Your Grace."

"I am not." He kept his voice low. "A diplomat would have said he savored your mother's opinions but held yours above."

She looked into his eyes for a long moment, and he imagined she leaned into him. Laughter from inside the house broke the spell, and Garrett pushed the notion aside.

"I must go dress for dinner and so must you. I will see you in the parlor." At a clipped walk, she scurried away and up the grand stairs.

Garrett sighed as he watched her go. Then he strode back outside, ran to the walnut trees and let out a scream of rage before he pounded the trunk of an innocent tree.

CHAPTER SEVEN

Aurora arrived in the parlor before her guests, and Bickford delivered a letter from her mother. She folded the letter and looked up as Poppy and Mercy entered.

Mercy hesitated. "Bad news?" She looked from Aurora's eyes to the letter in her hand.

"My mother is coming." The long sigh she'd been holding since she read the first lines of her mother's letter finally pushed out.

"Good God." Wesley said as he and Garrett strode into the parlor. "Whatever for?"

Aurora almost laughed at Wesley's dismay at once again being subjected to her mother. They had spent the better part of a fortnight together while Mother tried to bully her and Wesley into marrying. Meanwhile, it was Mercy who Wesley loved from the start. Mother had been less than magnanimous in defeat. "I'm not really certain why she's coming, but she'll arrive tomorrow or the day after."

"Forgive me, Aurora. I should have controlled my outburst. She is your mother, and as such, deserves my respect." Wesley scowled, but his eyes were sincere as he accepted a brandy from Bickford, the butler who had taken the reins at Whickette Park that morning.

Bickford was tall and stern looking, but kindness lay under his gruff exterior that reminded Aurora of Tipton, so he got the job with little discussion. He brought wine to the ladies and brandy for Garrett.

"Did I miss something?" Helen asked, waving off the offer of wine. "No thank you, Bickford. I find it affects me too strongly before I've dined."

Bickford bowed and his deep voice rang out. "I shall bring you a glass with dinner, madam."

Again, Helen thanked him before joining the others.

"The Dowager Countess of Marsden is joining us." Mercy kept her tone neutral, despite the fact that it was she who Aurora's mother tended to belittle most.

Cocking her head, Helen looked at Aurora. "Your mother, I presume?"

"Yes. She shall be here tomorrow or the next day. She is vague about her current location. We shall need to address each other more formally in her presence, or she'll make us miserable with her censure."

Poppy rolled her eyes. "If you think I'm going to my lady

and countess you for however long she plans to stay, you don't know me. Your mother will have to adjust."

Sighing, Mercy shrugged. "As you know, Poppy, with your mother-in-law it is sometimes easier to comply than to fight."

"It is always easier, dearest, but it is not right. I am not calling my closest friends by their title in a private house to appease a bigoted woman who hates me anyway." Poppy huffed. "There is no amount of formality that will make that woman like me, and I have no intention of trying. At least, not when Rhys is not here to take the brunt of her anger."

As there could be no argument, Mercy only smiled.

Helen watched with interest. "Why would the dowager not like you? I think you all delightful."

At that, Mercy brightened. "The dowager has never been an advocate for the Wallflowers of West Lane. Shall I see if Aunt Phyllis can join us? She is often a good match for your mother, Aurora."

The idea was appealing, but perhaps not fair to Mercy's aunt. "I hate to always put Aunt Phyllis in such a position. Though, I would like to see her. Let's first see how long Mother plans to stay."

Bickford stepped in with a silver tray holding a note. "This arrived by messenger, my lady."

Aurora took the note. "It's from Mr. Arafa." She read through the brief missive. "He asks if he might visit, as his business in the north has completed early, and he is anxious to see us and the site for the new school."

"How nice," Poppy said.

"The messenger awaits a reply, my lady." Bickford bowed.

Aurora stood and went to a small writing desk in the corner. She quickly told Geb to come as soon as it was convenient and that they were all looking forward to his arrival. She folded the note, addressed it to Mr. Geb Arafa, and handed it to Bickford.

Once the butler had withdrawn, Helen asked, "Mr. Arafa is from Egypt, is he not?"

Wesley said, "He is. He began as a close friend of Nick's." He cleared his throat. "The Duke of Breckenridge and we have all enjoyed his friendship since."

"I was in Egypt several years ago. It was spectacular." Helen's voice was far away as if she relived her time in Egypt. "I wish I had been able to spend more time exploring, but life brought me back to England."

Garrett had been quiet. Aurora returned to her seat. "Garrett, have you been to Egypt?"

He nodded. "For a month, and then I went to Palestine and several other lands in the region. I agree with Helen. It is a fascinating part of the world."

Clapping her hands, Poppy looked at him dreamily. "I long to see more of the world."

Aurora wondered if Garrett would eventually succumb to his wanderlust and leave England for far off lands again. A dull ache began in her gut at the thought and spread to her throat. She hated when he'd left before, and the idea that he might leave again worried her.

"The world holds many wonders, Poppy," he said. "But there is nothing so grand as coming home to England."

Poppy studied him then looked at Helen. "Do you agree with His Grace?"

"Oh yes," Helen said. "I would not trade my time abroad. It was an education to be sure, but the moment I put my feet down again on English soil my heart soared."

Mollified, Poppy shrugged.

Again, Bickford entered. "Dinner is ready, my lady."

"Thank you, Bickford." Aurora rose, as did everyone.

Garrett moved to her side and offered his arm to her and then to Helen, while Wesley escorted Mercy and Poppy to the dining room.

Aurora took the seat at the head of the table with Garrett to her right. As soon as they were seated, he leaned in. "I think your mother coming forces my hand to speak to you before she arrives. I imagine her presence will be a distraction."

"Does it?" Aurora's nerves leapt to her throat.

Her dismay must have been obvious as he backed into his chair by inches. "If you don't wish to talk to me regarding our interrupted conversation in the carriage after the ball, I will respect your wishes." He turned toward the soup placed before him, effectively ending the conversation.

Aurora didn't know what to feel. She'd bared her soul to him, and he should despise her now. At least, that is what she had always expected. Yet, he still wanted to confide in her.

Appetite gone, she picked at her food through dinner and attempted to follow the conversations and stories.

Just as the final course had been placed before them, the sound of the door knocker called Bickford away. A moment later he returned.

"Who is it, Bickford?" Aurora asked, glad for the distraction.

"A Mr. Renshaw." The butler looked from Aurora to Wesley. "I have put him in the parlor and told him you would join him for cake. Does that suit you, my lady?"

"Hades' breath," Poppy muttered.

"We shall be in shortly, Bickford. Thank you." Aurora

turned to Wesley and Mercy. "Should we have been expecting your cousin, Wesley?"

Wesley's neck grew bright red, and his ears turned nearly purple. "Absolutely not. I have no idea why he's sniffing around."

"Shall I send him to Plumbly to find a room at the inn or invite him to stay?" She focused the question to Mercy, as it was Mercy who Wesley's cousin Malcolm Renshaw had offended by attempting a seduction. He thought to discredit her and keep her from marrying Wesley, but Mercy had stuck him with a hat pin and ran. It was the habit of all the Wallflowers to keep a hat pin handy for just such occasions.

Mercy shrugged. "Malcolm and I have come to an understanding."

"He can stay at the inn," Wesley said through gritted teeth.

Aurora tried to hide her concern behind a serene smile and hoped she'd managed it. "Very well."

"Is it wrong that I am intrigued by all this drama?" Helen asked.

Putting his napkin aside, Garrett stood and offered Helen his arm. "If it is, we are both wrong, my dear friend. Let's go and meet the man who has ruffled all the feathers."

That wicked sense of humor was back in Garrett's eyes, and Aurora temporarily forgot that anything was amiss. It seemed that so many things were piling up on this trip to the country, she would be wise to stay on her toes.

With a dab of her napkin at the corners of her mouth, she drew a long breath, prayed for strength and followed the others to the parlor.

Wesley broke into a trot, surpassing them all to the confrontation with his cousin. At the tall ornately carved wood entrance, he pulled his shoulders back and flung open the parlor doors.

The maids had done a fine job cleaning the grand parlor. It had been well covered, but the ivory draperies had needed to be taken down and the dust beaten out of them. The tables were all hand carved dark woods, and the room boasted two conversation areas. One near the fireplace with a heavy, carved mantel had four large chairs, two at a side flanked by grand sofas. The upholstery was a mix of ruby red velvet and gold. The second seating area had matching furniture, but only a settee and two chairs with a chess set between.

Malcolm Renshaw stood admiring a painting of his and Wesley's great grandparents where it hung over the mantel. His broad shoulders filled his navy coat, and his brown hair lay in loose curls below the collar. At the sound of the doors slamming open, he turned. His full lips turned up wickedly, and his blue eyes danced with delight, perhaps at his cousin's surprise.

"What the hell are you doing here, Mal?" Wesley stormed to the center of the room.

Ignoring the irate head of his family, Malcolm went to Mercy. "Hello, cousin, you are as lovely as ever. I hope my arrival didn't interrupt your dinner or cause you a moment of distress." He bowed over Mercy's hand.

"Malcolm, what a surprise to see you. Did you come from the village?" Mercy made an attempt to hide her grin from Wesley.

"And he can go right back to Plumbly." Wesley ran his hand through his hair.

"I rode in from Thornsdown Manor. Shall I return to my dear younger cousins there?" The forced innocence of the look was too much.

Aurora had to stifle a laugh. Malcolm had outmaneuvered Wesley. Thornsdown Manor was one of the family estates that Wesley had recovered after his grandfather lost nearly everything. Currently, his two sisters were staying there with Mrs. Manfred their chaperone.

Wesley's eyes went dangerously dark. Any threat to his sisters' welfare couldn't be tolerated. "You have no business nosing around my sisters and no business here."

Once again ignoring Wesley's temper, Malcolm turned to Garrett. "Corwin, I didn't know you were here. Good to see you. I was sorry to hear of your father's passing."

"Thank you." After an awkward pause, Garrett said, "May I introduce Mrs. Hazlett-Barrow?"

Malcolm seemed taken aback by Helen. He blinked several times before clearing his throat and bowing. "My pleasure, madam."

"Sir." If Helen noticed his discomfort, she hid it masterfully. Her face and tone were mild and unaffected.

"Lady Marsden." He bowed to Poppy.

The skin around Wesley's collar was bright red, and his fist clenched and unclenched. "What are you doing here?"

The cake and refreshments arrived, and the ladies sat around a small low table.

Malcolm also sat. "I was only thirty miles away at your estate, enjoying the company of your sisters and Mrs. Manfred and they mentioned you were here. They said that Lady Radcliff had some notion of turning our family home into a school for girls. I came to see if this was true and perhaps dissuade her ladyship from such a course." He spoke with total nonchalance and favored Aurora with a smile.

Mercy spoke before Wesley could explode. "Did Esther and Charlotte tell you that Wesley and I have bought a share of the school and fully intend to be a part of the Castlewick School, both presently and in the future?"

Malcolm's expressive blue eyes narrowed, and his shoulders lifted with a long indrawn breath. "They did not, but it does not change my position."

Garrett sat on the sofa next to Aurora, and somehow his presence made her stronger. She shook off the notion that such an effect was possible just from his proximity.

Aurora took a sip of her wine. "Mr. Renshaw, why do you oppose my turning this house into a school?"

His expression warmed in a way that made Aurora slightly uncomfortable when he leveled his eyes on her. "I only wish you would give my family more time to raise the funds necessary to buy back our ancestral home, Countess."

Everything he said was polite and formal, but something in the way he looked at her sent a shiver down her spine. "Your cousin assured me that he was quite content with my plans, and as Mercy indicated, has partnered with me on this project. I have, of course, offered Wesley the opportunity to remove the family portraits if he wishes." She pointed to the couple above the mantel.

"That is very kind, Countess, but this house is important to the Castlewick title." Anger flashed in Malcolm's eyes, but it was gone so quickly, she thought she must have imagined it.

"I have been over this a dozen times with you, Mal. I have made my decision and have better use of the revenues from my estates than to buy this old place. It's too big to be anything but a burden if used as it was in the past. Unless you have the funds on hand, I suggest you leave this matter alone." Wesley drew a long breath and calmed as he sat next to his wife and took her hand.

Malcolm stood. "I'm sorry to have imposed. I will go to the inn in the village and return tomorrow to discuss the matter with you, Wes. Perhaps you will be in a better humor for listening after you've rested."

"Don't speak to me as if I'm some doddering old fool. I'm two years older than you and the head of this family."

Aurora looked at Wesley hoping he would give her some clue as to how much hospitality to show his cousin. She watched as he shook his head, looked resigned then nodded to her.

Maybe he worried that his cousin would go right back to cavorting with his sisters. Aurora hated to think of this rakishly handsome and roguish man being within ten paces of those sweet girls.

"Mr. Renshaw, may I offer you a room here? I'm sure you would enjoy staying in a house so dear to you, and it might be that we will convince you of the merits of the Castlewick School."

A wide grin spread across his face, and he bowed his head. "You are too kind, my lady. I look forward to hearing all of those merits from your sweet lips."

Oh dear. Aurora could see she'd have to keep her eyes open and her hat pin at the ready with Malcolm Renshaw in the house. He might be a danger to more than just Wesley's sixteen-year-old sisters. "Bickford, will you show Mr. Renshaw to a guest room?"

The butler stepped forward. "Follow me please, sir."

No one spoke for a long moment. Garrett seemed to have stopped breathing at some point during Malcolm's visit, and Aurora looked at him with concern for his health. "Garrett?"

Instead of replying to Aurora, Garrett turned to Wesley. "I think your cousin intends to court Aurora in an attempt to regain this house for your family. I can see you didn't know of his plan, but do you think him capable of ungentlemanly behavior?"

"Yes," Mercy said, before Wesley could respond.

"Mercy is right. Unfortunately, Mal will go beyond fair play to get what he wants." Wesley covered Mercy's hand with his.

"We shall have to keep a close eye on him." Garrett's knuckles were white from fisting his hands.

"I am not fond of being spoken about as if I were not in the room. Besides, I'm perfectly capable of taking care of myself." Aurora hadn't liked the look in Malcolm's eyes any better than they did, but she'd not be caged in her own home. "However, I shall be sure to keep my hat pin handy."

Mercy and Poppy nodded soberly.

"Hat pin?" Helen asked.

Poppy slid a large emerald from her coiffure, but only enough to show the long metal pin before she slipped it back in place. "The Wallflowers of West Lane have made a habit of keeping a sharpened hat pin within reach at all social events in case a man becomes too amorous and help is not available."

Hoping it wouldn't come to that, Aurora got up to pour more wine since Bickford was occupied and the footman had disappeared after dinner.

Helen said, "How intriguing you ladies are. This is turning out to be quite a visit to the new Castlewick School for Girls."

Indeed, it was.

CHAPTER EIGHT

Hours later, Aurora lay in her bed staring at the darkness. The new moon gave her no light as she got up and looked at the sky. At least the stars hadn't abandoned her.

After everything that had transpired, it was Garrett who haunted her thoughts and denied her sleep. It would have been more sensible to be worried over Mr. Renshaw's arrival, and all his bluster, or her mother's imminent visit. But Malcolm Renshaw didn't bother her, and her mother could be handled. She could bolt her door and carry her weapons. There were enough people in the house to keep her safe.

She had been unfair to someone she cared about. She'd not allowed Garrett to unburden himself. Garrett's secret kept her from her dreams.

Determined to make it right, she gave up on sleep, pulled on her robe and slid into her slippers. As she stepped into the hall, the house was quiet. Really, it was so large one could get lost with little trouble. Perhaps she could avoid her mother during her impromptu stay. She chided herself and let the notion go.

She walked past the wide landing overlooking the entry hall. The grand door loomed, but no one stood sentinel or wandered the halls. At Garrett's door, Aurora stopped.

It was foolish to wake him, yet she knocked softly. If he didn't wake, she would return to her own room and forget her stupidity.

Within a few seconds, the door swung open, revealing Garrett in his breeches, his blouse hanging loose around his hips. Without a cravat, a smattering of dark hair peeked from his open collar. His eyes widened at the sight of her. He stuck his head out the door and looked down the hall in both directions before pulling her inside. "Rora, are you alright?"

"I couldn't sleep," she admitted. "I was unkind to you. You whom I should never be unkind to. You may tell me anything, Garrett. I am your friend, and I want to know whatever you wish to tell me."

He hung his head for a moment and scrubbed his hand over his jaw. "With Renshaw in the house, I feared you'd been harmed. Come and sit."

"Mr. Renshaw is nothing to me. I'm certain his aims are not my virtue, which is nothing worth guarding."

His wardrobe stood open with his clothes for the next day already hanging in wait. On the dressing table lay his razor, cologne, and other masculine items. His bed linens were pulled back but not slept in. The candles were still lit, and a book lay on the small table near his chair.

What had she been thinking to come to a man's room in the middle of the night? Fear rushed in like an ocean wave and she was powerless to stop it. "I shouldn't be in here."

"Everyone is abed at this hour. The servants have all gone to sleep. Only you and I shall ever know you were here." He cocked his head, gazing at her with openness and trust. "Or is it me you are afraid of?"

Thinking about it, she realized she wasn't afraid of Garrett. Her fear stemmed from a man long dead and unable to hurt her. Even after so long, Bertram Sherbourn left his mark. Perhaps it was worse to harbor marks that couldn't be seen with the eye. At least the bruises and cuts had healed. The deeper wounds still festered. "You would never harm me."

He took one of her hands and rubbed her fingers. The touch was gentle and warm. He always knew how to comfort her. "No. I will never hurt you in any way, Rora. Why don't you tell me why you reacted the way you did at dinner?"

Unsure how to answer, Aurora reclaimed her hand and worried the lace at the edge of her robe. The bedroom furnishings were as elaborate as the rest of the house. Dark wood and mint green upholstery gave the room elegance. If it weren't so enormous, Aurora would quite like Whickette Park. "I'm not certain. Perhaps there has always been safety in secrets for me. Once you tell me yours, I fear my protection will be lost."

"You need no protection from me. However, if you truly

want me to stay silent, I will comply." His voice dropped, as did his gaze. Sorrow hazed around him.

It broke Aurora's heart. "Tell me, Garrett. Whatever it is, we shall deal with it together. We are friends."

Garrett stood, walked to the dark hearth and stared into the grate. He touched a small porcelain lamb standing on the mantel, adjusted it to the left then straightened his shoulders and looked at her. "And we shall always be friends, Rora. It is only that my feelings are more than those of a family or childhood friend, and I have come to the point where I can't push them aside any longer."

Her heart leapt into her throat and her pulse pounded. The room tipped slightly before righting itself. Aurora gripped the arm of the chair. "I don't understand."

A sad smile and solemn eyes were her punishment for the lie. "I think you probably do. But, so there are no misinterpretations or mistakes, I will speak plainly. I admire and love you, Rora. I have since before you went away to school. We were both too young then, and my feelings likely infatuation. But since, my feelings have not changed, only grown stronger."

"But you haven't even been in England for much of the last four years." Frozen in place, she looked for anything that could dispel his declaration.

Garrett knelt before her. "I left England because you were engaged to another man. Selfishly, I couldn't bear to see you married to another."

A wave of dizziness washed over her, and when it passed, she pushed aside his hands on her lap and stood, forcing him to rise and step back. Struggling to breathe, she pressed her hand to her chest. "I cannot. You are my friend. We are friends." She strode to the window, but the darkness gave no comfort. In a rush to the door, she stopped only when Garrett's hand touched her shoulder. He didn't keep her from leaving by force, only by need. His hand was gentle and comforting, never aggressive. His knuckles were scraped and scabbed over.

"Do not run from me, Rora. I will not harm you." Desperation rang in his voice.

Memories that had nothing to do with Garrett kept her still. But her husband was dead and Garrett would never harm her. She turned toward him. "You have harmed me. You have harmed us. This is not what I want."

He backed up a step, his hands in fists, the scrapes red and angry on the right one. "No. I am aware of that. You have decided that all men are worthless because Radcliff was a monster. You lump me in the same category as a man I would kill for what he did if he were alive to kill. Despite my love for you, in your eyes I am an animal just like Radcliff."

The venom in what he said brought her out of her panicked haze. Her instinct to flee broke. "You are nothing like him." Reaching forward, she took his hand and traced the rough skin at the scrape. Had he done this to himself after they talked? She thought so. His hand had been uninjured when they sat by the walnut trees. "But that doesn't mean I can change the damage that has been done. I will never marry again, Garrett. I will never allow myself to be a man's property again."

"You are determined to never know love then?" He kissed her fingers.

"The capacity to love the way you describe is lost to me. I cannot." A tear rolled down her cheek.

With the gentlest touch, he thumbed the tear away. "You love the Wallflowers, their spouses, your brother and many more. I think you even love me, though perhaps I flatter myself." His grin slipped.

"That is not the same kind of love." A steady stream of tears she could no longer control streaked down her face faster than she could dash them away.

He stepped closer and pulled her into his arms. She felt safe in his embrace. His lips pressed to her hair. It was warm and enveloping, as if nothing bad could ever touch her. "Love is love, Rora. We may express it differently when it is romantic love, but if you can feel it for your friends, you can feel it for a man. I am sorry that I am not that man." Dropping his arms to his sides, he added. "I am and will always be your friend. You may call on me at any time or visit me in the middle of the night when the notion strikes you. You will always be safe regardless of my desires."

His jaw relaxed and one side of his mouth lifted as he brushed her hair behind her ear.

"I wish you had declared yourself before I went away to school. Perhaps then, things... life might have been different." Regret flooded her, both for his delay in declaring himself and in the loss of his embrace. What might her world have been like had she married Garrett rather than Radcliff?

"I was just out of school, and you were only fifteen. I thought there would be time." He drew a sharp breath.

She didn't know when she had ever been so sad. A deep mourning for what had been lost overwhelmed her. "Time," she whispered.

He kissed her cheek the way her brother might. It was chaste and sweet and left a yawning hole in her soul.

"Go to bed, Rora. We will speak in the morning if you wish. Hopefully your mother's arrival will wait until tea."

Almost having forgotten, she groaned. "Mother. I don't

know what she's up to, but it can only add to whatever madness Mr. Renshaw intends. Good night, Garrett. I truly am sorry."

"You have nothing to be sorry for." He opened his door, looked into the hall to assure it was empty then stepped aside, and she walked down the hall to her own room.

In her room, she sank into the bed and cried. Loved her. *Garrett loved her.* She knew he was fond of her and thought he deemed her like a sister. But the look in his eyes tonight was not sisterly. When she thought back to other occasions, he'd not been altogether brotherly, yet she'd always been safe in his company. Remembering her wayward thoughts about taking a lover when they danced at Faith's ball, she shivered. The idea wasn't entirely horrifying.

Perhaps just to be held. But to ask a virile man to hold her and nothing more was madness, even if it was Garrett. Yet, he'd held her briefly in his room, and she'd been in no danger. In fact, his arms had been a balm to her tattered nerves.

She must be losing her mind to even entertain such a thought. Still, when his lips pressed to her cheek, it had been sweet and kind. When she was wrapped in his arms, she'd had a sense of comfort. And if she were honest, she longed to be in his arms again. Allowing fear to rule her was no way to live even if love were not possible.

If she'd been asked even a month ago if she could ever find comfort in the arms of a man, she'd have scoffed at the notion. Yet, as she lay awake, she missed the feel of Garrett holding her.

Of course, it was irrelevant. She'd never marry. She'd never give up the little she'd gained in her marriage. She owned Whickette Park, and since Wesley could not buy it back for his family, she would do with it what her heart desired. No husband would allow such an extravagance. She had the house on West Lane and an annuity that kept her quite comfortable.

She didn't need anything from anyone, and that suited her quite well. Mother's arrival would be a good distraction. Between her and the school preparations, she could avoid anything else. However, if she didn't sleep, her mother would rail about the dark rings under her eyes.

Closing her eyes, Aurora decided to keep her head, ignore any unpleasantness, and deal with whatever her mother had connived. It was only a matter of discovering agendas. Now she knew Garrett's, and it was not anything to be dealt with. She wouldn't love a man, no matter how much she liked him, and he deserved to be loved and adored by his wife. Her mother likely had divined another marital candidate, whom she wished to talk to Aurora about, and that could be pushed aside. Wesley would discover what his cousin was up to and deal with him. Her own plans were all that mattered, and no one was going to change her path.

As her mind drifted, she thought perhaps when they returned to London, she would help Garrett find himself a proper wife.

Aurora's eyes sprang open. Of all the young ladies who were available for marriage, she couldn't think of a single one who was good enough to be Garrett's duchess.

Frustrated, she closed her eyes and begged for sleep.

CHAPTER NINE

Garrett took a horse at first light and rode hard into the countryside. The day before had been one of the hardest days of his life. Learning what Aurora had endured while he wasted his time traveling the world had stirred rage inside him that he'd never known existed. She'd not pressed him for information about his damaged fist, for which he was grateful.

He hadn't know what to do with all the rage that grew inside him for not being there to save her. It had not been his place to come to her rescue, but remembering his lackadaisical romping around the continent nauseated him. All the while, she'd been in a private hell. He'd been the worst of friends.

He should have known or suspected, but how could he know? Her own brother had no idea, and he'd been in England the entire time.

When she'd appeared at his door in the middle of the night, all his fury had fled, and he'd been left with the wonder of being alone with her.

Despite the fact that she had rejected even the idea of their courting, he'd loved having her near and to himself. The scent of her so warm and fresh like wildflowers and honey. He could live on that alone for his lifetime.

He pulled the sorrel mare back, and they walked lazily down the lane toward the town of Plumbly. The weather was very fine, and many people were already rushing around the streets. Several were staring at a sign on the doors of a large hall. Garrett rode up to see what the fuss was about.

After dismounting, he tied the mare and walked to the doors. "An assembly," he read out loud.

"Yes, sir." A man of perhaps thirty with a strong chin and a coat that had seen many seasons gave him a nod and a smile. His teeth were crooked, but he had an affable manner.

"What is the occasion?" Garrett asked.

"We had a storm last Friday and had to cancel the regular monthly assembly. Tomorrow will be a fine time." He offered his hand. "I'm Grady Kinsmith. Are you staying up at the Park with her ladyship?"

Garrett took the man's hand. "Garrett Winslow."

Grady's mouth hung open. "Your Grace. I'm sorry. I didn't realize." He made an awkward bow.

"No need." Garrett waved off Grady's concerns. "Can anyone attend, or is it just for the local people?"

"We would be delighted if you and her ladyship's party would join us. It's just a country dance. I'm not sure you will find it as grand as you're used to, Duke." Grady looked around at the street, the carriage that rolled by, and anywhere but at Garrett.

"I think we should find it a fine evening out. I shall recommend the entire party join in the festivities if you're certain we wouldn't be intruding, Mr. Kinsmith."

Taken aback, Grady finally looked at Garrett. "Everyone is welcome. It would be no imposition."

Garrett tipped his hat. "Then I hope to see you tomorrow night, Mr. Kinsmith."

Another awkward bow from Grady, and Garrett climbed on his horse and rode toward Whickette Park.

As he topped the hill, the house came into view. He imagined Aurora busy inside making things ready for her mother or working with Helen to get the basics for the proposed school. Just the thought of her made him happy. He supposed that should no longer be the case since she'd rejected him, but it didn't seem to matter. She stirred his emotions no matter her lack of returning them.

Perhaps he was drunk from little sleep since his thoughts and Aurora's words had kept him awake all night. He would try to gain a few hours in bed after eating something.

The sound of a carriage made him turn in the saddle. The Marsden crest blazed on the side. It was unlikely the dowager had seen him. It was cowardly, but he trotted off the road and loped down the hill and out of sight. He had never cared for either of Rhys and Aurora's parents. They were selfish and treated Aurora as if she were somehow lacking. They had sent her away to school in Switzerland, an act for which Garrett had never forgiven them. And when the earl had announced his great match for Aurora even before she'd returned home, any respect for their father had been lost. It had been unfair to deny Aurora a season. She would have been a diamond of the first water that season, or any.

Garrett had booked himself on the first ship out of England. He was less proud of that decision now than he had been when he made it and saw the disappointment in his father's eyes.

He rode around to the stable out of sight of the drive. Once he'd unsaddled his horse and combed her down, he gave her water and food. "Thank you for a lovely ride, my dear."

A groom with mussed curls of dark brown and a bright smile poked his head in. "That there is Sheba. I wasn't sure if she'd been pinched, Your Grace. You get up early."

"Sorry about that," Garrett said. "I didn't sleep and needed some exercise. I think I have her settled, but if you wouldn't mind checking my work..." He waited for a name.

"I'm Ned. I'll see to her, Your Grace."

With a nod, Garrett left the stable and hurried toward the back of the house. Still unwilling to face Aurora's mother, he thought he might sneak up to his room and have a bath before having to deal with her.

He'd never been as thankful to his valet, Bronson, as he was when he found a breakfast plate of sausage, toast, and jam under a cloche on the table in his room and a bath ready to have hot water added, waiting for him.

Bronson pushed his dark hair to one side. "I shall have hot water brought up while you eat, Your Grace."

"You are a wonder, Bronson."

"Indeed, Your Grace."

He walked out of the room, and as promised, within twenty minutes, footmen with hot water arrived to heat the tub.

Garrett pushed aside the empty plate, took the last sip of tepid coffee and thanked them.

Clean and dressed, he was a new man as he went downstairs. He thought he would look around and see if the library was intact. In the hall, voices from the lady's parlor drew his attention.

Aurora said, "Do you understand what I'm asking?"

"I think so, my lady." A man's deep voice sounded from the open door.

Garrett stepped forward and looked in.

Bickford stood in front of the ornate lady's desk like a soldier called to a dressing down. "You want me to stay on here after the park is turned into a girls' school."

Aurora huffed out an amused breath and looked up at him from behind the desk. "Only if you feel you're up to the task, Bickford. If you're not comfortable, I will write you a letter of recommendation, and we shall part ways after I leave here."

The butler bristled. Perhaps he thought it ridiculous that he might not be able to handle a house full of female students. Once he'd recovered his stoic expression, he inquired, "May I ask, why you would wish me to stay on, Madam?"

Sitting back, Aurora gazed far away. "At my home in London, I have a very fine butler by the name of Tipton. He has done all in his power to protect me and my home under such circumstances that no man should have to endure. He has done so with diligence and honor. You remind me of Tipton. I need someone who will keep this house, this school, and the young ladies who attend and teach here safe. It is not an easy thing I'm asking."

If it were possible, Bickford seemed to stand even taller. "I think I should like to meet Tipton, my lady."

She grinned. "I know it's an unusual position to stand butler at a girls' school, but there will be a full staff that will need direction. I think you are a kind but firm hand to guide those who work here. You will know where to make rules to suit a school and when to break the customary mandates of a household."

After a moment, Bickford gave a nod. "It is a challenge, but I am up to the task. I accept the position and hope to do justice to your Tipton."

Standing, she offered her hand. "I know that you will."

There was a bare instant of hesitation before Bickford shook her hand. Then he bowed and left the room. "Your Grace," he said as he exited.

"Bickford." Garrett waited until the butler was out of sight before he stepped inside. "I think you have made an excellent choice. I hope he doesn't endure the kind of trouble that Tipton has these last years, but I think a house full of brilliant women is a challenge for any man."

Worry creased in her forehead. Likely she was recalling the troubles at the West Lane house with French spies kidnapping them last year. She took a breath. "I think he will do well."

Leaving the door open, he crossed to the sofa that sat to one corner, waiting for her to join him. When she sat in the rose-colored Queen Anne chair, he settled into the sofa's flowered silk. "I don't want there to be awkwardness between us, Rora."

Her shoulders relaxed. "Nor do I."

They would not speak of what had transpired the day before until she brought it up. He saw that in her gaze. Finding a subject they could begin with, he said, "I assume your mother arrived safely."

"She did and is resting. Though I suspect by the hour of her arrival that she didn't travel more than two hours today." Aurora drew a long breath and let it out slowly with her eyes closed.

Amused, he said, "It is rather elegant to rest after a journey and then appear for tea."

"She claims to have a surprise for teatime." Aurora rolled her eyes.

"How terrifying." Garrett smiled, but inside he worried over what Jemima Draper might have in store.

"I spent a good deal of the morning with Helen. We have decided the school will be kept to the east wing of the house. It has several parlors for classrooms and plenty of bedrooms. This end will be closed off unless I choose to visit or they hold a ball." She paused in thought. "A gentleman is coming this afternoon to give me a price on some modifications. I need to create a dining hall. I think the gallery can be altered for that purpose, and there are stairs down to the kitchen quite close."

She was a wonder, and he adored hearing how exciting

the project was for her. "It sounds like you have things well in hand."

"There is much to do. I need teachers." She brushed a strand of hair from her cheek.

"And students."

They both laughed.

One slim brow rose over her right eye. A teasing smile pulled at her lips. "To that, I have some news."

"Really? I am awash with anticipation." He was fully relieved that they could still banter and joke together.

Aurora walked to the desk. She picked up a letter and returned to where he'd stood, before they both sat again. "I've had a letter from the Marchioness of Dorsett. She actually sounds a bit at her wits' end with her husband the marquess. He is determined to send their twin daughters to the continent for school. He claims they are incorrigible, while her ladyship claims they have high spirits. She heard a rumor I was starting a school and would prefer to have her girls in England. I will write to her directly and have her send them. I would not like to see them shipped off to Lucerne as I was."

"I seem to remember you enjoyed your time abroad, and you met the Wallflowers." He knew for a fact that she had no regrets about her schooling.

She shrugged. "You're right, of course. I wouldn't change anything except the curriculum of my education. I should have enjoyed learning about science and math. Those subjects are only explored in girls' schools as far as it can help in running a house. I think Helen can manage two girls and I shall send out advertisements for a few more teachers willing and clever enough for the position."

"You believe cleverness is a requisite?" He had no idea if

there were other women of Helen's quality. Finding them would be a separate issue.

"Maybe not, but it would be helpful. Spirited girls can be a handful." She smiled and blushed a little perhaps thinking of herself when her parents sent her away.

"I was furious when your father sent you away to school. Did you know that?" He didn't know why he felt the need to tell her now, so many years after the fact. The thought blurted from his mouth before he had time to think.

She folded the letter and placed it on the table. "I didn't know, but you have always been a good friend to me, so I am not surprised."

"I went to my father, who told me to mind my own business. Though I suspect he disapproved of your father's behavior in most instances."

"Your father was a kind man." Her smile was warm with old memories. "He was right, of course. It was none of your business, and there was nothing you could have done about it. My brother tried and failed. Besides, as you said, I loved my time at school."

A knock on the door was immediately followed by Bickford's entry. "My lady, the Duke of Hexon has arrived. He claims he was invited by the Dowager Countess of Marsden."

Aurora stood with a sigh. "I suppose this is my surprise. Bickford, can you ask the maids to make up one of the nicer rooms for His Grace? Is tea ready?"

"It is nearly so, and I can ask Mrs. Lyme to speed things up if you like." Bickford referred to the cook.

"No. Don't trouble her if it's already in progress. Have the room made up and escort His Grace into the west parlor. We shall join him directly. And would you please inform my mother that her guest has arrived?" Aurora returned the letter from the Marchioness to her desk, took a breath and turned to Garrett. "Shall we?"

He offered his arm. *Hexon, of all the arrogant asses. Why was Aurora's mother so dim when it came to the selection of husbands for her only daughter?* "Do you know the Duke of Hexon?"

"I have never met him." She brushed out her skirt. "Do you know him?"

"We were in school together." A knot developed in the center of Garrett's chest. "Of course, he was not a duke then. Of course, neither was I. You may find him likable."

She glanced at him as they walked arm in arm down the hall. "I have no idea how you mean that, but I suspect you do not find him so."

"He is rich and has a fine estate. His debts are paid, and he keeps a house in London." What more could he say? It wouldn't do to defile a man's reputation, especially one he'd not spoken to in ten years.

Lady Marsden flew down the stairs. "My wonderful surprise arrived early."

"So I've been told, Mother. You might have said, so I could have a room readied."

Brushing the notion that a duke's arrival might inconvenience anyone, Jemima turned to Garrett. "Your Grace. How nice to see you. Have you been in the country long?"

He bowed over her hand. "Not long, my lady. The pleasure is mine."

"We shouldn't keep your guest waiting." Aurora nodded to the footman, who opened the parlor door.

Jemima practically gushed with glee as she floated across

the room to Hexon, who stood looking out at the front drive. "Hello, my lady. I didn't realize you had yet to tell Lady Radcliff of my arrival."

"You were a surprise." A warm smile pulled at Jemima's lips.

Aurora stepped forward. "A very pleasant one, Your Grace. Welcome to Whickette Park." She made a curtsy and looked a bit too happy to meet Hexon.

Despite the newest bout of jealousy roiling in his belly, Garrett couldn't brood. "Nice to see you, Hexon."

They shook hands. "Winslow. Oh, it's Corwin now, isn't it? My condolences on the loss of your father. I met him on several occasions in Parliament. Though we rarely agreed, he was a true gentleman and a very smart man."

"Thank you. He hated your politics but told me once that you had a good head on your shoulders. High praise from my father." Garrett hated to admit that, but there it was. Father had liked Hexon despite his politics and his arrogance.

"That was kind of him." He gave a nod then turned to Aurora. "I also didn't realize the house was filled with your friends. I hope you are in earnest that I am not an unwelcome intruder."

"You are most welcome. Tea and the others will be here in a moment, and you'll see we do not take ourselves too seriously. All are welcome."

After tea, Garrett fled to the gardens. He'd tolerated Hexon at school, but he'd not considered him a rival then. Now it was clear that Aurora's mother had plans to arrange a match between Hexon and Aurora. And not even his emotionless Aurora could hide her attraction to the dreadfully handsome duke.

He rounded an overgrown patch of some flower or other and found Wesley staring out over the hills.

"I'm sorry to disturb you, Wes." Garrett turned to walk away.

Wesley said, "No need to go. I was just thinking about summers here when I was a boy. It will be good to see children at play here again."

"Then you're not as upset with Aurora's plans to convert your ancestral home into a school as your cousin?"

"When I decided Mercedes Heath was the only woman I could ever marry, I let this place go. Even if Aurora wouldn't marry me, and I have it on good authority she never would have, I could have found a rich wife and perhaps come to a price with Aurora to have Whickette Park back. I've never been happier in my life than I have been these last few months as Mercy's husband. This is only a house. I have enough of those." Wesley pointed to a large tree in the distance. "That chestnut tree produced the finest nuts. The boys from town and I would run there and eat until we were sick."

"I'm glad you're content, but what of Renshaw?" Garrett meant it. He liked the friendships he shared with Aurora and her Wallflowers. It was like having a large family to be a part of their group. He'd missed family when he was traveling.

"Malcolm will come to his senses. He has some crazy

notions about this place and some old family legends of buried treasure. It's ridiculous, but he's determined. He'll go as far as making a bid for Aurora's hand, and now with Hexon here, I suppose Lady Marsden is up to her tricks again and will now try to wed Aurora to Hexon." Wesley started down the path toward Garrett, and they proceeded together.

He was going to have to do something about the growing jealousy inside him. "I'm sure that is her purpose."

"Won't work, not for Mal or Hexon," Wesley said it as if it were a fact.

"No?"

Shaking his head, Wesley plucked a yellow bloom as they walked. "Does Hexon seem like the type to allow his wife to have a project like the Castlewick School? A school where girls are taught subjects like mathematics and science. I know for certain Malcolm doesn't think that highly of women to allow such an indulgence."

"Perhaps the lure of becoming a duchess will win her over."

Wesley gave him a sly smile that seemed to say *it didn't work for you*. But he said nothing on the subject. "I heard from the groom that the dance at the assembly had to be postponed due to weather last week and will be held tomorrow."

"I learned that myself when I rode to town earlier. I thought it might be fun to attend," Garrett admitted.

"It is fun. I shall mention it at dinner tonight and see who is game." They continued toward the edge of the gardens. "Shall we go back and have a game of billiards before we have to dress for dinner?"

"I didn't realize there was a game room." Garrett followed him the way they had come.

He leaned in and whispered. "It's well hidden." He let out a good laugh. "My grandfather often hid in there from Grandmother. Though I suspect she knew exactly where he was."

"Women usually do." Garrett would always be willing to have a wife who was smarter than him. Aurora's blue eyes smiled inside his mind. He shook the image off and entered the house. He could use some time without her nearby. Perhaps he could get his emotions under control. Perhaps he could fight everything his heart wanted.

CHAPTER TEN

When Aurora's mother burst into her room before the assembly, Gillian gave her a sympathetic look and slipped out of the room.

"What do you make of Hexon?" Mother gushed as she sat on the edge of the bed. Her gold gown shimmered in the afternoon sunlight. Despite her constant worry of the state of her daughter's widowhood, she was still lovely, and Aurora accepted that the nagging was out of love. But also, out of a desire to have her friends admire her success.

Aurora turned from the mirror. The gray cat that she'd

named George, after the king, jumped into her lap. Not wanting to be covered in fur, she gave him a loving pat and placed him on the floor. She'd picked a bright blue gown with cream lace. Gillian put her hair up in a simple chignon with only one strand of pearls. "Mother, I think the duke is perfectly nice, but I have no idea why you invited him here."

Rolling her eyes, Mother threw up her hands. "He is looking for a wife, of course."

Of course, Aurora thought and had to force herself not to imitate her mother's eye roll. This working trip to the country was turning into a bit of a circus. "You do know why I have come to Whickette Park, Mother."

She waved her hand about, the bracelets at her wrist jiggling. "Some ridiculous notion about a school."

"And do you think the Duke of Hexon would wish to have a wife who sponsors and runs a girls' school?" Aurora thought perhaps she could lead her mother to her own conclusion rather than just give her the standard *no*.

"Of course, he will not. You will marry, become a duchess and give up this foolishness." Rising, her mother brushed out her skirt and raised her chin in a challenge.

Aurora stood as well. "I have no intention of giving up this school. I also have no intention of marrying the Duke of Hexon. You should not have come here, and you were grossly out of line to invite a guest, whom I have never met. You forced my hand on both counts, and it is very unladylike, Mother."

"Don't you dare speak to me like that. Who do you think you are?"

Keeping her voice soft, Aurora stepped closer. "If you were anyone else, I would have been quite rude yesterday at tea. But you are my mother, and Hexon is your guest."

Attempting to remain calm and not escalate an argument with Mother, Aurora took a breath. "Now, I am going downstairs to meet the others. I have to say I'm a bit surprised you decided to attend the assembly. You did not enjoy the event when last we were in Cheshire."

With a shrug, Mother said, "Last time the goal was only an earl. Now you have two dukes vying for you, Aurora."

There was no point in continuing the conversation. Her mother heard only what she wanted to hear. Aurora stepped around her. "Try not to embarrass me, Mother."

Hexon waited at the bottom of the stairs. Aurora had to admit he was extremely good looking with a shock of blond hair, stunning blue eyes, and warmly tanned skin. He was broad of shoulders and narrow of waist. She imagined many women would be quite taken with him. Plastering a smile on her face, Aurora greeted him. "Your Grace."

"You are a vision of loveliness, Countess." Something in his smile sent a warning bell ringing inside Aurora.

Mercy said, "I think we are all ready. The carriages have been brought around."

With Poppy, Mercy raised her brow at Hexon who had little choice but to step back and let Aurora complete her journey down the steps.

Poppy's eyes narrowed. "We shall need two carriages. Is her ladyship joining us?"

"I believe so." As soon as she said it, her mother descended the stairs.

"Grand. You will ride with us." Mercy took her arm and led her to their carriage where Wesley waited to hand each lady up. Poppy rode with them too, assuring Hexon would not be able to ride with Aurora. As soon as the carriage was moving, Mercy crossed her arms over her chest. "I know she's your mother, but that woman is remarkably dense, Aurora."

"It's so unlike you to say so, Mercy." Poppy grinned.

Mercy's smile was serene. "I'm a countess now, I can say what I please."

"Mother wants me married because she deems that a good marriage is a successful life for a woman. She believes what most of society believes." Aurora leaned her head back and closed her eyes against the wave of guilt that she always associated with disappointing her mother.

Wesley's soft voice broke into her thoughts. "Aurora, you told me you would marry no one. Have you changed your mind?"

She had told Wesley she'd never marry, and she'd meant it. He had wanted to court her but had fallen in love with Mercy. Still, she could do what a good daughter would do, and her mother would leave her in peace. A knot of pain banded around her heart. She took several deep breaths and thought of Garrett and how kind he'd been even as she disappointed him. "I have not changed my mind. I have no interest in Hexon. Besides, something about him doesn't seem right to me."

Mercy sighed. "Thank goodness you said so. I get a very uncomfortable feeling around him. He bears watching."

"Really? He seemed perfectly normal. I mean arrogant, even for a duke. But what do you mean, dearest?" Wesley took his wife's hand and kissed her fingers.

"I'm not sure. At least with your cousin, Malcolm, we know he will take what he wants and propriety be damned. Hexon is not so easy to read." Mercy shook her head and drew her brows together.

"I also thought something was amiss with him," Poppy

said. "But I thought you would all say I was being too critical."

A deep frown tugged at Wesley's full mouth. "So, all three of you think His Grace is unsavory in some way?"

The three Wallflowers nodded.

Aurora said, "I couldn't say why though. It's just a feeling."

"Still." Wesley didn't move to open the door as they pulled up to the assembly hall in Plumbly. "If you all have this instinct, I shall stay alert. Women's intuition is nothing to sneer at."

Mercy smiled brightly, and when they alighted from the carriage, she kissed his cheek.

Poppy took Aurora's arm. "Perhaps it's time to teach your mother a lesson about interference and ferret out the truth about His Grace at the same time. I think showing your mother that not every man is worth having, even if he has a lofty title, might be worth the trouble."

Adoring Wallflower schemes, Aurora grinned. "What did you have in mind."

The second carriage pulled up, and Hexon stepped down before it had fully come to a stop.

"Let's talk in private after the ball. I shall come to your room and tell Mercy to join us." Poppy put on a fake smile that was completely out of character for her, and to anyone who knew her, would seem ridiculous.

Garrett gave her an amused look. "Is everything alright, Lady Marsden?"

She took his arm. "Oh yes."

He led her inside and Aurora heard him ask her for the honor of the first dance.

It had been a while since the Wallflowers of West Lane had pushed a lord of the realm into revealing more than he wished. Aurora liked the idea of teaching her mother a lesson, and just maybe, it would be the end of all the maternal matchmaking.

The man himself approached. "This is a quaint gathering."

She thought Hexon probably meant beneath him when he said quaint, but she ignored it. "I have found these assemblies vastly entertaining."

A tall man with bright blue eyes approached. "Lady Radcliff, how nice to see you again."

It took Aurora a second to remember the man's name. "Mr. Underhill, how do you do? May I introduce His Grace, the Duke of Hexon."

Mr. Underhill's eyes widened for a moment, but then he made a brief bow. "A pleasure to meet you, Your Grace."

Hexon nodded but said nothing.

His silence annoyed Aurora. As if he felt too important to speak to Mr. Underhill, a mere farmer, but still a gentleman. "I heard that some bad weather was my good fortune, sir."

Mr. Underhill smiled. "Indeed, my lady, and we all feel quite fortunate for it." The start of the minuet paused his conversation. A slight blush warmed his cheeks. "Would you care to dance, my lady?"

Before Hexon could claim her, and she could see his eyes narrowed at Mr. Underhill and his mouth opened to say something, Aurora took the farmer's arm. "I would be delighted."

Once they were a few steps away, Mr. Underhill leaned in. "I hope I have not created a problem for you, my lady."

Aurora grinned. "Not at all. I'm happy to have such a fine dance partner, and I'm certain His Grace can manage to find someone thrilled to dance with him."

Thick eyebrows rose over his bright eyes, and amusement

tugged at his lips. "Perhaps you would do me the honor of the second dance as well then."

A warm laugh bubbled up inside Aurora, and she couldn't help but let it out. "Perfect, Mr. Underhill. It could only be better if the second is a waltz."

Without hiding his own amusement, Mr. Underhill bowed. "I shall see that it is, Lady Radcliff."

Having nearly an hour of her time taken up with two lovely dances with a man who was a complete gentleman and wanted nothing from her but to enjoy the evening, Aurora was happy. Her cheeks hurt from laughing at all Mr. Underhill had to tell her regarding a little calf on his farm that was constantly getting into mischief.

When he walked her to the refreshment table, she said, "I think I should very much like to meet this calf and see your farm, sir."

Garrett handed Poppy a lemonade. "Are you planning to see more of the area, my lady?"

"Oh, Garrett, this is Mr. Underhill. He owns a farm and has been telling me some wonderful stories. I think I should like very much to see more of the area."

Garrett bowed. "Nice to meet you, Mr. Underhill. Garrett Winslow."

Wide-eyed, Mr. Underhill bowed. "The Duke of Corwin? The pleasure is mine, Your Grace. I didn't realize our little assemblies would be getting so grand."

Wesley came over and shook Mr. Underhill's hand. "Nice to see you, John."

"My lord. I hope you are well. Word reached us here that you have married. May I wish you great joy?"

"Thank you."

Mercy joined them and smiled.

"I think you have met my wife." Wesley beamed with pride and love.

"Of course." Mr. Underhill had danced with Mercy when last they were in the country. "My lady, it is good to see you again."

"And you. What is this I heard? Are we going to visit your farm?" Mercy smiled, clearly delighted.

Aurora noted the shock on Mr. Underhill's face. She was certain the farmer had never received such a party of guests before. "We don't wish to impose, sir. I'm sure you are far too busy to be bothered with us."

He recovered himself. "Not at all, my lady. From what I've been told, you will be opening a school at Whickette Park. That makes you a local, and if you wish to see a working farm, I'm happy to show it to you. I'd be happy to help you in any way I can."

In a few moments the issue was settled, and they planned to visit the Underhill farm after church on Sunday.

Aurora endured a dance with Hexon and one with Malcolm Renshaw before the evening wound down to the final dance. Where Hexon was arrogant, Malcolm was cunning. Neither was as charming as Mr. Underhill.

Hexon couldn't fathom why Aurora wanted to see a farm. She declined to respond to any of his queries as it was also clear he required no response when he was spewing his view of the world.

As the last waltz started and Garrett bowed before her, she was surprised by her own delight at the notion of being in his arms. Garrett's warm smile seemed to bring happiness with it and that joy flowed into her easily.

"May I have the honor of this dance, my lady?" Garrett held his hand out.

"Thank you. I thought you'd never ask."

He led the way to the center of the dance floor and took her in his arms. "I would have asked sooner, but your mother has been occupying most of my time. I have been ordered to make you stop all this nonsense. I think that's how she put it."

Aurora sighed. "The school, refusing to marry, or going to visit a local gentleman's farm? What is my current crime, pray tell?"

"All of the above." Sympathy warmed his already kind eyes.

"And will you follow my mother's commands?"

They made the turn, and he hesitated an instant before guiding her back into step. "I should think you already know the answer to that, Rora. I would never tell you what you should or shouldn't do. You are fully capable of determining your own mind. Besides, I love the idea of the visit to a farm, and the school will be marvelous."

"Would you tell my mother that?" The entire business with her mother was exhausting. She felt her life had been spent avoiding, dodging, or nay-saying her parents. Now her father was gone, and her mother had gotten far worse.

Garrett's hand tightened on the center of her back. "Do you honestly believe it would help if I told her that?"

"No." She let another sigh escape. "What did you say?"

"That it was none of my business, and I thought the school was a wonderful idea. I also said learning a bit about how local farming is done successfully could mean the difference between the school being profitable and self-sustaining, or costing a fortune." One side of his mouth turned up.

She had trouble pulling her attention away from his lips

but caught herself. "And what of marriage? Did you voice your opinion on that subject as well?"

"I only said, you were a grown woman and would not wish my interference on such a personal decision. To which, your mother said, 'Tish, tosh, and poppycock.' I think I repeated that correctly."

"You know," she started, but then thought perhaps she shouldn't say more.

"What is it?" He saw inside her, like he was the only person who really knew her.

Of course, that was ridiculous. She had three best friends who knew all there was to know about her. Still there was that look that pierced right through her. "I have only one regret. I would have liked to have had a child. A little life that depends on me, loves me, and I would lavish with love. I would do it better than my parents. I would never censure a child for having opinions or wanting to read a book rather than attend a tea."

"I'm not sure what to say, Rora." His throat bobbed as he swallowed. "I think you would be a wonderful mother."

The music drew to a close, and Aurora brushed a tear from her eye.

It had been the last dance, and the crowd began streaming out of the assembly hall.

Without any way to avoid it, she had to ride with Garrett and Hexon, but thankfully Helen was in the carriage and not her mother. "Did you enjoy the evening, Mrs. Hazlett-Barrow?"

"Very much." Helen beamed. "It reminded me of the balls from my childhood. Everyone was so kind and full of joy for the night."

"I wonder if you couldn't bring some of the older

students from time to time as a special treat." Aurora liked the idea of her school being part of the community, as Mr. Underhill had intimated.

Helen nodded. "Perhaps. We shall see how we get on with studies, my lady, and decide about entertainment at a later date."

"And these students," Hexon began, his face twisted in disgust, "they will be daughters of good families?"

Eyes narrowed and shoulders pulled back, Helen met his gaze. "If by good families, you mean that they will all be the daughters of rich titled men, then no. At least not entirely. We will make room for bright girls from any kind of upbringing. We have already discussed setting up a scholarship for one or two girls a year. We are not unreasonable and know we shall have to have mostly paying students, but—"

"But nothing. Your school will fail," Hexon announced. "It is doomed from the beginning with such inane thoughts of charity. What do you think will happen to those poor girls who attend alongside a duke's daughter? I'll tell you what; they will be badgered and teased. You will be subjecting those girls to horrors they are ill-equipped to endure. Shame on you."

Eyes flashing with unreasonable rage, he turned to Aurora. "And you—"

Garrett put up a hand for silence. "I think you've said quite enough, Hexon. You know nothing of what young women of good families with small pocketbooks can and cannot endure. You are speaking out of turn and should silence the impulse."

Hexon's tanned skin burned nearly purple with rage as they made their way up the hills toward Whickette Park.

Having a great deal to say on the subject, Aurora chose to keep silent. The arrogance of the man was not to be borne.

Even Helen looked ready to burst, but she too kept quiet. It was the wiser course, but not at all the easier one.

As soon as the carriage stopped, Hexon leapt out without waiting to help the ladies down.

Garrett said, "Well, that was uncomfortable. At least he was quiet after his tirade."

"Only thanks to you, Your Grace." Helen stepped down with Garrett's help. I know he's a duke, but must he be so, so duke-like?"

Aurora took Garrett's waiting hand, and they both watched Helen bustle into the house. "She's right, of course."

"I'm a duke." He looked slightly affronted.

"You are a gem," she said and left him standing at the carriage. Her legs were tired from dancing. Her mind was tired from scheming. She would go directly up to her room and pray for a good night's sleep. The Wallflower meeting could wait for tomorrow.

CHAPTER ELEVEN

After the late night at the assembly hall, Aurora didn't rise until Poppy swept into her room. "I have called for our breakfast to be brought up to your room. Mercy will join us in a moment."

Mercy glided in. "You went to bed so quickly we decided not to bother you last night."

Aurora sat up in bed and brushed her hair out of her face. "It was a long night."

George jumped up on the bed and snuggled into her lap

for a pet and a scratch under his chin. A loud rumbling purr followed.

"I saw you dance with Hexon. Did you learn anything?" Poppy sat at the small table by the window and peeked out the curtains, allowing the sun to stream in.

Mercy pulled the curtains back, flooding the room with light.

"I learned he is even more arrogant than we first thought, and he has a bit of a temper, but not during the dance." Aurora got up and pulled on her robe. She went to the water closet to relieve herself. When she returned, she told them about the ride home from the ball.

"Hades' breath. He has nerve to attack Helen. He was into the punch at the assembly quite a lot." Poppy's eyes narrowed.

"It's a pity your mother was not in the carriage to see this side of him." Mercy sighed but then added, "Though, your mother might not see anything wrong with his scolding a woman of no title."

Aurora started to drag a chair from the corner so they all three could sit at the table.

Poppy jumped up to help her and they managed the task.

"My mother would not have said anything about it. Still, I don't think his temper was within reason. It was far more vicious than the situation deserved, even if he disapproved of the school and our plan to have more than the wealthy attend."

"You don't think he would do more than scold, do you?" Mercy crossed her arms over her chest and narrowed her eyes.

"I don't know. Once Garrett put him in his place, he sulked the rest of the drive." Aurora hadn't been afraid, but she gave that credit to Garrett, not her faith in the fact that Hexon was a decent man.

Poppy opened her mouth, but the door opened and Gillian and a girl from the kitchen brought through two large trays of breakfast.

With a loud mew, George scurried out the door.

At the aroma of yeasty bread and savory sausage, Aurora's stomach growled. "Thank you, Gillian."

"Enjoy your breakfast, my ladies." Gillian shooed the wide-eyed girl out as she left the ladies to eat and talk.

As soon as the door closed, Poppy reached for a piece of toast. "I wonder that Helen didn't put him in his place."

"I think it was in deference to Garrett rather than her desire to halt any confrontation. She looked ready to burst with indignation." Aurora spread fresh jam on her toast.

Mercy filled her plate with coddled eggs and sausage. "I don't imagine Helen is accustomed to holding her tongue. She's going to be a very good headmistress: fair, in control, smart and wise. I'm glad Garrett brought her to you."

"I agree." Aurora sipped her tea. "Poppy, tell me what you have in mind to teach Mother a lesson?"

Mouth full, Poppy chewed, swallowed, then drank some chocolate. "In order to show your mother how terrible her taste in men is, we shall have to get Hexon to show his true self in front of her. Also, his lashing out at Mercy, Helen, or me will not be enough. She thinks very little of any of us. He will have to lash out at you."

"This is sounding too dangerous," Mercy said, putting down her toast and giving Poppy a scolding look. "I'm not going to rile up a duke who might be violent just to prove a point."

Aurora shuddered at the thought of having a man harm

her in the way her husband used to. But she was no longer that girl, Hexon wasn't her husband, and she had friends who would protect her.

Poppy rolled her eyes. "We won't leave her alone. One of us, Wesley, or Garrett have to be with her at all times. Ideally, we want to push him far enough that he behaves badly in front of my mother-in-law. She might not believe it if she doesn't see it."

"There is the possibility that the Duke of Hexon is a perfectly respectable gentleman, and will not crack even under the pestering of Wallflowers." Aurora continued, "Many men can behave themselves under extreme situations."

Shrugging, Mercy said, "For short periods of time perhaps. If he's a good man, he has nothing to fear. If he's the kind of man we suspect, at the very least he'll have this coming to him for his behavior toward Helen."

Aurora nodded. "I don't like anyone under my roof having to endure what she did last night. It had been such a pleasant evening up until then."

"I wish Faith were here. She's always so clever about things." Poppy stuffed the last of her toast into her mouth.

They finished their breakfast and chatted of the assembly. There was no need to discuss how to rile the duke. The Wallflowers of West Lane had plenty of experience annoying people who deserved it.

Garrett sat with Helen at breakfast. "The other ladies have decided to eat above stairs?"

"It would seem so." Helen buttered a piece of toast. She kept her head down and didn't look up at him when he spoke.

"Are you angry with me or with Hexon?" Garrett knew that Hexon had taken a horse and gone riding after breaking his fast. He expected Wesley would join them at some point in the meal. It was better to get whatever needed saying out while they were alone in the breakfast room.

Finally, she pulled her attention away from the plate. "I'm furious with that arrogant ass and even more angry that I was not permitted to tell him so."

"I apologize, Helen. I didn't want things to get uglier inside the carriage, and I don't know Hexon well enough to be sure of his reactions."

Her red hair was arrested into a tight bun and she pierced him with her green eyes. "I am capable of fighting my own battles, Garrett, and you should be well aware of that."

He'd overstepped. "I am, and I apologize."

"If I call him out for his prejudice now, I'll sound like an unreasonable banshee." She shook her head. "I need to school myself in letting annoyances go. This will be a test of my resolve."

"You are too good, Helen. You really are. Why is it some man has not scooped you up and married you?" Garrett teased.

She favored him with a smile. "You would not ask, and those who did were not worthy of my regard."

"Alas, my heart was already taken." He let the mood be light despite the truth of his statement.

Wesley walked in. "Good morning! I think it will be an interesting day."

Garrett gave Helen a wink and when she grinned, he turned his attention to Wesley. "Why do you think so, Wes?"

"The Wallflowers are plotting."

A knot formed in the pit of Garrett's stomach. "What are they up to?"

Shrugging, Wesley took a plate and filled it from the dishes on the buffet. "They keep their own council when they are like this. Mercy won't tell me anything. If Rhys were here, he might be able to wheedle it out of Poppy or his sister, but they won't tell the likes of us." He gave Helen a long look. "You might be able to find out."

Helen picked up her coffee, sipped and then looked at Wesley over the rim. "Well, even if that was so, I would not divulge a confidence."

Garrett chuckled. "I suppose we shall just have to wait and see how the plot unfolds."

"I hope Geb arrives soon. He will be a fine addition to our party." Wesley sat with his plate.

Cocking her head, Helen narrowed her eyes. "I'm a bit surprised that Aurora's mother tolerates Mr. Arafa."

Wesley laughed out loud, nearly spitting his coddled eggs across the table. He wiped his mouth and apologized. "She detests him, but it is of no real significance. He's a fine man and part of our happy circle of friends. I'm sure Aurora would say he is far more welcome than her mother. Though I suppose I shouldn't say it aloud."

"As it is just the three of us, no one will be offended by the truth." Garrett loved to see Jemima Draper in a fit over silly things. She was one of the most bigoted people he knew and with no reason for her biases. She fought in no wars and lost no one close to her in war. Her prejudices were based in ignorance. Though, Garrett found all such evils tended to be the product of stupidity.

Garrett put down his cup. "I'm going for a walk if either of you would like some exercise."

Wesley chewed a mouthful and shook his head.

With a sigh, Helen rose. "I have some letters to look over. Her ladyship and I are meeting in half an hour to discuss our first students."

"Very exciting. I'll be in the near gardens if either of you should change your mind." With a bow, Garrett left.

Shuddering at the thought of whatever the Wallflowers might be up to that required a private breakfast in Aurora's room, Garrett made his way to the garden. He had thought of leaving Whickette Park at the end of the week, but that was before Hexon and Malcolm Renshaw arrived. He'd not remove himself while men of questionable character were so near to Aurora. Though, he imagined she could take care of herself.

Since he was on his own for the morning, he climbed the hill to the walnut trees. The place made him feel like a failure for not protecting Aurora, not that she'd been his to protect. These thoughts led him to realize what an ass he was for sparing a thought to his own failures when Aurora had suffered so much.

"Am I disturbing you, Garrett?" Poppy's day dress had a brown and green smudge near the knee area. She cocked her head, waiting for an answer.

"Not at all. Did you injure yourself?" He turned fully toward her and pointed at her damaged skirt.

Waving off his concern, she looked down at the stain. "I

stumbled. My poor maid suffers much from trying to keep me in clean dresses and gowns."

He forced a smile, his mind still on what Aurora had shared with him when last he was in this stand of trees. He looked back over the rolling hills. "It is quite pretty here."

"Yes. This is my first time in Cheshire. It's very nice. Have you come up here to think on something? I feel I have disturbed you." Poppy remained on the outskirts of the trees as if she might go back to the lower garden at any moment.

He turned to her. His thoughts a jumble of do's and don'ts. "May I ask you a question, Poppy?"

Stepping into the circle, she nodded. "Of course."

How to begin? He paced to the edge of the trees. "I don't know what to ask."

"Mercy told me there is an ancient circle of stones close by. Would you care to walk and see it? Perhaps you can find the words while we walk." Poppy's face was open and friendly as she smiled warmly at him.

"Did Mercy tell you the direction?" He liked the idea of a destination rather than the maddening stagnation.

"To the west a mile, perhaps two."

He bowed. "If you are up for the exercise, I would be pleased to accompany you."

When they reached the hollow between the first two hills, Poppy said, "I think Rhys will join us next week. Will you be staying long, Garrett?"

"Honestly, I hadn't planned to, but I'm hesitant to leave now." He forced himself to release the fists he'd been clutching. His knuckles ached from the strain.

"You don't like the Duke of Hexon." She said it plainly and not as a question.

He shrugged. "I don't know him well, but he and

Renshaw have agendas that may be dangerous to certain parties. I'm certain Aurora told you and Mercy about Hexon's outburst in the carriage last night."

"She did," Poppy confirmed, frowning. "So, you will stay. Is that what you want?"

The weight in his chest was like an anvil pressing down. "What I want seems to have little bearing on the matters at hand."

Stopping, she stared at him. "I'm sure that's not true. Is that why you were brooding in the walnut trees?"

"Was I brooding?"

She shrugged. "It was what it looked like to me. However, if you do not wish to stay, then go. Wesley will keep everyone safe from unwanted attentions, if need be."

"Staying here with my friends does not trouble me. I'm happy to have a good excuse to stay."

"But?" She prompted.

"I may have done something foolish and caused a strain between myself and someone I care about." It was the truth, but he'd left enough out to feel he wasn't exposed.

"I see. And you were going to leave to resolve the issue, but now you feel you must stay?" Poppy maintained a good pace as they headed west.

"Not exactly, but close enough." The pressing weight did not lessen with Poppy's misinterpretation. If anything, it got worse.

"Is the rift with a very close friend? I mean to say, is it someone you believe cares for you as well?" She squinted into the distance.

"I believe this person's feelings for me are strong and true." Half-truths and part of a story would have to do. Sun shone from behind them as it climbed the sky and glinted off the gray pillars half a mile ahead. "I think those are your stones."

With a gasp, Poppy rushed forward, skipping toward the monoliths. She stopped when she reached them but didn't enter right away.

Picking up his pace, Garrett joined her at the edge of the circle. "It is quite something to stand with these ancient stones and know that others stood in the same place so many years ago."

She stepped inside the circle and pressed a hand to one of the stones. Twelve in all, they were in different stages of decay, but still there was something alive about this place. It made one lower their voice as if it were a church.

Silently, Poppy went around and touched each stone before she returned and stood in front of Garrett. She whispered, "May I be frank?"

Taken aback, he almost laughed. "I much prefer it."

"If the person you care for cares for you, they will understand and forgive whatever error you made. They will have forgiven you, as I can't imagine it was much of a faux pas. You are always very considerate and thoughtful. However, if you wish to give me more information, I will offer my advice."

He stepped out of the circle, not sure why it bothered him to speak of such things within the stones. "I divulged my heart to someone who does not or perhaps cannot share my feelings. I think it has put a strain on our friendship."

Poppy's eyes were wide as saucers. "I could pretend I don't understand your meaning. Would that make you more comfortable?"

Letting out a long sigh, some of the weight lifted from his chest. "Not particularly."

"Good." She grinned. "I'm not good at subterfuge."

Even he had to laugh at how true that was. "Go ahead. Let me have the full force of a Wallflower's censure."

There was a tree not far off, and they walked to it. "I don't censure you for loving Aurora, Garrett. I think you could not love a better person. No one deserves to be loved as much as she. She needs someone who will worship her and whose highest priority is to make her happy. I know you would do that."

His face must have shown his shock at her directness.

With a giggle, she brushed at the ruined spot on her skirt. "I see how you look at her. Don't look so surprised that her closest friend would notice."

"She is not of a like mind." His heart actually might break like some stupid sod in a novel. How he had come to this pass, he didn't know.

"I'm not certain that's true. Aurora doesn't think she wishes to marry. Marriage to her means losing everything she's gained as a widow. It means turning all of her possessions over to a man, trusting he will not abuse all she has relinquished."

Garrett hadn't even considered assets beyond his passion and ardor for Aurora. "Why must it be one thing or the other?"

"I beg your pardon?" Poppy's mouth made a little *O*.

"Why must I get all of her assets or none? Why should any of that matter when a match is made?" Frustration rang in his voice.

"There are laws to that effect. When a woman marries, all her property and even her body belongs to her husband. It may not be fair. In truth, it is most definitely not fair, but it is a fact." Poppy cocked her head, studying him.

"You married, Poppy, and I have never known a more independent girl than you." His voice held more accusation than he intended.

She held up her hands in a helpless gesture. "I fell in love and knew that Rhys would keep me safe while never smothering me. He is the other half of me. Besides, I had very few worldly possessions to lose."

A notion formed in Garrett's head. "So, if I could make Aurora see that I would not steal what she owns or make her a possession, she might consider me."

"I think she will fight you at every turn, Garrett, and you would be happier in the short term to find a nice woman with a good fortune to be your duchess." Sorrow filled Poppy's eyes. "However, if you really love Aurora, and you're willing to suffer the trials of courtship with a woman who has suffered much, and no longer thinks she can love, you are the perfect man for my friend and need not fear the wrath of the Wallflowers." She winked.

Something that felt a bit like hope bloomed inside Garrett, pushing aside some of the hurt that weighed on him. "I don't know what I will do, Poppy, but knowing you approve of me is very comforting. I know how protective you Wallflowers are of one another."

"I can't help you with your quest." She seemed to have known what he would do.

Standing, he offered her his hand to help her up. "I understand. I do hope you will keep this conversation to yourself though."

"You can trust me, Your Grace. You have my support, just not my assistance. Aurora will have to work it out without any nudging from my direction." Poppy walked beside him back toward Whickette Park.

They reached the gardens near the house speaking of Geb's arrival and then her expectation of Rhys finishing his business in London and joining the party. It was a pleasant walk back, but Garrett was completely distracted by the possibility of courting Aurora.

Could he court her? Would she see him as more than a brotherly friend? He needed time to think it through.

Excited with news, Aurora had searched the house for someone to tell, but found everyone except her mother had gone out. Mother would not have appreciated her news, so she rushed out to the garden in search of a friendly face.

Walking toward her looking like old friends were Poppy and Garrett.

Poppy grinned when she spotted Aurora. "We walked to the stone ring. It's quite something, Aurora."

"It is amazing. I visited when Mercy and I traveled here

before." She loved Poppy's enthusiasm. "Garrett, did you find the site worth visiting?"

He inclined his head. "I am always astounded by the longevity of such places. The company was quite good as well. Lady Marsden and I had a good talk and a fine bit of exercise. I can't think of when I've had a more pleasant and illuminating morning."

Raising her brows, Poppy turned back to Aurora. "You look as if you have news as well, Aurora. Were you looking for us?"

"I was in search of a friendly face. Only my mother remains in the house, and I don't think she would find my news as exciting." They took the path to a small fountain surrounded by white roses.

Aurora and Poppy sat on a stone bench while Garrett stood near the fountain.

"Well, don't keep us in suspense for Zeus's sake. What is your news?" Poppy fussed with a grass stain on her pale blue day dress.

"Helen and I have had a letter from a Miss Stein. She is coming from London with excellent references. She says she can teach both mathematics and science." Aurora felt ready to burst with excitement at finding someone brilliant enough to teach at her school. She'd thought poor Helen might have to teach on her own.

"Wonderful news! I had no idea there were so many ladies with that kind of education. How did you find her?" Garrett sat on the stone edge of the fountain with his ankles crossed in front of him. Many men would be appalled at the idea that a woman's mind might be as keen or keener than a man's. But not Garrett.

Aurora shook her head. "To be honest, I thought the

search would be more difficult, but I sent word to an employment firm for women. They mostly place companions and nannies, but Miss Stein was available and fit our needs."

"When does she arrive?" Poppy grinned.

Frowning, Aurora lowered her voice. "She should be here in a day or two depending on when she left London. Do you think there is any chance of the duke leaving before she arrives?"

"Not if your mother has anything to say about it." Garrett cocked his head to the side as if he heard something.

"What is it?" Aurora asked.

"I think a carriage is arriving." Garrett stood.

Poppy jumped up. "Oh, perhaps Mr. Arafa has arrived early."

Standing, Aurora didn't see how Geb could have gotten to Cheshire so quickly. She'd only received his note the night before last. He wouldn't be hiding out in a nearby inn, like her mother. "I had better go and see."

Flanked by Garrett and Poppy, she rushed to the house. Having people who would stand by her, no matter what, tightened her throat as she strode down the hall, through the grand entry to the front door, where Bickford stood at the ready.

Bickford opened the door to allow them out and then stood like a sentinel in front of the open passage.

A very fine carriage stopped, and two footmen jumped down in fine, though dusty, navy blue and white livery. One opened the door, which was emblazoned with a coat of arms.

Garrett lowered his head. "That is the Marquess of Dorsett's carriage."

Aurora's heart pounded. Had the Marquess come to

berate her for offering education to his daughters? She was suddenly very relieved to have Garrett at her side. Not that she couldn't defend herself, but it was nice to have a duke handy when faced with an angry marquess.

The finely dressed footman opened the carriage door and stood with his hand out to help someone alight.

A small hand took his, and a girl of perhaps twelve with brown curls hopped down, followed by another with similar curls but in a dark honey gold.

Aurora stared at the carriage door, but no one else alighted. She stepped toward the girls, who looked varying degrees of terrified. "Hello. I am Lady Aurora Sherbourn."

They both looked up at the footman, who was perhaps twenty. He gave them an encouraging smile and a nod.

The girl with the darker hair stepped forward an inch or two. "I am Wilhelmina Belgrove, and this is my sister, Petra. Our father is the Marquess of Dorsett. Mother said we were to come here for school."

Hoping her eyes were not wide with the shock she felt, Aurora forced a smile. "I see. I did have a letter from the Marchioness, but I didn't realize you would be arriving so promptly."

Tears began to tumble down Petra's cheeks.

Poppy ran forward and dragged the girl into a hug. "Now there's no need for that, my dear. You are safe and very welcome. We're just surprised to see you so soon. It does not follow that your early arrival is unwelcome. Come, we'll have some tea and biscuits and arrange for a room for you both."

One tear pushed out of Wilhelmina's eye. "She's just sad that mother sent us away, but it is still better than father putting us on a ship to the continent."

Aurora took Wilhelmina's hand. "Come inside and tell us

all about your trip. I will have a room made up, and all will be well, just as Lady Marsden said. Do you prefer to stay with your sister, or would you each like your own room?"

Poppy was already past Bickford with Petra.

Garrett waited at the steps with one hand on a stone lion. His smile was warm and his eyes full of amusement.

Another tear, and Wilhelmina said, "Mother sent a letter."

"Then we shall read it. Come inside now." Aurora walked with the child toward the door.

"I have the letter," the footman said as he pulled it from his coat and handed it to Garrett."

"I will see that her ladyship gets it. Can you bring in the young misses' trunks?" Garrett asked.

The footman bowed. "Can we rest here tonight? We have to head back, but the horses need tending."

"I'm sure it can be arranged." Garrett nodded to Bickford, who inclined his head.

Aurora let the warmth of knowing Garrett would take care of those details while she dealt with two scared girls roll over her for a moment before she entered the house with Wilhelmina.

They sat in the parlor, and both girls cried quietly while Poppy fussed over them. Aurora sent for Helen, hoping she would do better at calming the girls. They were only about twelve, much younger than she and the other Wallflowers had been when they'd been shipped off to school. What was their mother thinking?

The scene took her back to the frightening moments when she and Poppy first set off for Switzerland. They hadn't returned to England for three years. At least these girls would only be a two-day ride from home.

Home!

That was the answer. She knelt in front of the two girls on the settee. "Petra, Wilhelmina, I know you are sad because you are away from home, but you may now consider our Castlewick School to be your second home."

Garrett stepped into the parlor with Helen right behind him.

Wilhelmina looked up. "But this is a school."

"It is true," Aurora admitted. "But not an average school and not one where we'll pack a hundred girls into the space and have one or two of you learn something. Here we shall have ten or twelve young ladies, and each will learn all they can gather in. You will live in this house with teachers, maids, a housekeeper, and butler. We have footmen, and the town of Plumbly is not far. You will always have a home here when you need it. Even after your time here is finished, you shall always be welcomed home when you come to Cheshire."

Standing, with her throat clogged with emotion, Aurora looked at Poppy, who was grinning from ear to ear. Helen raised a brow, but beamed.

Petra stood and turned slowly to look around the parlor. Her doe eyes turned up to Aurora. "Then when we are old and perhaps married, we might still return here to visit if we wanted?"

"This is your home, and you will always be welcome to it." Aurora took her hand and smiled down at her.

Garrett crossed the room. "Tea is on the way. May I introduce your headmistress, Mrs. Helen Hazlett-Barrow."

Wilhelmina joined her sister in standing, and they both made pretty curtsies.

"Hello, ladies. You are our first students, and we are a bit unprepared, so we shall have to figure all of this out together.

I hope you will help me as other young ladies arrive in the coming months."

Suddenly, as if realizing they were to play an important role, the girls stopped crying.

Tea arrived with a mountain of sweets.

Poppy cried out with joy at the sight of the treats.

Both George and the orange cat, dubbed Tiger, strolled into the parlor and investigated the new arrivals with keen interest.

The girls were happy to sit on the floor with the purring furballs.

Handing her the sealed envelope from the Marchioness of Dorsett, Garrett smiled, and it went right to her soul. Had he always been so good looking? She didn't think so. Nor had he always looked at her so warmly. He should be furious with her, but instead, he was her friend, as he had always been. There was comfort in knowing he would stand with her no matter her decisions.

She blew out a long breath and broke the seal on the letter. Inside was an account of recent events that must have been written in a hurry. Aurora folded the letter and tucked it inside her waistband to read fully later. She didn't want her temper to rise while the twins were present, and she'd seen the words *shipped off* and decided she'd better wait.

A young, curly-haired maid, Beth, stepped inside the parlor.

Aurora said, "Yes, Beth?"

"If it pleases you, my lady, the young misses' room is ready, and I'd be happy to show them up. I thought they might be tired after such a journey." Beth had a sunny disposition, and her cheeks were flushed.

Bickford stepped inside.

"You are right, Beth." Aurora turned to Petra and Wilhelmina. "Ladies, will you go with Beth? She will get you settled in your new room."

Offering them each a hand, Beth was exactly the kind of well-meaning girl who would be a comfort to these displaced children.

They stepped out.

"Bickford?"

"My lady?"

"Can you see if a suitable housekeeper can be hired locally? It would be nice if the school were a help to the community as well. However, if you do not find someone, I'm willing to send an advertisement to London." Aurora settled next to Poppy.

Bickford straightened. "I think the neighborhood can provide what we need, my lady. I'll inquire right away."

Once the door was closed, Helen said, "So we run it like a house, make it a home and teach them what we know. And what if we find we are not up to the task for one child or another?"

Aurora smiled. "You are being modest, Helen. You are up to the task, and I have high hopes for Miss Stein to join the staff."

Helen frowned. "I wonder that the Marquess of Dorsett would be happy with Miss Stein teaching his daughters."

"Because she may be Jewish?" Poppy looked about to blow up into a volcano of all that was wrong with the world.

Holding up a hand, Helen rushed to say, "I am not bothered, but you know some people will be. Even some of the girls may already harbor these types of prejudices."

Anger that would have no outlet rose up and simmered in Aurora. "They will have to get over it here at the Castlewick

School. That type of narrow thinking will not be nurtured, whether or not Miss Stein is a fit for the position."

Mollified, Poppy relaxed. "What was in the letter, Aurora? Any clues there?"

She'd almost forgotten about the Marchioness's letter. Pulling it from her waist, she opened it again and read aloud. "Lady Radcliff, I send you my daughters, Petra and Wilhelmina. They are high spirited and often make mischief, but I feel it is only my failings that have made them less the young ladies their father would prefer. Actually, he would have preferred I'd have given him a son, but alas that was not our lot. A ship was to leave London on Thursday, and the Marquess was determined the girls be shipped off. He was already making arrangements for transport to a school in Germany. It's so far. I couldn't bear the thought. I convinced him the two day's drive to Cheshire was quite far enough and the girls could leave immediately. I hope to come and see them in a few months if I can get away. They are good girls, and I hope you will not beat them often. Yours gratefully, Lydia Aasberg, Marchioness of Dorsett."

"Beat them!" Poppy's cheeks were red as a beet.

"Who is being beaten?" Mercy asked from the door with Wesley at her side.

"No one," Helen said, not looking much less furious than Poppy.

Aurora sighed and folded the letter. "No one, indeed. We have enjoyed the arrival of our first students while the two of you were out."

Wide-eyed, Mercy rushed in and sat. "Have we? Tell me everything."

"Poppy will tell you." Aurora's head, full of too much

emotion and responsibility, felt ready to burst. "I've got a bit of a headache. I'm going out for some air."

Garrett followed her out. He offered his arm but said nothing as they walked the garden path.

It was nice to be silent but still have company. Yet she broke the silence. "I don't think they can be more than twelve."

"The footman confided that they are eleven, but will turn twelve in September. What do you suppose they might have done to enrage their father so?" Garrett's tone was light, but concern still rang in his question.

She shrugged. "More than likely being born girls was enough. Perhaps they are high spirited as their mother claimed. We'll know soon enough. For now, they are scared little girls who deserve a safe place to grow up and become young ladies."

"They do, and you have given it to them, Rora. You should be very proud of yourself."

That he was proud was warming and heady. "It just came to me all at once that I was looking at the school the wrong way. We don't need dozens of girls who will learn to smile when they want to rage, though that does come in handy."

"I often feel you learned that lesson a bit too well," he said softly, in almost a whisper.

Smiling, she gave his arm a squeeze. "Society doesn't like it when ladies lose their temper or laugh too loud."

He stopped and stepped in front of her. His eyes blazed and it unsettled her. His throat bobbed as he swallowed. "Society can be damned. I would give my right arm to see you melt with joy or rage or any emotion. Your stoicism borders on the morose, Rora. Are sorrow and bitterness all that is left inside you?"

Unsure what to say to the truth of that, she said nothing. She held her expression still and watched as his turned from discontent to understanding.

"I see." Garrett turned and strode away from her.

How could he understand? Passions led a person down a hole they might never get out of. She had long ago turned off those parts of herself. She'd let it slip a bit when she'd told Garrett about her marriage, but now she was more herself. Or, at least she was the person she could get from day to day as. The girl she'd been before had left her long ago and there was no getting her back.

She walked the paths and put aside those lost years to consider her school and all she could accomplish. Thinking about all the angry and hurt girls at the Wormbattle School for girls, herself included gave her more ideas. It was critical that Whickette Park be run like a home where girls learned all they could.

"Am I interrupting a deep thought?" Malcolm smiled as he stepped toward her on the path.

The entire visit was becoming like a farce. How many men would show up before she returned to London. "I was doing some planning in my head, Mr. Renshaw. How are you enjoying being here?"

"I love the area." He fell into step beside her.

Glad she'd had her hair dressed with two long, sharp hairpins she had to make an effort not to roll her eyes. "It is lovely. My sources tell me you believe there is some kind of hidden treasure on the property, sir."

He stopped, a darkness crossed his face filling his eyes with anger but it passed, and he gave a sharp laugh. "I assume your source is my cousin and the countess."

"Wesley told me you think your grandfather hid

something valuable here. I see no point in being coy, Mr. Renshaw. If there is some treasure that you feel inherently belongs to your family, I will not lay claim to it." Maybe he would be satisfied and go away.

He leaned against a maple tree at the end of the path. "Why would you say that, my lady? Do you know what is hidden?"

The tone of his voice sent a chill up her spine. "It is my understanding the value of the treasure is unknown. At least, Wesley doesn't know, and he thinks it some myth started by your grandfather to stave off bill collectors."

"You are very lovely, Lady Radcliff." He crossed his arms over his chest and looked at her from beneath hooded eyes.

This didn't bode well. "Thank you. You needn't flatter me. You may have any treasure you find that is not cataloged in the estate."

He stepped closer. "You don't think I am in earnest? Is it not possible that I have developed feelings for you?"

Determined not to back away or run, Aurora held her place. "I don't care if you are or you are not, sir. I am not interested in being courted by you or anyone."

"Hexon is a duke and you seem less than thrilled with him. I thought perhaps I might be a better fit for a lovely widow determined to run a school in my ancestral home." While his words were like syrup, his tone was chilling.

Without bothering to hide it, Aurora pulled a long pin topped with a sapphire from her hair and held it aloft. "You would no more let your wife run a school than Hexon. You may sell your lies elsewhere, Mr. Renshaw. If you wish to continue to stay here, you will cease any pursuit of me or my person. If you think Mercy was brutal with her pin, you will find me twice so. I suggest you keep your charms to yourself, be a gentleman and search for whatever it is you think you might find here at Whickette, or I will have you removed permanently. Do I make myself clear?"

His eyes narrowed on the pin. "You ladies are quite something." His posture relaxed and he shook his head. "You will find no danger from this corner, my lady. If you were interested in being courted, I would have been honored to throw my hat in the ring. I learned my lesson with Mercy. I'll not make that mistake again."

Lowering her hand, she gave him a nod. "Good. I'd hate to ruin a perfectly good day by drawing blood."

Aurora strode back to the house and, at the veranda, slid the pin back into her hair.

CHAPTER THIRTEEN

Garrett had been an ass. He knew it, and he wished almost immediately to have taken back his words and his disappointment. He kicked at a stone on the road from Plumbly. He could see the kind, passionate woman inside Aurora, but didn't understand why she held her so tightly behind a mask of calm indifference. One moment he was prouder than he'd ever been of anyone and then she made that comment about ladies hiding their feelings to appease society and it was as if his insides had turned out.

Helen had to pretend to be a man to get the education she deserved.

Miss Stein, whoever she was, would have to struggle to gain employment and acceptance because she is Jewish.

Mr. Arafa was accepted to his face and then talked about behind his back in many circles, because of his heritage.

And Aurora –sweet, smart, beautiful Aurora—would hide her passionate nature to keep her mother and men like the Duke of Hexon from seeing inside her.

Staying and watching Hexon and Jemima try their manipulation, would be torture for Garrett, but he couldn't leave her with Hexon in the house.

He returned in time to dress for dinner. The door opened before he'd passed the lions guarding the entrance. "Bickford, what have I missed?"

"Miss Stein arrived early and is being interviewed these last two hours." Bickford raised a brow. "I have hired Mrs. Court to be the housekeeper. I hope she will prove herself worthy. And Mr. Arafa arrived about thirty minutes ago."

"My word. A man walks into town and misses a lot around here." Garrett's spirits lifted. "Are you holding dinner until her ladyship is available?"

"We shall delay if necessary. The young misses have decided, having been given the option to dine in their room tonight, to instead dine with the adults. I hope you won't be put out." A hint of worry rimmed the butler's eyes.

"Hexon threw a fit, did he?" Garrett shook his head.

"It was not pretty, Your Grace." The confidence was given in a voice hardly above a whisper.

"They seemed like good girls. It's good they not stay alone in their room all night. I assume they will have rested from their journey and be full of lively conversation for the meal."

Garrett could hardly wait to see how such a dinner, with such a wide variety of guests would turn out.

Bickford gave a bow. "Bronson has already gone up to see to your clothes for the evening, Your Grace."

So many females to protect and defend. He was already exhausted, as well as amused. For most needed no protection beyond their own wits. Taking the stairs two at a time, he anticipated a lively evening.

Garrett washed and dressed in his black coat, gray waistcoat, and a crisp white shirt. If the night was to be interesting, he thought full formal attire was needed. The parlor was fully lit, but only Hexon stood in a full brooding pose with his hand on the mantel.

Bickford poured him a glass of wine from a crystal decanter and handed it to him.

"Thank you."

With a nod, Bickford stood tall and silent while they awaited the rest of the party's arrival.

"This is some household, eh Corwin?" Hexon shook his head and downed his brandy.

Thinking of the variety housed under one roof made Garrett grin, but he controlled his elation. "It shall be an interesting evening and the days to follow will not fail to amuse."

"What is she thinking?" Vexation laced Hexon's question.

"What is who thinking?" Though Garrett knew full well it was Aurora, there was no need to help his competition along.

Turning to Garrett, Hexon straightened his shoulders and narrowed his eyes. "She's a countess. If things go as planned, she'll be a duchess. I can't have a wife who runs a school. Duchesses don't have employment and certainly not with this type of schoolmistress. And did you see the..." he paused and pulled a face. "Woman who came in today?"

"I have not had the honor of meeting Miss Stein." The familiar anger Garrett often fought back when faced with ignorance rose up from his center.

"Miss Stein." He said her name as if it were a curse. "This is England. She has no place here."

"I think Miss Stein was born in Sussex, Hexon. However, your misguided petulance aside, I would suggest you be a gentleman to all of her ladyship's guests. If she is to be a duchess, she shall not change for your benefit." Garrett might have agreed that Aurora would be a duchess, but he'd be damned if he'd stand by silently if she showed the least inclination toward Hexon. Calming himself, he was reminded that Aurora had no interest in marrying anyone, let alone this bigoted pig.

Hexon's face burned bright red, but he had no opportunity to respond as Wesley, Mercy and Geb entered, engaged in a lively chat.

Happy to have better company, Garrett crossed to meet them. "Mr. Arafa, how good to see you again. I hope your journey has been a pleasant one."

"Just some business in the north. I was pleased that her ladyship allowed me to sojourn here for a few days before I return to London." Geb's smile was easy even as he noted Hexon staring from the mantel.

Unable to ignore the duke, Garrett held back a sigh. "Mr. Arafa, may I introduce His Grace, The Duke of Hexon. Your Grace, Mr. Arafa is a great friend of her ladyship's and mine."

Mercy said, "Mr. Arafa is a good friend to us all."

With a curt bow, Hexon eyed Geb. "Sir."

"Your Grace."

Mercy took Geb's arm. "You travel without Mr. Kosey? I was hoping to play a duet with him."

"I'm afraid he was needed in London when we left Parvus. He and Mrs. Bastian are busy with getting some rooms ready for shipments I have waited months for. It could not be helped." Geb waved off the offer of wine from the butler.

"Are you in shipping, sir?" Hexon took the wine that Geb had refused.

Wine and brandy, this was going to be an interesting night indeed. Garrett wouldn't let anyone be caught alone with a drunk who had a bad disposition to begin with.

Geb tilted his head. "I collect artifacts from my home and the surrounding countries. I find there are many here in England who appreciate these items."

"You must make a great deal of money selling these trinkets to members of society."

Garrett didn't like the tone of Hexon's voice. "I thought the price of my very fine rug to be exceedingly fair."

Whatever more might have been said, it was stopped by the arrival of Aurora, her mother, Poppy, Helen, and a dark-haired woman, who must have been Miss Stein. The women sparkled like jewels, with Aurora the brightest of them all. Her sky-blue gown showing just a hint of her curves, and Garrett had to swallow down his desire to rush to her.

There was no need, and she ushered the woman on her

right over immediately and introduced Miss Stein to everyone. "We have had a long talk this afternoon and decided a position at the Castlewick School where Miss Stein will teach science and Mathematics suits us all."

Garrett said, "Congratulations, Miss Stein. I'm sure you will be a great asset to the school."

A huff sounded from where Hexon stood with the dowager. He had another glass of something he drank down in one gulp.

Jemima Draper might have been keen on getting her daughter married to a duke, but even she could see the danger of a man in his cups before dinner. "Are you ill, Your Grace? You look very bad. Perhaps you should take to your bed. We shall have dinner sent up to you."

"I am never sick," he slurred out and put the empty glass on the table. It fell over and Bickford smoothly saved it from crashing to the floor.

Helen sipped her wine. "Oh dear."

"Hera's eyes, perhaps the young ladies should be kept from the parlor at present." Poppy put her wine glass on a coffee table and she and Helen left the parlor.

Miss Stein sat in a small pale pink chair with curved feet and watched the goings on with wide-eyed interest but no sign of fear.

"I'm not ill." He narrowed his gaze on Miss Stein. "I'm expected to dine with the likes of this and him." He turned his attention to Geb as he snatched another brandy from the table where Bickford had poured for Wesley.

Neither Geb nor Miss Stein made any reply or gave any indication they were shocked or insulted by his statement.

Aurora's neck turned pink, but she kept her voice steady. "You are not required to eat at all, Your Grace. You are here because my mother invited you without my foreknowledge. You will not dine with us this evening. You will go to your room where a plate will be sent up to you."

"You cannot speak to me like this." Hexon stepped forward.

Garrett set his wine aside but made no move to stop him. Aurora was a grown woman and would not appreciate being coddled. He'd not allow any harm to come to her, but he would not imply she was incapable either.

Mr. Arafa eased a step closer, as did Wesley.

Mercy lifted a gold statue from a side table.

Without the slightest indication of fear, Aurora arched one brow. "I can and I will. You should be grateful you are not tossed out this moment. I will not allow your kind of ugliness in my school for young ladies. Here we will teach by example and that will include respect for those who deserve it by virtue of deed, not title. You are not worthy to eat at my table in your current condition and temper."

"Aurora," Jemima gasped.

Aurora turned her head sharply and the ferocious look in her eyes silenced her mother.

Hexon's bloodshot eyes narrowed. "I will ruin you."

"Your Grace, you can remove yourself, or you will be removed. The choice is yours."

As if he'd only just noticed Garrett, Geb, and Wesley being ready to manhandle him, he turned and noted Bickford and two footmen standing by. With only the slightest wobble on his feet, Hexon cleared his throat and pulled back his shoulders. "I have a touch of a headache. It may be best if I retire for the evening."

Once he was gone, Aurora's shoulders slumped slightly before she pulled them back again and turned to Miss Stein.

"I'm humiliated beyond words and so very sorry. I hope you do not think I would have put you in such a situation knowingly, Miss Stein." She rushed to Geb. "Or you, my dear friend."

Miss Stein had warm honey skin and full lips. She smiled. "I have endured far worse, my lady. Do not trouble yourself."

"You should not have been subjected to such ugliness here. I do not know how I shall make amends." Aurora took her hands.

"I do have a question," Miss Stein said.

"Of course, anything." Aurora sat beside her.

With a wicked smile, Miss Stein looked at Mercy. "What exactly were you going to do with that statue, Countess?"

With a shrug, Mercy returned the metal figure to the table. "I had very exciting plans to smack a duke on the head if need be."

"I hope my head is safe, Mercy." Garrett rubbed his head.

The room erupted in laughter.

Aurora's mother drew a long breath and threw her hands up in the air before letting them fall to her sides with a slap. "We are ruined. You heard him, Aurora. He will make things very hard on you. He will return to London and spread terrible rumors, and he's a duke so people will believe him."

Of course, what Jemima predicted was a possibility, but Garrett didn't believe it would come to pass. He turned to the butler. Bickford stood like a sentinel without expression or comment regarding the scene he'd witnessed. "Bickford, how much had His Grace imbibed before we arrived in the parlor this evening?"

With only a slight raise of his brow to indicate shock or surprise, Bickford said, "His Grace appeared a bit worse for his trouble when he returned from the village this afternoon. He took a bottle of brandy to his room when he went up to change. I cannot speak for how much of that was partaken."

The footman standing near the door cleared his throat.

Narrowing his eyes, Bickford addressed the footman. "Andrew, do you have something to add?"

Blond hair the color of butter was pulled back from Andrew's young face. His bright red cheeks stood out in stark relief of his light skin. "Pardon me, sir. His Grace called for hot water and I carried it up earlier. He was near... um... asleep when I brought the bucket and the bottle stood at half on the dresser."

"Thank you, Andrew." Bickford sounded at once grateful and disapproving. It was a skill only a really good butler could manage.

Garrett couldn't help his grin. "I think we shall be safe enough from Hexon. He will sleep for some hours. Bickford, please see that a plate of food is brought up this evening. Send a footman," he added as an afterthought. He didn't want any women; servants or guests, subjected to Hexon in his current condition.

With a barely perceptible nod, Bickford left the parlor.

"I don't suppose it's worth worrying about anyway. There is nothing we can do about it if he does cause a scandal." Aurora shrugged.

"This is my fault. I'm sorry. It never occurred to me a man of his status would behave so abominably." Jemima Draper melted into a chair looking small and frail. It was hard to imagine she'd actually learned a lesson, but for the moment she was contrite.

Poppy peaked in. "Is it safe to bring the young ladies down?"

"I think so," Aurora said. "His Grace was unwell and has gone up for the night."

Doing a terrible job of hiding a derisive laugh, Poppy said, "Indeed. I will inform the headmistress that the coast is clear."

In retrospect, it was impressive how quickly the ladies went to protect Wilhelmina and Petra. They were like soldiers silently doing what needed to be done, while Mercy gripped her weapon ready to defend Aurora and anyone else. Garrett had never thought of women as champions, but clearly, he'd never really looked. His perspective shifted and he thought himself better for the new knowledge.

Bickford entered. "Dinner is ready whenever you are, my lady."

"I think we are all ready for a change of scenery and topic." Aurora stood and blew out a long breath.

Garrett offered his arms both to Aurora and Miss Stein. "May I escort you ladies in?"

Looking back at her mother, Aurora leaned in. "Thank you, Garrett, but I wonder if you would see to my mother? I don't think she will respond to my assurances right now."

He made a low bow. "I am at your service."

There was something warm in her eyes when she smiled at him. It made him wary *and* gave him hope. Perhaps it was his own wishes that worried him.

Once the others had exited, Garrett went to Jemima who still sat slumped in the chair with her forehead in her hand. "Lady Marsden, may I escort you to dinner?"

"I cannot imagine my daughter wants me at her table."

Garrett sat in the chair adjacent to hers and leaned his elbows on his knees. "If that were true, she wouldn't have sent me to escort you in. Aurora may not always agree with you, but she does love you."

Looking up, Jemima's eyes were filled with tears. "I would not have wished harm to come to my girl. I didn't know about Radcliff. You must believe me."

"Of course." Just the mention of that monster, made the hair on the back of Garrett's neck stand up.

"I think Aurora may have gone to her father for help, but they were already married, what could he do. It was too late and nothing could be done. It was Rhys who told me after Radcliff was dead." She shook her head. "But Hexon..."

Not sure what to say, Garrett let her talk without interruption.

"He is always so gentlemanly. He's a duke. I know this house is unusual, but to become so angry. I would never have guessed it. Do you think he would have become violent?" She looked at him with wide, desperate eyes.

"I don't know, my lady. I think he was far too drunk for company and if his goal was to wed Aurora, he didn't like all he'd discovered about her in the past few days."

A tear escaped and she brushed it aside. "Why don't you seem put out by the idea of a lady born to an earl and widowed by another making herself less by fostering a school for girls?"

"I am in favor of anything that makes Lady Radcliff happy." Garrett gave her the truth, but no more.

Staring at him, she seemed intent on studying his face. After several beats, she shook herself. "Are you certain Aurora will wish me to dine with her tonight?"

He stood and offered his arm. "I have not a single doubt."

To Jemima's credit, she hesitated long enough to show

sincere doubt and remorse before taking the offered arm and allowing him to escort her into the dining room.

"Have I missed anything?" Malcolm fixed his cravat messily and tucked it inside his collar as he rushed in.

Poppy covered her grin with her hand. "Nothing of note."

Wesley placed his napkin on his lap. "Hexon is nursing a headache and won't be joining us."

Malcolm gave a nod and went to the empty chair across the table.

Aurora sat at the head of the table with the school's only students on her right and left. She spoke to Petra and only gave him a hint of a smile when he held the chair for her mother to the child's left.

In her element, Aurora made the girl smile and giggle over the soup of chicken and greens. White soup was often made with pork and Garrett assumed that in deference to both Geb and Miss Stein, she had instructed the cook to serve a chicken broth instead.

Within a moment, whatever Petra said intrigued Jemima enough to join in the conversation.

The strain on both girls' faces eased and as dinner commenced their fear was replaced with smiles.

CHAPTER FOURTEEN

Aurora sat in the conservatory long after the others had gone to bed. It was full dark and cloud cover kept any light the moon might offer at bay. She had a single candle to light her way. She really liked Whickette Park. It would make a fine school, and her plan to keep the number of students small and the school open minded felt right. Other than Hexon, everything about the plans and planning was good and rewarding.

Even the early and unexpected arrival of the Aasberg girls seemed to be well timed. She'd not expected their arrival and that of Miss Stein to trigger the drunken temper of the Hexon, but even that scene had come at the right time. The Wallflowers hadn't needed to instigate anything. Hexon showed his true colors without the least help from her friends. It would be some time before she could make amends to poor Miss Stein, but at least her mother would no longer foist the duke's attentions on her. If she was really lucky, maybe it would be the end of any matchmaking attempts by her parent.

She just couldn't see herself allowing another man to lord power over her. Garrett's warm smile and kind eyes flashed in her mind. He said he wanted her, and it hadn't been easy to reject him. Yet, fear grew at the notion of ever marrying again.

Footsteps sounded in the gallery which led from the front parlor to the back of the house and the glassed conservatory. Perhaps she should blow out her candle and stay hidden from whoever was striding so purposefully across the floors. A man, certainly. Not likely a servant. Could Hexon be sober enough to walk so decidedly already?

Probably not.

Garrett, Geb, Malcolm, or Wesley then. Though she couldn't imagine Wesley would leave his wife's bed to wander the halls in the middle of the night.

She fingered the sapphire end of her hat pin in case it was Malcolm, but she felt certain the sound of the gait was Garrett. Her heart did a little jump knowing it was likely Garrett making his way toward her.

He stopped in the doorway. "I wish you would not sit here alone with certain gentlemen still under this roof."

Without his cravat tied and no coat, the full breadth of his wide shoulders filled the threshold. A dark smattering of hair peeked from the open collar. Concern darkened his eyes even in the light of the three-candle candelabra he held aloft.

"How did you know I was not in bed?" Aurora leaned back on the arm of the long settee. It was one of two matching pieces that stood filling the center of the conservatory. The navy-blue cushions had seen better days, but the furniture was comfortable and the color rich against the marble floors.

Garrett entered, put his candelabra on the floor to the right of the settee and sat next to her. "I didn't. After the scene in the parlor, I couldn't sleep and thought to ease my worry by having a look around the house. Just to make sure Hexon hadn't gone on another drunken rage."

Everything Garrett had done in the past few days showed a man who was thoughtful and kind. He'd accepted her decisions, let her fight her own battles and stood ready to join her cause if needed. Had he always been so attuned to her needs?

Brushing the thought aside, she turned her attention back to the dark. "It was ugly, but it's better to know his true character sooner than later."

"Were you warming to your mother's idea of him courting you?" Something dangerous crackled in his voice.

"No." She shifted to face him. "I never even considered the idea. However, now Mother knows his character and he will likely leave the county sooner rather than later."

"What will you do if he does not intend to vacate with haste?" Garrett made the inquiry lightly, but that steel remained in his tone.

Aurora had thought a lot about this problem. "What will you do?"

"I am not master of this house, Rora. I am happy to deal with Hexon for you, but not without your leave to do so."

"Do not all men take charge and barrel through a lady's problems as if they had a right to do so?" She was poking a dragon and she knew it, yet she couldn't stop herself.

He filled his cheeks with air and blew it out slowly. "I will not be lumped in with all the men you speak of. It is unfair for you to put me into some category of male bullies you have conjured in your head."

Guilt swelled inside her. "It is. I apologize."

As if she hadn't spoken, he continued. "I understand the propensity, Rora. Your father was a bully and even Rhys can be pushy."

"His wife has him well in hand," she laughed.

"Indeed." Garrett let a smile slip before turning serious again. "What you have told me of Radcliff shows he was a monster. I am not any of those men. You are a bright, resourceful woman of an age and situation where you can act and speak for yourself. I am only curious as to how you will deal with the duke should he not remember his behavior or choose not to remove himself from Whickette."

"I will ask him to leave." Her stomach turned but she was resolved.

"May I ask another question?"

She nodded.

"If it had been Hexon or Renshaw rather than me tonight in the dark, what would you have done?" He watched her with those intense light brown eyes.

"I surmised it was you long before you arrived at the door. Hexon's steps would not have been so steady after all his drinking, and Malcolm has a slower gait. Besides, he and

I came to an understanding this afternoon. However, if I was in danger, I have weapons at my disposal."

"Do you?" There was amusement in Garrett's voice.

She touched the sturdy metal figure of a dog on the table next to her, looked Garrett in the eye and slid a long hat pin from her coiffed hair. "This usually is enough of a surprise to give a lady time to run or at the very least find another weapon or even to land a well-placed kick."

Garrett took the pin by the large ruby and studied it. He touched his finger to the sharp end and grinned. "I had no idea young ladies were so resourceful, but I suppose I should have known. Is this type of armament common?"

"I couldn't say, but the Wallflowers of West Lane are generally thus armed and exceedingly careful. Wesley's young sisters have begun to keep a hat pin handy too. You would be surprised how often men who call themselves gentlemen forget themselves." She took back her pin and slid it carefully into her hair.

"It is difficult to imagine you using it, but before today, I couldn't have imagined Mercy taking up a statue to bludgeon a man. However, now I can certainly visualize the event. I've never been thus attacked by a woman." He leaned his elbows on his knees, his grin in place.

Aurora liked the way his hair curled slightly at the collar and she wondered if it was soft or coarse. "I'm pleased to hear you have never taken liberties that might cause a lady to protect herself or her virtue."

"I prefer a lady be willing and enthusiastic," he chuckled.

Something knotted low in Aurora's stomach. "Have you had many lovers, Garrett?"

Now he sat straight and fidgeted. "I'm not a virgin, Rora, but to say more would not be gentlemanly."

It shouldn't bother her if he had a dozen mistresses. Yet, the idea sent a cold chill to her bones. "I suppose I should retire for the night. It was kind of you to check the house. In fact, all your actions today have been very helpful. Thank you."

He stood and offered his hand to her. Once she took it and rose, he kissed her fingers. "It is nothing. Anyone would have done the small things I managed. It is nothing to send the servants to prepare rooms and stand ready when a peer acts an ass."

It was more than that, but she wasn't ready to discuss how his help had affected her. "Well, I appreciate it none the less."

They walked through the fine gallery to the parlor before making their way to the foyer and up the stairs. He was a steady force beside her through the day and part of her wanted the feeling to continue.

She stopped in front of her door and looked at him in the candlelight. It was hard to catch her breath while her heart beat so quickly. "I think my brother will arrive with Faith and Nick tomorrow."

Something sad passed through his eyes. "Then with Rhys here and Hexon gone, I will likely take my leave the following day."

Overcome with worry and fear, which she couldn't explain, she gripped his hands. "You must have other commitments that you've put aside for me. I'm sorry to have kept you from more important matters."

Leaning in, he kissed her forehead. "Oh, my dear Rora, there is nothing more important to me than you. However, I will leave the day after tomorrow. I have business in Scotland and then in London."

It was hard to know what to do or say. She didn't want him to leave her. The idea of being in her own room alone and without comfort suddenly scared her. It was ridiculous since she'd been without male company for over two years and had not enjoyed a moment of her husband's company. Yet, this was not Radcliff and the events of the day had left her feeling fragile. "I understand, but I will miss your company."

He tipped his head to one side and studied her. "Will you?"

"I may not be capable of returning your generous feelings, Garrett, but that does not mean I don't enjoy your friendship and company." There. She sounded perfectly competent.

Those beautiful lips tipped up and he looked stunning in the dim hall outside her bedroom. "Good night, Rora."

"I have brandy." The words blurted out of her mouth before she could stop them.

"I beg your pardon?" He had half-turned to continue down the hall, but stopped and returned his gaze to hers.

Gathering her bravery, she closed her eyes a moment and drew in a long breath. She couldn't go on as a sad lonely widow. Opening her eyes, she found him staring at her. "In my room. I have brandy. Would you care for a glass?"

"Are you inviting me into your bedroom, Rora?" Something dark and dangerous vibrated in the low tone of his voice.

She nodded and spoke quickly. "For a drink. I'm not ready to sleep and it has been a long day with much to keep my mind occupied."

Wordlessly, he reached behind her and opened her door.

The newly oiled hinges were silent and a small fire lit the well-appointed room.

Swallowing down her nerves, Aurora turned and entered. It was the master's chamber that Aurora had claimed. It was her house after all. It took a concentrated effort to keep her eyes off the large bed with heavy drapes as Garrett closed the door and sealed them inside. "It's more masculine than I would choose, but it's a nice room."

Aurora walked to the table where a crystal decanter stood with two glasses. She poured and only startled slightly when Garrett came close to put his candelabra on the table.

The scent of soap and fresh air hung on him in the most alluring way. She missed it when he moved away to add a log to the fire. Late summer brought with it cooler nights.

As the log sparked, Garrett stood watching the flames with one hand on the mantel. "I'm more than a little surprised you would invite me into your room."

Steeling her nerves, she crossed to him with the glasses and handed him one. "I'm not some maiden aunt. I'm a grown woman."

Eyes full of passion, he put the glass on the mantel and faced her. "Oh? Are you inviting me in for more than a drink?"

She put her own glass next to his and the move brought her an inch from him. She craned her neck to look at him. "To be honest, I don't know what I want. I didn't wish to be alone. Does that make me very selfish?"

"No." The word came out on a breath, and he ran his knuckles along her jaw. "You are never selfish. I have to warn you though; if you have some notion of offering yourself in hopes that I will be too gentlemanly to accept, you are mistaken. I will not be strong enough to resist such a gift."

"You've had many lovers. Perhaps I could be just one more." Her pulse pounded so hard in her ears; it was a wonder he didn't comment on the noise. She'd given no thought to sex in the years since Radcliff died. At least not until these last months when Garrett had come back into her life. Before Radcliff's death, sex had been an event to dread when he was sober enough to manage and when he wasn't he often beat her for his deficiency.

"I never said that, and you could never be just anyone, not to me." He leaned in a fraction and the heat of him swept over her.

Her breasts ached and awareness sparked between her legs. "I think I'm aroused by you, Garrett."

His hand slid around her back and wrapped around her waist, easing her forward to feel his passion. "Why do you sound as if that's such a surprise?"

Standing stock-still, she caught her breath. "It has never happened before."

Like the wings of a butterfly, he let his lips graze her temple. "Never?"

"Once, when we danced at the ball, I thought perhaps I should consider taking a lover." She admitted though her cheeks flushed.

His smile stretched. "You danced with me and considered taking someone else as a lover? I don't know if I should be flattered or offended."

"Considering our current proximity, it would be better if you were flattered." Her voice lost its steadiness as fear worked its way into her bravado.

"Shall I help you out of your gown, Rora?" Soft assuredness warmed his voice.

With a nod, Aurora turned her back to expose the laces of her gown. "I'm a little afraid, Garrett."

His hands stilled. "I would never hurt you. You must know that."

"I know and if it were anyone else, I would not mention my trepidation. You have always been one of the few people I trust. I thought you should know." She tried to calm her breathing but despite her resolve to relieve her desire, she couldn't separate the act from her past.

Once her gown was untied, he slid the fabric down and kissed her shoulder. "You are in control, sweetheart. Look at me."

She turned and watched as he pulled his shirt over his head. Her heart skipped with excitement and not fear at the sight of his broad chest with a dark smattering of hair, muscles that tapered to his abdomen and disappeared beneath his breeches.

"You look very fine." Reaching to touch him, she pulled back a moment before her skin met his.

Garrett snatched up her hand and placed the palm on his chest. He reached behind and slid the hat pin from her hair. "You needn't skewer me. Your command will be enough should you wish to stop."

Unable to help herself, she grinned back at him. She stepped out of the puddle of her gown. With only her corset and shift, she felt exposed, but not afraid. This was nothing like the times whenever Radcliff had invaded her bedchamber. Running her fingers over his small nipple drew a sharp breath from him. There was power in bringing pleasure and a strange satisfaction she'd never expected.

Wishing her voice could be steadier, she forced out her desire. "Will you untie my corset?"

Before she could turn, he wrapped his arms around her and drew her close enough for her to place her cheek on his warm hard chest while he worked at her laces. When they fell to the floor, he discarded the boned restraint and carried her to the bed.

Like a piece of fragile crystal, he eased her to the mattress. "You are so beautiful."

Unable to move or breathe, she stared as he toed off and discarded his boots and his breeches went next. Completely naked, he stood beside the bed. His warm skin glowing in the firelight. His shaft stood proudly from his body.

Panic bloomed in her chest. "I don't know if I can do this." She rolled to her side and pulled her knees up to wrap her arms around them.

The bed dipped and Aurora stiffened, but then his arms wrapped around her while his body formed to hers. "Shh. Do not make yourself uneasy. You are in charge. Remember? You can tell me no and that will be the end of it."

"You wouldn't be disappointed?" Tears choked her.

A low rumble of laughter brightened the mood. "I would be extremely disappointed, but not angry or regretful. I want you, Rora, but if it is not mutual, it would be nothing. You said you were aroused. Has that feeling left you?"

"No." The truth of her denial was surprising. "But the act has held nothing but pain and shame for me in the past."

He kissed her back.

A thrill spiraled to every inch of her flesh.

"I am so sorry, sweetheart. Lovemaking should be full of joy and pleasure and love when possible."

As she relaxed, her body formed to his like pieces of a puzzle long separated. "I have no knowledge of what you describe."

A low whisper along with a kiss vibrated at her ear and with it her body roared with need. Garrett said, "You have a choice, my dearest. You can trust me enough to show you how precious this can be, you can tell me to go, or I can hold you for as long as you wish and nothing more."

No anger. No disgust. He laid out choices, two of which would leave them both unsatisfied, as if the decision was truly hers. Doubt flooded her. "Surely, you will not be satisfied with any but the first."

"I would hold you through the night and be happy to do so. But I'll not lie and say I do not wish for more. I want to show you how much can be shared in a loving bed. But the decision shall always be yours, this night and always." He placed one brief kiss behind her ear.

"I'm afraid, Garrett, but I do trust you." She tried not to tremble but failed as her words shook.

Another kiss, this time on her cheek. "How about we drink that brandy now?"

Shocked and relieved, she sat up and watched him walk across the room to the mantel. His rear, round and firm, was as fine to look at as his front. She blushed but scanned down to his very muscular legs.

He didn't turn as he clasped both glasses. His shoulders rose and fell on a long breath. "Why don't you slip under the covers?"

Happy to cover herself, she did as he suggested and sat with her back against the carved wooden headboard. She propped up a few pillows behind her and tried to hide that she watched him walk back gloriously naked.

A knowing smile on those lips that made her more and more curious, he handed her a glass before sliding under the sheet and propping up his own pillows. He sipped. "I wonder that you haven't seen a naked man before with the way you gawked at me."

Nearly sputtering out her brandy, she wiped the drip from her chin. "I have," she protested. "However, you look much finer than the one I have seen before."

"My ego is properly fed, and I feel quite good about myself," he laughed. "What I have been privileged to see of you, is also very fine."

She took another sip. "It is not that I fear you, Garrett. I wouldn't wish for you to think my trepidation is a reflection on your character. It is the act itself that I vowed never to endure again. And yet..."

Sliding lower, he held the glass in one hand and propped his head on the other. "And yet?"

Aurora drank down the remaining liquor and let it burn down her throat before she put the glass on the side table. She slid down, propped her head on her hand and faced him. Ignoring the warmth that flooded her cheeks, she confessed, "I have a need burning inside me. I didn't even know it was there, but it has grown within me for a few months now. I find the longer I am in your presence, the more I want to know how to relieve this yearning."

Garrett blinked. "I have no idea what I expected you to say, but that was not it. Good lord, Rora. He put his drink aside and ran his hand over his face. "You do not make this easy and you will make me think far too much of myself."

"I don't think that is likely." She knew him well enough to know he'd never become vain or have false pride. Still, she liked knowing he'd enjoyed the compliment.

Tracing a finger along her cheek, down her neck and then down her arm where it lay atop the blanket, he said, "You needn't decide tonight."

His touch set her skin on fire and the need that had pooled between her legs grew with renewed force.

"No? I suppose you will go and have a good laugh at what I put you through." She pushed back tears. "You will leave in two days and my ridiculous fear will be forgotten."

Garrett's eyes burned as he leaned forward. "There is nothing to laugh about. I may go, but being here with you is an honor, Rora. Do you think I love you less for having feelings and needs that are natural and just? That you thought to explore those needs with me is a tremendous gift."

Before she could form a single word, he pulled her bottom lip between his and then the top. His tongue touched the crease between her lips and repeated the gentle suckle on her bottom lip.

No kiss had ever been so sweet and so erotic. Unable to help herself, she gasped from the shock of desire that lit her entire body.

"Are you afraid?" he asked against her lips.

She shook her head.

"Kiss me back then."

Following his lead and her instincts, she moved her lips on his. It was like being kissed everywhere at once. His tongue touched hers and her lower abdomen clenched with want of more. Unable to resist, she slid her fingers into his hair and found it soft as China silk.

He moaned at her touch, and his pleasure drew even more desire. It was hard to catch her breath and she didn't want to. Pressing close to him, she let all her soft curves align with his hard edges.

He cradled her head, coaxed her to tip right and deepened the kiss.

Sighing with steady pants, she clutched his arm, his shoulder and then his back. When his hand wrapped around her bottom and pulled her against his arousal, she groaned with need but felt no fear. "Garrett?"

Leaning his forehead against hers, he drew in long breaths. "Rora, if you will let me, I would like to show you pleasure. I can be satisfied to give you what you long for this night. Will you trust me?"

"I don't understand." She wanted to know what he meant, wanted to give him something of herself.

His fingers were rough with small calluses as they caressed her hip, then down the back of her leg and to her knee. Every inch of skin he touched burned and she wanted to cry with the joy of it. He touched between her knees, separated them before sliding up and massaging the inside of her thigh.

The need at her core grew almost painful as did her fear, but she wanted to know, to give. She would give him this for loving her. Even if she couldn't love him the way he deserved, he would have some piece of her.

As he skimmed up to her center, she stiffened and clamped her knees shut. Waiting for him to pry them apart, she held her breath.

Instead, he ran one finger along the top of her clenched thighs to the space above where she'd been hurt in her marriage. He was gentle and her legs relaxed as if she were not in control.

Pausing, he asked. "Are you alright, sweetheart?"

"I don't know." Her voice was rough and strange. Her hips lifted to his finger.

"The instant you wish it, I will stop. Do you understand?"

She nodded, eyes squeezed shut.

"Look at me," he whispered and stilled that delicious alluring finger.

Forcing her eyes open, she was rewarded with his steady admiring gaze. Her body thrummed with untapped desire mixed with the fear that had been beaten into her. Yet this man would never harm her.

He lowered his head and kissed her collar bone before pulling loose the ribbon of her chemise. The lightest tug and the warm air touched her breasts. He traced the tip of his tongue around her nipple.

Aurora gasped and clutched his back while her other hand gripped his hair and pulled him closer.

A low moan and he pulled the sensitive peak into his mouth.

Her back arched off the mattress, wanting more and not knowing how she'd never known there was this kind of delight. Tears spilled from the corners of her eyes. "I didn't know."

Lifting on his elbow, he kissed her lips. "It's okay." He kissed away her tears. "You're okay."

Her breasts full and her thighs quivering, she pressed against him, needing more but not knowing how to ask.

Staring into her eyes with so much love, he slid his hand between her thighs and parted her folds. His finger slid along her crease with gentleness that sent her hips rising from the bed.

She cried out as he touched her center. He muffled her cries with his mouth and captured every moan, groan and scream of delight. All the while, his finger circled and teased then dipped barely inside.

"Rora, I want to taste you. Can you hold that delicious

tongue long enough for me to heighten your pleasure?" He pressed tiny kisses to her cheek, chin and the tip of her nose.

She covered her mouth with her hand. The idea of the house knowing they were behaving so wantonly would be too much embarrassment to handle.

Garrett chuckled before he kissed his way down her neck. Suckling each breast in turn, her body thrummed with something wild and spectacular. Her insides tightened like the string of a bow pulled and ready to fling its arrow. Rib by rib, his lips and tongue fired delight before he dipped his tongue into her navel and she had to pull a pillow to her mouth to stop the cry from escaping

It was just as well for when his mouth covered her most sensitive place, she could not have stopped the scream of pleasure that escaped and was caught by the pillow. Still, the pressure built inside her while his tongue made magic between her legs. Lips and tongue teased and delighted until she thought she might explode. Her body pulled in on itself and let go with a release that rocked her. She shook with unimaginable pleasure. Her hand released his hair and with both she clutched the pillow as waves of pleasure rolled over her.

Garrett drew the pillow away and pulled her into his arms as the ecstasy ebbed and withdrew. He whispered words of love in her ear, but her mind was too absorbed in the experience to recognize the meaning.

arrett might never be as happy as he was at this moment holding Aurora in his arms after bringing her pleasure. "Are you alright, dearest?"

With her cheek pressed to his chest, she nodded. "I had no idea."

The tears in her voice shocked him and he pressed two fingers under her chin to lift her eyes to his. "You must have known what happened during your marriage was not normal."

"Of course. And my friends claimed the act held pleasure, but I..." Crystal eyes shone back at him, she blushed and buried her face against his chest. "Thank you, Garrett." She shuddered. "Would you like to take your pleasure now?"

His heart missed a beat even as his shaft reacted to the idea. "Tonight was for you. I shall be content with your joy."

Pulling her head back she met his gaze. "That hardly seems fair."

"If you will let me hold you for a few more minutes before sending me to my own bed, I will have more than I ever dared hope for." He knew he was ruined for all other women after tasting Aurora and hearing her pleasure. Causing her to show emotion and scream out her orgasm would be a memory held in his heart for a lifetime. Yet she had told him she would never marry and those words rang in his mind and had to be pushed aside before they ruined his perfect moment.

"I don't mind you holding me a while longer." She encircled his waist with her arm.

He longed to propose, to demand she marry him. However, he knew she would reject him and it would be his undoing. Perhaps he needed to be patient. He closed his eyes against the wave of possessiveness that flooded through him.

The first light of a new day shone through the east facing window.

"I must go." He kissed the top of her head. "The servants will wake soon and I shouldn't be caught leaving your room."

She sat up and pulled the sheet up to cover herself. "And you must leave tomorrow?"

If he stayed, would she invite him to her bed again? Would she soften to the idea of a lifetime with him? He did not want Aurora as a mistress or a lover for a time. He longed for her for a lifetime. "I should go to Scotland and see my steward. You will be safe once Hexon is gone."

"I would like to spend more time like this." Her blush was enough to turn any man to mush.

The truth was harder than he expected, but she deserved as much. Still, he held back. "I don't think delaying my travels is a good idea. I only stayed this long to ensure you and the others in the party were safe."

"I see." Her usual calm mask fell into place. "I shall see you later today then."

"Of course." Pressing his lips to hers, he let her warmth fill him once again. "You really are the most magnificent woman, Rora. Never let anyone force you to settle. You should have everything the world has to offer."

With a brief look into those startled eyes, he left and found his own bed for a few hours of sleeplessness.

Garrett went down to breakfast room, where Hexon nursed a bad head. With a nod to the other duke, he took a plate and filled it. His night of pleasure left him hungrier than usual. "Can you see if there is coffee, Bickford?"

"Of course, Your Grace." Bickford took the empty carafe and exited.

Hexon's plate was empty save half a piece of dry toast. He

sipped a cup of tea. "I suppose I made an ass of myself last night."

Nodding, Garrett said, "You did. Do you remember it all?"

"Not as much as I should and more than I wish to." Hexon held his head in one hand and put the teacup down. "I'm not inclined to approve of the group under this roof, but it was not my plan to act ungentlemanly."

"I'm afraid whatever your plan was, it failed miserably." Garrett ate a large piece of sausage.

Hexon's skin looked a bit green and he looked away from Garrett's plate. "I shall leave as soon as my stomach settles enough to travel. I don't suppose a bid for Lady Radcliff's hand would be welcomed now."

Continuing to indulge in the food on his plate despite its effect on Hexon, Garrett said, "If it makes you feel any better, you had little chance before your display of intolerance and temper."

"I'm a duke. I thought all women wanted to marry a duke." Hexon nibbled a small piece of toast and forced down some tea afterward.

Garrett shrugged. "Lady Radcliff is not like other women. I have known her since childhood and she has always marched to a different tune. I hope you will not follow through with your ridiculous threats of ruination. If you should travel that path, you will have to deal with me. I am very fond of this family and will not tolerate anyone doing them harm."

Hexon pressed his napkin to his mouth and then waved it in dismissal. "Whatever I said, I don't recall. I don't approve of this school or the type of friends her ladyship keeps, but who am I to ruin a widow. I think arriving at her mother's invitation might have been a misstep."

With a shrug, Garrett said, "The first of many, Hexon. You will have no problems finding another lady of good fortune who will be more to your taste."

Grumbling, he stood and left the breakfast room holding his head.

Bickford brought coffee and poured a cup for Garrett.

"Thank you, Bickford." Garrett had a thought. "Perhaps you might see if the cook has something for the Duke of Hexon's head and stomach. The sooner he's feeling better the sooner he will be on his way."

Eyebrows raised, Bickford nodded. "I shall see to His Grace's well-being myself."

Garrett laughed over a fork full of coddled eggs.

"You seem pleased this morning." Helen stepped in and took a seat to his left.

His mind slipped immediately to his night with Aurora, but he said, "I suppose I shouldn't be pleased that Hexon is under the weather, but I'm only human."

A footman brought her a cup of chocolate and a plate with toast.

"Thank you, Ben." Helen pulled the crock of butter from the center of the table and spread some on her toast. "Does his illness mean His Grace won't be leaving?"

Shrugging, Garrett ate the last of his eggs and leaned back in his chair with his cup of coffee. "I hope not. Bickford is caring for him. Let us hope the butler knows his remedies for a night in the bottle."

Aurora strode into the breakfast room. "Ben, I overslept. Is there coffee still."

"Yes, my lady. A new pot just brewed for His Grace." The tall blond footman, poured a cup and set it at the head of the table.

"Thank goodness." She sat and sipped.

It was impossible for him not to stare at her rosy cheeks and perfectly smooth hair. In a violet day dress, her eyes were bright and he wondered if it was the effect of the night or just the color of the dress. He'd like to think he was the cause for her added radiance.

"I'm glad you needed coffee as well, Garrett." She grinned over the rim of her cup.

With a nod, he said, "I'm happy to have obliged."

Helen's gaze shifted from one to the other before settling her attention on Aurora. "You're looking very sunny as well, my lady."

"It's only us here. Won't you call me Aurora?"

"As you wish."

Aurora sighed. "I suppose I've woken in a good mood. Do we know if Hexon is on his way to... wherever dukes go?"

"Not yet, but I think it eminent. He did seem regretful for his behavior if not apologetic." Garrett put down his empty cup.

"I suppose that shows some intelligence, but too little too late."

Another footman bustled in with some kind of fizzing liquid, looked around then sprinted out and up the servants' stairs.

When she'd chewed and swallowed her bit of toast, Helen drank down some chocolate. "He was very keen on you, Aurora. Did he ever have a chance at winning you? If he'd behaved in a more gentlemanly manner, could he have won you?"

"No." Aurora practically spat out the word. "I had no interest in the Duke of Hexon, nor would I ever have. The men my mother sends are not all bad catches, but they are not for me. After all, Lord Castlewick was one of Mother's finds and now look how happily he is married to Mercy."

Helen stood. "We have some work to do to make the old nursery into a classroom. I thought that would do for as long as we have only two students. I want to spend some time with the young ladies today and find out their interests. If this is to be the type of school that enhances the minds of women, we need to do things differently than a random finishing school."

Once Helen strode out looking very pleased, Garrett said, "Are you well this morning, Rora?"

Her cheeks pinkened. "Quite well."

"I plan to stay today and quit Cheshire tomorrow morning. It will give me a chance to see Rhys and the others when they arrive, and you will have no need for me here. I'm happy the school will work out." His longing to tell her again that he loved her and wanted her for all time, had to be tamped down. More would have to change than a night in each other's arms to alter Aurora's resolve.

Staring into her cup, she said, "I shall be sorry to see you go."

His heart leaped in his chest. "I will be sorry to leave you."

A great commotion sounded from the foyer complete with barking dog and Faith's voice raised in a scolding. "Rumple, no!"

Faith walked in. Her hair had sprung loose from its bindings as she pulled her bonnet off. "Good gracious, you're still at breakfast. Are we too early?"

Aurora accepted the kiss from her friend. "Not at all. I overslept and stole in for a bit of coffee."

Garrett stood and bowed. "If you are hungry, I think there is still sausage and coddled eggs to be had."

Searching the sideboard, Faith said. "I wouldn't mind a cup of chocolate."

Ben said, "Right away, madam." And scurried from the room.

Faith sat across from the seat Helen had vacated. "We stopped in town last night and stayed at The Smoker. It's a nice little inn."

Aurora gasped. "Why didn't you come to Whickette directly? You were so close."

The door opened, admitting Nick and Rhys. Nick dropped his gloves and hat on the chair near the door where Faith had left her bonnet. "We couldn't come in so late and intrude on your planned dinner. Is there no butler?"

Garrett shook hands with both. "Bickford has his hands full with a... situation this morning."

Rhys kissed his sister's cheek. "I heard mother was bringing Hexon to court you. Is he the situation?"

"We should go to the parlor and shut the door. I'll tell you all you have missed." Aurora drew a long breath and her gaze caught Garrett's.

Not all, he thought.

Garrett used spending time with the new arrivals as an excuse to be near Aurora. He knew he had to leave, but it wasn't going to be easy.

"Must you leave tomorrow, Garrett?" Faith asked while they all sat in a conversational grouping of two settees and four overstuffed chairs.

He nodded. "I'm afraid so. I put off my travel north for long enough. I believe I shall let out my Scotland home. I've no need for it now that I've inherited. If I can find a good tenant and my steward will check in quarterly, I can take an item off my list of worries."

A carriage rolled to a stop outside. Nick eased to the window as if an attacking force might be arriving. "It would seem someone is taking his leave today."

The words were only just out of his mouth when the door opened and Hexon stepped through. He bowed. "Lady Radcliff, I must take my leave of you."

Aurora walked to the duke and curtsied. "I hope your travels will be safe, Your Grace."

Scanning the room full of onlookers, Hexon opened his mouth to say more, then stepped back and bowed to the room. He turned and skulked out.

The carriage pulled away a few moments later.

Poppy sat with Rhys on the settee so close they might have been one being. After their short separation, she seemed unwilling to allow any space between her husband and herself. "At least that's one less thing to worry about. We'd hardly begun our plan. I suppose he wasn't really worth the effort."

Rhys narrowed his gaze. "Did the three of you run the Duke of Hexon off?"

"Certainly not." Aurora gave her brother a wicked grin. "As Poppy said, we'd hardly started when his narrow mind and bad habits had him tripping over his own feet. Besides, I'll not marry and even if I considered it, it won't be to anyone Mother brings calling. No offense, Wesley."

"None taken." Wesley grinned and put an arm around Mercy's waist.

Shaking his head, Rhys sighed. "Is mother in a bad temper over the situation."

Aurora took up the metal statue that had nearly been used as a weapon. She seemed to consider the weight and put it down again. "Surprisingly not. Mother was just as disgusted by Hexon's display as the rest of us."

The door opened revealing Helen, Miss Stein, and Malcolm. "I beg your pardon," Helen said. "I didn't realize you had more company, my lady."

They stepped back intending for she and Miss Stein to leave.

Malcolm walked in smiling. His entire attitude different from when he first arrived.

Aurora rushed to the ladies. "Not at all. Come and join us. I want Miss Stein to meet the rest of my friends and then since the weather is fine, I thought we might collect the girls and go for a walk."

Malcolm shook hands with Nick and Rhys. "Shall I go find Mr. Arafa for the walk?"

"Is Geb here?" Nick asked.

Garrett nodded. "Arrived two days ago."

"This is more house party than school, Rora." Rhys laughed, but stood and crossed to meet Miss Stein.

Once introductions and the finding of the rest of the party was completed, they strode into the garden and headed up the hill toward the stone circle.

Wilhelmina and Petra ran ahead while Faith, a great hater of walking, lagged behind with Nick by her side. The others made their way in a large group within reach of the girls and chatted about the plans for the school.

Garrett let his gait slow so that there was distance between the larger group and the lagging Duke and Duchess of Breckenridge. He wasn't certain she'd want to speak to him, but his heart jolted when Aurora slowed enough to walk beside him. It took a force of will to keep from holding her hand so he clasped his behind his back. "It seems Wesley is very keen on this venture of yours. It was good of you to include him."

Rushing up to keep the girls on track, Wesley made some comment that caused a bout of giggling.

"It has all worked out." Aurora clasped her hands to her elbows in front of her. "I didn't know you planned to let Thwackmore, Garrett. Are you in financial difficulty?"

"I am not, but it seems such a waste to leave the place empty. I rarely used it when it was my only country holding. Now I have two others that will need my attention. It seems a wise course to keep the Corwin holding for use, and let out the baronetcies until I may have a son to inherit."

A sorrow crept into her watery eyes. "You will have to marry then."

"Of course. I have responsibilities, Rora. You must realize." He wanted to grab her up and tell her he would only ever love her and beg her to marry him.

"Yes." She pulled her shoulders back. "Of course, you do. I don't know why I said that."

There was that mask she wore so well, tightly holding back her emotions. But he had seen those bonds break when he held her in his arms. If he lived ten lifetimes, he would never forget the passion he'd seen inside his Aurora.

Time for a change of subject, lest she run away. "What did you do to Renshaw. He's practically simpering with congeniality."

Indeed, Malcolm was laughing and joking with the others as if he'd never been in a bad temper or demanded the notion of the school be put aside.

Aurora shrugged. "It seemed he'd not wanted to court me any more than I wanted to be courted. I gave him leave to search for his family treasure. If it is not cataloged with the possessions of the house, he has my permission to keep whatever he finds for his family. It seems this has made him content."

"He's an unusual man." Garrett couldn't help his relief at one less suitor to worry over.

They walked in silence for a few minutes. The others had nearly reached the stones while Nick and Faith were far behind, leaving the two of them virtually alone.

Aurora cleared her throat and looked at him. "I don't want you to think your leaving is wanted."

Heart in his throat, he said, "I will see you when you return to London. I shall call if you will inform me when you arrive."

"We all return in a fortnight." Her throat bobbed in several swallows. "I hope you will come to call. I shall miss you. You probably think me a fool."

"I am deeply touched that you might miss my presence when you have so many friends around you, Rora. You may call on me any time." He wished with all his heart, she would call on him to be her company, but he knew full well, she would not.

The girls squealed with delight as they ran around the ancient ring of stones.

"Spirited girls," Aurora said grinning.

"Much like you were. Why do you suppose people have children if they don't want them to act like children?" Garrett wondered aloud, not expecting an answer.

"For the same reason you must marry." There was a bitterness in her voice he'd never heard before.

Touching her arm, he halted her then waited for Nick and Faith to pass them by.

Faith did a poor job of hiding a grin.

Anger and disappointment swam inside him. "Aurora, my duty aside, any child of mine will be loved." He reined in the anger, but his frustration couldn't be harnessed completely. "I would marry you. I long to marry you. It is you who have proclaimed it impossible. I declared my love long before last night. You know my wishes and I respect yours. Please don't blame me for my obligations to my title and family. It isn't fair."

CHAPTER SIXTEEN

It wasn't fair. He was right. Still, Aurora bit her lip to keep her emotions tightly reined. "You're right. I set the standard and have no right for rancor. I wish you only happiness, Garrett."

They continued forward to join the group.

"Thank you, Rora." There was strain in his voice and she had put it there.

It pained her, but the idea of binding herself to another man for the rest of his life, was too terrifying. "I'm certain whoever you marry will be a fine lady and we shall all be good friends."

Suddenly nauseous, she rushed forward and joined the others, ending the conversation.

"How long have these stone stood here?" Petra pressed her hand to a stone, her large brown eyes full of wonder and curiosity.

Wesley sat cross legged on a humped bit of earth. "Some say thousands of years."

Wilhelmina leaned against a tall stone. "I hardly think that could be possible."

"Why not?" Miss Stein asked.

"I don't see how such primitive people could have organized and moved such great stones." The dark-haired twin seemed very sure of herself.

Esther Stein smiled and sat on the ground. Her dark blue day dress fluffed out around her legs. "I see your point, Miss Wilhelmina, but England's best scientists believe these stones date perhaps as much as four thousand years ago. No one knows how the people of that time might have moved such mammoth stones. It is intriguing, don't you think?"

Staring around her, Wilhelmina seemed to give the notion her full attention before sitting with her eyes narrowed in concentration. "I cannot fathom it."

Petra sat beside her sister. "What could they have meant to do with these circles?"

"Another good question, Miss Petra." Miss Stein was in her element. "Perhaps prayer or ritual. We don't know for certain."

"There are some Roman ruins down the hill. Not quite so old, but perhaps fifteen hundred years old or more." Wesley pointed in the direction of the ruins.

Both twins sprang up. "It is like an archaeological dig, Mina," Petra said with great excitement.

The girls ran down the hill skirts flying out behind them.

Standing, Wesley laughed. "I shall go and make certain they don't actually begin digging."

"They are quite bright." Mercy sat near Miss Stein.

"I agree. Both girls are full of interesting questions." Miss Stein pushed her hair behind her ear where several strands had escaped in the breeze.

Faith plopped down and sighed as if the walk had nearly done her in. "I hate to walk."

Giggling, Mercy sat as well. "Miss Stein, may we call you Esther when the children are not in hearing. We are a very informal group as long as none of our parents are present. Since the dowager remained at the house, it would be good to feel more intimate."

"I would be flattered, my lady." Miss Stein blushed and looked extremely pretty doing so.

"Mercy," she corrected.

Geb leaned on one of the stones then straightened and placed a palm against the hard surface. "They have a kind of life to them, do they not."

"I think so too." Mercy nodded. "I find the phenomenon as interesting as the girls. It's fascinating to think who might have erected these, and for what."

Helen found a fallen stone and sat on it as if she were still in the parlor. Her back was straight and she crossed her hands over a knee. "There is speculation that these were holy places for the Druids. Of course, little is known about them."

"It would be an interesting study," Geb thought out loud. His gaze shifted to Helen.

"Indeed." Helen's cheeks pinkened but she changed the

subject. "There are a great many mysteries in the world that could make for a lifetime of study."

"I think I would enjoy a lifetime of study." Geb nodded to the group, cast his gaze on Helen again then walked off toward the girls and Wesley.

Esther stood. "I shall make certain the girls are not driving his lordship mad."

Rubbing her foot, Faith said, "I like her a lot. She gave them only enough information to pique their curiosity. Rather brilliant."

Aurora had noted the same thing. "I think this will work out quite well. Helen, you must let me know if you need more help. I have no idea how many students we shall attract but I think for now we shall be happy with these two despite our intention of waiting a month or so."

"I will keep you informed, my... Aurora." Helen smiled.

They soon returned to Whickette Park for luncheon and though they were late, had a very good meal with Mother who was in disturbingly fine spirits.

Aurora went to her room to rest and think. She hated that she might have hurt Garrett, but how was it to be helped?

The rap at her door of three knocks, a pause, and then a fourth, told her a Wallflower wished to enter.

"Come in."

Faith stepped inside. "I thought we might have a chat."

Sitting at the small round table in the window niche, Aurora longed for a long chat but was wary of whatever thoughts had brought Faith to her. "Are you in need of council, or am I?"

Letting her giggle free, Faith said, "That depends." She sat and took Aurora's hand where it lay on the polished wood. "What is going on between you and Garrett?"

Lying to a Wallflower was impossible. She had over the years occasionally kept her own council, but to lie would only mean Faith would prod further until she had the full truth. "I'm not entirely sure. He has declared himself. I have told him I shall never marry."

Eyes wide and golden in the afternoon sunlight streaming through the window, Faith gawked at her. "He told you he loves you?"

Aurora nodded. "That was his secret. The one that had me so worried after your ball. He told me he has loved me since we were children."

"And you could not tell him you returned his feelings?"

A pang of regret knotted inside Aurora. "No. He is aware that I greatly esteem him, but to profess a love that cannot end happily seemed too cruel."

Faith cast her gaze down at the table. "Poor Garrett. How heartbroken he must be."

"Do not think me uncaring, Faith." She allowed her distress into her voice. "I would love him if I could. Of all the men in the world, he is the only one I regret hurting in such a way. I just can't."

Aurora stood and went to the window. She could just view the grove of walnut trees from there. Several people milled around in the garden. From below, she faintly heard Mercy playing pianoforte. The world went on as if nothing was amiss and yet, she was misplaced. Adrift. She gripped her stomach in hopes of stifling the clutching pain.

Faith's arms came around her. "Do not fret so, Aurora. If you cannot love him, there is nothing to be done about it. I'm certain you have been kind and Garrett didn't immediately quit the house, so he must forgive you. In fact, by the way the two of you were talking today, I thought perhaps you had become lovers."

Every muscle in Aurora's body tightened.

Faith pulled her around to face her. "Have you been lovers?"

Tears flooded Aurora's eyes. "In a manner of speaking, I suppose we have."

"He didn't do anything you didn't wish, did he?" Venom dripped from Faith's question.

Aurora shook her head. "No. Of course not. He gave me a gift. I know now that I had been misled by Radcliff, and lovemaking can be a pleasure to be savored."

"I am happy for you, Aurora." Faith smiled, but sorrow filled her eyes. "Still, you don't wish to think about marriage."

Pulling away, Aurora crossed to her bed and gripped the wooden post. "It is one thing to take a lover or two, and quite another to turn one's life over to a man. I can never imagine I will want to entrust my existence to a man again."

"But you may share his bed again?" Faith raised a brow.

Her feelings and her fears had warred the entire day over this very question. "I don't know. Garrett is kind and wonderful, but he is a duke and will have to marry. When he does, whoever his bride is will become a part of our lives. It shall be far too awkward as it is. An ongoing dalliance would only make things worse."

"Hmm. I see your point." Faith took Aurora's hand and led her back to the table where they both sat. "I am happy that you have found some pleasure with a man. Perhaps now, you can let go of the other memories that haunt you so. I know you can never forget. I cannot, and those things were not done to me. However, perhaps this is a welcomed step toward you letting joy back into your life, Aurora."

Garrett's dark-honey eyes filled her vision. He had given her joy and more. She'd trusted him. It was more than she'd ever hoped for. "Perhaps. Time will tell, Faith."

*D*inner was lively. There were more ladies than gentlemen, but that didn't harm the enjoyment. Petra and Wilhelmina were full of energy, though well mannered.

They spoke of little else but the standing stones.

Wesley said, "Our students convinced me to write a letter to the Royal Scientific Society to obtain the papers currently available regarding the stones around England. I have no idea what will be turned up, but I think it a fascinating project for the young ladies."

"Interesting." Helen sipped her soup.

A deep frown marred Wesley's handsome face. "I hope I haven't overstepped, madam. I only meant to help."

"Not at all, my lord. I am only intrigued that you have the connections that might produce those papers and get them sent here."

Geb put his spoon aside. "I find this entire thing most interesting. This school will be a model for how to truly educate."

"Because the ladies may study some archeology?" Esther Stein asked, her voice taking a sterner tone.

Waving off her censure, Geb said. "I am most certain you will teach your students all the courses that will make them as bright and smart as their contemporaries. But to also feed the imagination is a rare treat. Curiosity breeds dreams and dreams innovation. I predict great things to come from a new generation of young women."

Satisfied, Esther's mouth drew up in a lovely smile. "I see your point, Mr. Arafa."

"We shall do our best to make that a reality." Helen drew a deep breath and kept her gaze from meeting Geb's. "I deeply hope to change the way women see themselves, even if it is one girl at a time."

Esther nodded. "We cannot change an entire culture of men who think women simple and ornamental, but if we can teach women to believe themselves more, then one day the world will have to see the same thing."

"Present company excepted." Nick laughed. "My exposure to the Wallflowers of West Lane has cured me of any notions that women are inferior to men."

"I should hope so," Faith said meeting her husband's warm gaze.

Aurora loved a lively conversation and reveled in the banter.

Garrett sat next to Mother. "What do you think of a new kind of education for young ladies, countess?"

Aurora held her breath.

Jemima dabbed the corner of her mouth with her napkin. "A good education is always an asset. I still think these girls," She pointed to Mina and Petra, "will have to marry. They will need to know how to run a house and it never hurts to know how to paint, sew, and play an instrument. However, I think a better understanding of the world and all it has to offer can only enhance a life and a good marriage."

Meeting her mother's gaze, Aurora couldn't help the

flood of joy that filled her. She'd never thought she'd see the day when Mother would evolve beyond what was expected. Though, she held no hope that Jemima would stop trying to marry her off.

It was a perfect evening.

After dinner, the twins were sent to their room. Helen and Esther both excused themselves, claiming to be tired.

The other ladies went through to the parlor for cake and wine while the men went to a gaming room on the other side of the house. As soon as Garrett was out of her sight, Aurora felt his loss deeply. Telling herself she was acting the fool did no good.

"Mother, you seemed very content at dinner this evening. I suppose you're not missing Hexon's company." Aurora handed her mother a delicately painted blue and white plate with a piece of cake.

A rare smile pulled at Jemima's lips. "You were right about the duke, Aurora. I'll not pretend he could have been redeemed. I would not wish you to be married to a man who cannot control his drinking habits or his temper."

With an effort, Aurora said nothing about Radcliff's bad habits. It was her father who had chosen her husband and not her mother. When Father was alive, Mother had little to say in defense against him. Perhaps she might consider that her mother's marriage was not much happier than her own. "I'm relieved you see that."

Mother swallowed a bite of cake. "That does not mean I have given up on you marrying again. You are far too young and beautiful to never marry. Besides, I know you want children of your own and you would be a wonderful mother."

There, she had played the final card. Aurora couldn't

deny her desire to have children and she would always morn her inability to get with child while married. Nothing good had come of the union with Bertram Sherbourn, the Earl of Radcliff. Swallowing the bitterness of regret, she shrugged. "I appreciate your confidence in my mothering abilities. However, those talents will have to be spent on the children of my closest friends."

Poppy blushed, which was a rare sight.

Faith narrowed her eyes. "Poppy?"

"I wasn't going to tell you until we were back in London." Poppy's grin spread wide.

Mother jumped up nearly toppling her plate before she steadied herself and placed it on the table. "I'm going to be a grandmother?"

Nodding, Poppy's eyes went wide when her mother-in-law grabbed her up in a tight hug. Poppy patted Jemima's back awkwardly. "I'm glad you're pleased."

Recovering herself, Mother backed away and cleared her throat. "Well, of course I'm pleased you shall finally do your duty to both my son and his title."

Aurora stifled her amusement and pulled Poppy into a hug. She whispered, "High praise from Mother." Then in full voice, she added, "I'm so happy for you and Rhys."

"Thank you."

The five of them spoke of redecorating of the nursery both in the country and the one in London. Poppy had many plans and for the first time Mother didn't gainsay any of her ideas. Perhaps a small step for the better had been taken between Rhys's wife and his mother.

Aurora hoped for Poppy's sake that was true.

*L*ong past the time everyone took to their beds, Aurora stared up at the ceiling. The warm night left the grate cold, and she had opened the window, but little breeze helped to cool her. But it wasn't the heat that kept her up and she wouldn't pretend otherwise. It was unhealthy to lie to oneself.

It did no good to deny that she wanted more time with Garrett. She liked having him near, liked the steady tone of his voice and the way he always knew how to help without charging in and taking over.

Unfair as it was, she couldn't give him her heart. At eighteen she'd dived into her marriage fully expecting to love her husband and by the morning after her wedding night, she knew it could never be. Her heart had died that night and nothing could revive something so stale and dark.

Rising, she grabbed her wrap from the end of the bed. What harm could it do to say goodbye in private? She trod with light steps down the hall, took a deep breath at his door and knocked lightly.

If he was sleeping, he'd likely not hear the rap.

The door swung open. Garrett stood bare-chested; legs exposed with just his breeches on. Startled, he took her hand and pulled her in before checking the hall as he'd done the first time she'd come to his room. He closed the door making hardly a snick as the latch caught, then he slid the bolt. "Rora, couldn't you sleep?"

"No. Why are you half dressed?" It came out far more distressed than she intended.

He laughed. "I'm in my room and it's quite hot. I couldn't sleep and was attempting to read. Though with little success."

A book sat on the cushion of the chair near the hearth with a lighted candelabra on the small table. A glass of something amber awaited him as well. "I didn't mean to disturb you. It's only that I wanted to say goodbye without the others present."

"You came in the middle of the night to my bedroom to say goodbye?" He picked up the book and tossed it into his open trunk, which stood filled near the dressing room.

She sank into the other chair and put her head in her hands. "It sounds quite feeble even to my own ear. I just wanted to see you. To thank you."

"Thank me?" There was surprise in those two words.

So much, Aurora looked up from her palms. "Yes. You gave me a great gift last night."

He held up a hand and sliced the air to stop her.

Staring, she didn't know what to do. She'd upset him, but she couldn't fathom how. Still, she'd never witness such command from Garrett. It was clear he could take charge and overwhelm when he wished. A rumble of fear tightened her belly.

CHAPTER SEVENTEEN

*S*he'd come to thank him. Good God could anything be more absurd? "I do not require your thanks, Rora. Last night was a gift for you, but also for me."

Eyes as wide as a frightened doe, she stood and moved toward the door. "I shouldn't have come. This was foolish."

Wishing he had the right words and less temper, he stopped her by pressing his hand to the door. His body grazed hers. "I would never harm you, dearest. Not even when you are this offensive."

Turning, she stomped her foot. "How have I offended?

Before last night I thought relations between a man and me could only involve pain and mortification. You showed me something beautiful and asked nothing for yourself. Does that not deserve some kind of thanks?"

Wrapping his arms around her, he put his chin on the top of her head and let the soft scent of roses from her hair fill him and take away his rancor. "No, but I am glad to have given you something, considering what you shared with me."

"Why can't you speak plainly." Frustration cried out in her voice even as she pressed her cheek to his chest.

Awkwardness aside, he took her hand. "Come and sit and I will be as plain as I can."

She followed him and sat.

Garrett sat, then stood and paced. Finally, he knelt before her and kissed her fingers. "I want more from you, Rora. More than you're willing to give." He held up a hand to stop whatever apology she was planning to make. "It's not your fault. I love you and you cannot return those feelings. You are attracted to me, and you trust me, but while those are lovely things, they would not bind us in the long term. I'm going to Scotland and then London. I'm not going to renew my desires for you after tonight. I have bared my soul and cannot keep the wound opened indefinitely. I am honored and delighted that last night meant something to you. Seeing you in such a state of bliss will always be the finest moment of my life."

Her lips parted and the sight of her sweet tongue forced him to close his eyes.

Blinking, she said, "Should I leave you?"

"Do you want to leave?" Despite his resolve, he longed to hold her, to give them one more night. It could only harm his heart. Yet the memories he'd take with him…

She shook her head. "I do not want to leave you tonight. I want... I don't know how to ask for what I want." Her cheeks turned the most charming shade of pink.

Resting his head in her lap, he closed his eyes. "I'm not strong enough to say no to you and honestly, I don't want to. I long to hold you in my arms and show you delights. I wish you'd never married that monster, but I'm selfishly pleased that you've only known carnal pleasure with me."

"I'm glad it was you." Aurora ran her fingers through his hair. Taking his hand from where it clung to her thigh, she lifted it and kissed each finger.

The sweetness of the gesture was too much. Garrett wrapped his arm around her waist and pulled her to the edge of the chair. Then standing, he lifted her in his arms and padded to the bed.

Placing her on the mattress, he followed her down, laid beside her and wrapped his arms around her. "I wonder if I might just hold you for a while?"

"You only wish to hold me?" she asked in a stilted voice.

Smiling against her neck, he kissed her pulse. "I want more, but for a time, I would delight in having you in my arms."

She relaxed, toed off her slippers and ran her foot along his bare calf. Intimate and sensual, her body fitted to his and she gave a sigh of satisfaction as she caressed his arm at her waist. "This is lovely, Garrett. Another first for me."

Part of Garrett reveled in the firsts he could give to her and share with her, but a larger part grieved for all she'd endured and suffered. His ability to share these firsts stemmed from a miserable three years with an animal not worthy to lick her boots.

"What's wrong, Garrett. I can feel your tension."

He propped up on his elbow so he could look at her. "I'm sorry. I let my mind wander to thoughts of Radcliff."

Something haunted flitted through her gaze and then she settled her attention on him "It might be best if we left him out of the bedroom. I know the information is new to you and thus very fresh and discomforting, but he has been dead nearly two years and the death sentence that was my marriage is communed. I should have told you sooner and for that I am truly sorry."

Hair braided for bed, the plait lay on her shoulder. He toyed with the end pulling the soft tresses free. He would never have the pleasure of brushing her hair or watching her grow with his child inside her. He wouldn't have lazy mornings spent in bed or long nights by the fire talking. "I will do my best to keep my thoughts on you and nothing else."

"I shall endeavor to help you focus your attention." Her smile was sweet and wicked at once.

The braid freed, he ran his fingers through her soft hair and let the silky strands fall through. Memorizing every inch of her that he hoped to carry with him after he left her. "You are so lovely."

"I wonder if I might touch you?" She met his gaze. Hope and fear in her voice, she didn't shy away.

With all she'd endured, she was the bravest person he knew. "I am yours, do with me as you will." He rolled onto his back and put his hands behind his head.

Aurora faced him and pressed a hand to his chest then put her ear to his heart. Her hair fanned out across him.

A touch of a breeze spilled through the open window. The coolness was a welcome relief.

She toyed with the fall of his breeches.

"Do you want me to undress?" His voice strained with even the notion that she wanted to touch him intimately.

Clearing her throat, she turned her head to look at him. "I think I would."

He closed his eyes and drew a long breath then eased out from under her and out of the bed.

Never taking her eyes from him, she watched as he loosened the fall and stepped out of his breeches. Aurora's cheeks pinkened.

When she stepped from the bed, he thought she'd been frightened away and would leave him standing naked and aroused. To his surprise, she let her wrapper fall to the floor and pulled her shift over her head.

He'd never imagined she could be more beautiful than the woman in his dreams, but she was perfection. Every inch of her like something out of a dream. He placed a hand over a pink, puckered scar at the front of her right hip.

When his eyes fell to the spot, she traced a finger over the mark. "Remnants from my marriage. I landed on a sharp stone on the fireplace in the parlor at West Lane. There was a tremendous amount of blood. When he saw it, he ran from the house. Tipton called a surgeon. The wound had to be stitched. Radcliff didn't come home for a fortnight. I considered the injury a reasonable price for sending him from the house."

Perhaps Radcliff couldn't be banished from their privacy as yet. Garrett knelt and kissed the scar. "Where else?"

Her fingers brushed through his hair. Turning, she lifted her hair and revealed a jagged white scar at the edge of her hairline from her ear to her nape. "This nearly ended me. It happened a few months before his death. I can't remember exactly what happened. When I woke, I was in bed. Mercy,

Poppy and Faith were with me and Radcliff had fled. Tipton told me he came looking for me when he saw the master pale and rushing out the door. He found me in my bath, I think I might have drowned if not for him. I can't imagine his shock, but he's never given me anything but loyalty."

Garrett rose and kissed that mark as well. He longed to destroy Radcliff and regretted the man was already in the ground. "Are there more?"

She pointed to a slim scar that ran across her thigh in the back and ended at the front. "This was a knife. It was a dinner where he'd gone into a rage. I tried to run, but he stabbed me from behind. When I turned in shock, the cut went around. He dropped the knife, but didn't run. He beat me until I lost consciousness then went to his club."

Tracing his fingers along the raised mark, Garrett let one tear slip. "I don't know what to say."

"I've been terribly disfigured. You must be horrified." She stepped away and reached for her shift.

Garrett stayed her hand by taking it and kissing his way up her arm. "You are perfect, Rora. These are nothing but bad memories."

"I am damaged beyond the scars one can point to, Garrett." Her tight voice pained him more than any revenge he'd been denied.

Wrapping his arms around her, he pressed kisses on her forehead, her cheek, her jaw. "Those can heal just as the other's did."

"But the scars." She choked back emotion.

"Scars are strong, dearest. They leave a mark but make the damaged places stronger on the outside and within." He ran his hands up and down her back. He memorized the curve of her spine and the swell of her hips. The arch of her neck where it met her shoulder revealed another smaller scar and he pressed a long kiss there.

"Garrett, I would not stop you if you wished to bed me. I should like very much to give you pleasure." Her palms cupped his back at the shoulder blades but she didn't move them to caress him. She touched him as if afraid of what she might unleash.

Turning so that he could sit on the bed, he pulled her to stand between his knees. "I would treasure making love with you. However, the bedding must be mutual and if you wish you may take charge."

"Me?" Her eyes were wide and the large dark pupils reflected the candlelight.

He took her hands and placed the palms on his chest. "You're afraid and understandably. You trust me, but still think the act will bring you shame and pain. I wish for you to be empowered not afraid in this and in all things."

"I don't know what you want." She ran her knuckles along his stubble-covered chin.

Joy filled him. He couldn't explain it. With all she had suffered and all he had lost with that suffering, she was his for this night and he was hers. He let his hands rest at the swell of her hips. "I have already had more than I ever dreamed. However, if you'd like to kiss me, that would be wonderful."

She cupped his cheek, and her smile lit her eyes as she lowered her lips to his. Timid, a feathery brush of her bottom lip to his top then her top to his bottom.

Holding still was a kind of wonderful torture. Garrett's fingers tightened of their own accord, but he resisted pulling her in.

Agonizingly slow, she sank into the kiss and opened her

mouth on his. Their tongues danced and swirled leaving him breathless and achingly hard. She broke the kiss panting and pressed a string of kisses down his neck, ran her thumb over his nipple and nipped the lobe of his ear.

Garrett slid his hands over her soft round bottom.

Gulping air, she tossed her hair over her shoulder. "Will you lie on the bed."

He rushed to comply, part of him still expecting her to run from the room and leave him to pleasure himself and dream of a golden-haired goddess.

Instead, she climbed on the mattress and straddled his hips. "Will you touch me?"

Pulling her forward he took one nipple in his mouth and caressed from her neck, down her spine to her bottom.

Aurora cried out and arched her back.

"Rora, your other guests are in this hall and likely have their windows open as well. While I love to hear your pleasure, you may want to muffle those cries. I wouldn't want your brother calling me out at sunrise."

A warm giggle filled the heated room. "I will try." The words hardly out, she pressed her center along his shaft and moaned. Pressing both hands to his chest, she pushed herself up and eased along his shaft again, but this time bit her lip to silence her cry.

She lifted enough to center herself and slid her body onto him in one slow, painfully erotic move.

Garrett elevated to meet her but despite the wondrous torture, he let her set the pace. Slow and steady, she rose and fell. Her eyes closed and her lip clenched between her teeth, she arched her back and rode him like the goddess she was.

His control slipping, he pressed his thumb to her sensitive bud smoothing circles and heightening her pleasure. Everything inside him longed to feel her body squeeze his and when she tumbled over the edge, he pulled her down and kissed her screams to muffled moans.

Unable to stop the flood of pleasure, he pulled free and spilled his seed between them.

Holding her tight, he pressed kiss after kiss to her face, along her jaw, to the tip of her nose. "You are all things good and beautiful."

They were both covered in a sheen of perspiration as the final shocks of pleasure rippled through them.

She settled against his side with her head on his chest. "Why can nights like this not be enough?"

He sighed. "Because I want more than your body. I want your company, your mind, your heart and your soul."

A tear slid down her cheek. "I don't have all of that to give."

"You underestimate yourself, my darling. But I will go to Scotland and see you in London in a few weeks." He tamped down the sadness rushing to fill him to the brink.

Brushing the tear aside, she pressed her lips to his chest. "Why did you not stay within me?"

His longing to do so was so great, he let his heart calm before he answered. "If you found yourself with child, you would be forced to marry me. I do not want you trapped into something you cannot want."

"You are a good man, Garrett. I don't deserve your goodness." Her arms tightened around his waist as if her body claimed him even if her heart and mind would not.

The belief in his goodness might be an exaggeration, but he reveled in hearing her say so and tucked the memories deep inside to carry with him. He kissed the crown of her head. "Thank you, Rora."

She pushed up. "I should leave you to sleep." It came out more question than statement.

"Or you might stay here and sleep in my arms a while," he suggested.

"Sleep?" Grinning, she rested her chin on her hands stacked on his sternum. Her eyebrows rose high.

He shrugged. "If you give me ten minutes and you wish it, we might do more than sleep."

Hugging him, she giggled. "I wish it very much. I've just discovered being in a man's bed can be a delight. It hardly seems wise to rush away."

Rolling her to her back, he didn't know if he'd ever been as happy. He'd think about consequences on the morrow. "You are a very wise woman. I have always thought so."

CHAPTER EIGHTEEN

Aurora sneaked back into her own room just before dawn having woken to Garrett's gentle kisses and soft voice. It hadn't been easy to leave him, but it would be worse should her maid find her missing or his valet find her in his bed.

Her body still sang with pleasure from the night. Glorious sensations sprang from his fingers, mouth and every part of his hard, beautiful body. Nothing her friends had told her did justice to what she'd experienced. And, nothing about lovemaking with Garrett resembled the violence of her marriage.

Crawling into her bed, she let that knowledge filter in and tucked it away as sleep took her and dreams filled her mind with light brown eyes and brown hair streaked with red in the light.

The sun streamed into the room when she woke to Gillian padding around with wash water and towels.

"Is it late, Gillian?" Aurora pushed her hair back from her face. The sleeping braid a distant memory.

"Nearly half past ten, my lady." Gillian put the towel next to the wash basin then poured steaming water from a white pitcher into the bowl.

"Is the house up?" She swung her legs over the side of the bed.

Gillian closed the window as the morning had brought cooler temperatures. "Some of the men have been up and broken their fasts. Miss Helen and Miss Esther walked into town with the young ladies to investigate a book shop. The other ladies are not below yet and, of course, His Grace has left for Scotland."

Pain shot through her chest and she swallowed down any outward display of distress. "I didn't realize he would leave so early. I suppose it rude of me not to see him off."

"It was quite early, my lady. I doubt His Grace expected anyone to be up and about at that hour." Gillian placed Aurora's slippers on the floor in front of her. "I'll be back after you wash to help you dress. Will the peach day dress do, my lady?"

"Yes. That's fine. Thank you, Gillian." Once her maid closed the door, Aurora put her hands over her face and pushed down the grief of his leaving. He had business and she had rejected his proposal. Of course he left. He must have called for his valet after she'd gone to her own room to have left so early. There was nothing keeping him, she'd seen to that.

Brushing aside her self-inflicted troubles, Aurora slid into her slippers and got out of bed.

$\mathcal{A}$ week past Michaelmas, and it had done nothing but rain in London for days. Aurora's mood matched the saturated fall weather. The fire was lit in the parlor at West Lane and she stood staring into it. It was Tuesday so at least she had her friends coming for tea.

The sound of a carriage in the street told her someone was arriving before Faith's voice sounded in the foyer as she asked after Tipton.

"I'm very well, Your Grace," the butler said.

Faith walked into the parlor. "You look deep in thought, Aurora."

Plastering a smile on her face, Aurora turned. "Not at all,

just getting the chill off. Do you suppose it will ever stop raining?"

Faith cocked her head and stopped in her tracks. "Are we relegated to speaking of the weather or are you going to tell me what's troubling you?"

It wouldn't do to get into a long conversation about things that could not be fixed or altered. "I think for now, we will stick with the weather."

The look from Faith was almost as bad as a scolding. "If you wish." She tugged off her gloves and tossed them on the settee. "I missed our tea last week."

"I would have thought you'd be sick of me after all the time at the school." Aurora sat.

Faith's eyes widened then narrowed, and she placed her hands lightly on her knees. "Oh you are in a cross mood. You know very well that I am never sick of you."

Poppy made a ruckus as she always did before she entered. "It is terrible weather." She stopped. "Why do you both look so horrid?"

"Do we?" Faith raised a brow.

Mercy glided into the parlor. "Oh dear. Should we forgo the tea and go straight for the brandy?"

Right on time, the tea arrived and they all remained silent until the footman had gone and the door closed.

She wanted to crawl out of her skin. With practiced movements she poured the tea and told herself to gather her wits. "It is the weather is all. I'm sick of London rain."

"Is that all?" Poppy asked. "I thought perhaps you were missing a certain duke and that had your temper up."

Bobbling the pot, Aurora splashed tea on the tray. She flashed a look at Poppy. "Garrett is my friend and nothing more. We have been friends since childhood. I don't know why you all are making so much of his being at Whickette Park. He came to convey Helen and Poppy."

"And stayed far longer than the delivery required." Mercy smiled as she added milk to a cup on the tray.

"He was concerned about Hexon, and his concerns were valid as it turned out. However, regardless of his feelings or lack thereof, I am in London and he is in Scotland."

"No, he's not." Poppy spoke around a biscuit.

Aurora nearly dropped her tea in her lap and had to steady the cup in the saucer. Her china was in peril, she feared. "What do you mean?"

"He called on Rhys and I two days ago. He's been back in London for several weeks." Poppy licked crumbs off her fingers.

Heart pounding in her ears, she couldn't believe he was in London and hadn't come to call on her. But why would he? She told him their dalliance was at an end. He was clear that he would not renew is regard. That was what she wanted after all. "Strange he didn't come here."

Mercy sipped her tea then spoke over the rim. "I heard a rumor at the theater last night, but perhaps I should keep it to myself."

"You should not." Poppy plunked sugar in her tea and lifted the cup. "What did you hear?"

With a brief shift of her gaze to Aurora, Mercy waited for some sign.

Unsure if she wanted to hear or not, Aurora stayed silent.

Mercy said, "It seems the mothers of eligible daughters in London are in a frenzy about the Duke of Corwin seeking a bride."

The pain that pierced her chest had no explanation. "Garrett will marry?"

"It seems so." Faith had been oddly quiet, but now she directed a hard stare at Aurora.

Poppy narrowed her gaze, but then changed the subject. "We are to attend the Mercer ball on Friday. Are you going? I heard Lady Mercer has redecorated in a Grecian style. I'm sure it's absurd, but you know I love to see the latest trends and laugh at them."

"Grecian? Is that a trend?" Faith pulled a face.

"I think Lady Mercer hopes to start one and take the credit." Poppy nibbled on another biscuit.

"Nick and I were planning to attend. He has some business with Lord Mercer and his lordship sent a personal note." Faith walked to the window. "I hope the weather will be better. The streets are terrible after all this rain."

"I suppose it will be a distraction." Aurora sipped her tea and wished she could go up to her bed and wallow in the idea of Garrett and his wife coming to call one day. She would have to be cordial, of course.

Mercy broke into her daydream. "Whatever you are thinking, Aurora, it has formed a crease between your eyes. Are you certain you don't wish to discuss it?"

Waving it off, she said, "I have procured some whisky from Scotland. You are forbidden from asking how I came by it. Let's just say it was a gift." She crossed to the small cabinet at the far end of the parlor and pulled out glasses and scotch for four.

Mercy's aunt had sent the bottle with strict instructions not to tell anyone she'd been procuring such things from their neighbors to the north. Evidently, it wasn't as refined as other libations. Aurora quite liked it and a little burn might east the ache pressing on her chest.

"What shall we toast?" Poppy lifted her glass.

Faith gave the scotch a sniff and grinned. "Let us toast our friend Garrett. To his finding a bride who deserves him." She lifted her glass high. "To the Duke of Corwin and his bride to be."

Mercy and Poppy repeated the toast.

Aurora drank down the entire glass in one belt. No amount of burn would push aside her pain.

The Mercer townhouse was in Mayfair. The rooms were awash with candles lighting every corner. It was extravagant, but Aurora supposed her hostess wish to show off her attempt at all things Greek including enormous white pillars around the ballroom as if they were standing in the Parthenon. At the far end of the room stood a statue of Zeus. It was at least eight feet tall, and no covering of cloth or stone hid the details of his form.

"Gracious," Aurora said.

Poppy's mouth hung open. "I would say Zeus's beard, but I suppose my colorful epithets are entirely misplaced now."

They both burst out laughing and even Rhys let a low chuckle slip.

The music began and Rhys took Poppy's hand. "Dance with me, my dearest."

Aurora melted back to the side of the room and watched the minuet take shape. The familiar sight of Garrett forced her to hold her breath lest she gasp out loud. She shouldn't be surprised by his presence. She knew he was in town. Yet the sight of him stirred something inside her.

He was in a black suit but his waistcoat was a patterned gold brocade that was very fashionable.

His hand met that of his partner and Aurora had to turn away and compose herself. Mary Yates smiled and simpered up at him.

It shouldn't matter. It was only a dance. Garrett had not offered for Mary as far as Aurora knew. Oh, God, not Mary Yates. Anyone else. Well, not anyone, but certainly not Lady Mary Yates.

A torrent of nightmares from her days at the Wormbattle School for Girls rushed back. Mary Yates had been a year ahead. She had taken an instant dislike to Aurora and her friends and made life very hard for a time. She'd labeled them wallflowers at their first dance. Poppy, Faith, Mercy, and she had fought back by embracing the title and making it their own. Unsatisfied, Mary had stolen papers and handed them in as her own. She taken Faith's diary and read it out loud to the assembly. Once, she'd loosed a goat in the Wallflower's room. The poor animal had been terrified and destroyed everything, leaving the room in such shambles every linen, paper and stick of furniture had needed replacing. Luckily, the beast hadn't had time to get inside the wardrobes and their clothes had survived.

Of course, the Wallflowers had done their fair share of mischief, but they had been provoked. Mary Yates was unfeeling and malicious. She was not good enough for Garrett.

"I see Garrett has taken to the dance floor." The bite in Mercy's tone could not be mistaken. "We have only just arrived. I hope you weren't alone long."

Aurora kissed her cheek. "No. I came with Rhys and Poppy. They have gone to dance."

Spotting the statue, Mercy covered her mouth. "I think our hostess has taken the Greek style a bit too far."

Unable to help herself, Aurora said, "Why would he dance with that horrible woman?"

"Mary is rich and very pretty on the outside, Aurora. Garrett may not be privy to her true character." Mercy spotted Faith and Nick and waved at them across the room.

She was right, but that didn't make seeing him dance with Mary less offensive. "Where is Wesley?"

"He went to get me some punch. I heard that Lady Mercer is very proud of her punch."

Aurora pointed across the room. "I heard that too much of that punch and you will take off your clothes and dance with Zeus over there."

Giggling, Mercy said, "I shall pace myself."

The minuet ended and Garrett bowed to Mary before taking her back to her mother to the left of Zeus. With a word and another bow, he disengaged himself and walked from the ballroom.

It wouldn't do to run after him, but a large part of her wanted to do just that. Waiting until the next dance began and her friends took to the floor, Aurora told herself she needed air as she walked down a hall to the door that led to the veranda.

After over a week of rain the skies had cleared the day before, leaving London feeling fresh and clean.

The statues of female gods lined the wall. From Hera to Artemis and so many more. The expense of such a ridiculous display had to have been outrageous.

Garrett looked up at Demeter with her full bosom and

hand outstretched with barley clutched in it. His black coat stretched tight across his shoulders.

"I think Lady Mercer has outdone herself." Aurora stepped beside him.

The way he drew in a sharp breath made her think she might have startled him. "Hello, Rora."

"How are you, Garrett?" So much awkwardness and simple talk when there was so much she wanted to say, but couldn't.

"I'm well. I had planned to call on you next week." Still, he kept his gaze on the statue and then further into the torch-lit gardens.

She shrugged. "How long have you known Mary Yates?"

Turning, he looked at her for the first time. "I have only just met Lady Mary. I can see and hear that you know her better."

"We were at school together." She tried and failed to keep the rancor out of her voice.

Closing the few feet separating them, he said, "Is it Lady Mary particularly, or would any woman I danced with garner such a disgusted tone in your voice?"

Aurora faced him and breathed deep the warm scent of soap, the outdoors and Garrett. The exquisite breath of him made her head swim. "I cannot say for sure to the rest, but it is most definitely Mary Yates in particular."

With a sad smile, he stepped back. "She is quite pretty and comes from a good family."

She could go on for hours about Mary's flaws, but what good would it do? "She is both of those things. Was your trip to Scotland fruitful?"

"I have advertised to let the house. I took time to meet with all my tenants so I could explain the situation. I was gone far longer than I intended, but it was a good trip. I'll not return for some years. My steward will handle interviews with any good prospects to take the lease. I'm sure it will all be well in hand." He said it all as any friend might inform another.

His tone gave the comfort of a friend and made her miserable at once. "I'm glad for you."

"Are things well in Cheshire?" he asked.

"Helen has it all under control. We have three additional students, and they all get on very well. I hope it shall all work out. I will return in the spring unless something urgent should arise."

"You returned after the expected fortnight?" Perhaps he was tired of conversation and so made light talk.

"We did. There was nothing keeping us in the country once the lessons began in earnest. I think Helen was happy to see us go so she could get the girls into a routine." Aurora hazarded a look at him. Those eyes that had so intrigued her stared back with confusion or questions. She didn't know and was too cowardly to ask.

"I'm glad to see you, but I must return to the ballroom. I'll call during the week, Rora." Garrett turned and rushed away and into the house.

Aurora found her way inside, but the coolness of their exchange broke something inside her. The dining room was crowded with revelers, each taking their turn at the giant crystal punch bowl at the center of an elaborate table.

Pushing him away was for the best. She'd told herself that a dozen times, so why did it hurt so much?

Mary Yates entered the dining room and strode over. "Lady Radcliff, I was surprised to see you here."

"Lady Mary, how nice to see you. Why did you find my

presence a surprise?" Unable to tolerate chatting without some other reason for being there, Aurora followed the queue for the punch bowl.

The smirk twisting Mary's mouth told a foul tale of what was about to pour from it. "It is all about town that your bid for not one, but two dukes of the realm have been thwarted. I should have thought you would have preferred to stay out of sight for a while."

Aurora reached the bowl, and with painful slowness, filled a glass without letting a drop fall from the ladle. She turned to Mary and took a sip. "This is quite good."

Turning her nose up, Mary said, "You don't deny the rumors?"

As precisely as she'd filled her cup, Aurora stepped to Mary with such determination that Mary's eye's widened, and she stepped back. "I need not deny anything, Lady Mary. You are likely the source of the rumors, and I'll not satisfy your wicked curiosity. I am the Dowager Countess of Radcliff, and that is title enough." She took another sip. "While I'm flattered you've taken such an interest in my future, I beg you not to trouble yourself. I am quite well and independent."

"When I am the Duchess of Corwin, I shall ruin you and the rest of your little band." Mary's mouth twisted, making any attractiveness fade.

The very idea of this witch marrying good, kind Garrett nauseated Aurora. With an act of will, she kept her expression placid. "You forget that one of my little band is already a duchess and the other two countesses. I feel certain our reputations will survive whomever you persuade to marry you, Mary. I would suggest that you hide this nasty bent until after the vows are said. You're so twisted up with hate, I doubt anyone would have you if they saw you now."

Realizing she'd let her mask slip, Mary relaxed her face and a smile touched her lips. Her eyes remained full of hate. She pointed to Aurora's half-finished punch. "You should monitor your drinking, Lady Radcliff. No one likes to see a widow getting sloppy in public. Imagine the rumors."

Ignoring the line of people, Aurora turned back to the bowl and topped off her glass. "Thank you for your concern."

With Aurora's stare leveled at her, fear flashed in Mary's eyes, and she hurried from the room.

Once she was gone, Aurora apologized to the guests waiting their turn for punch and wound her way in the other direction and back into the garden. She drank down the delightful punch and considered how to refill her glass without having to wait again.

CHAPTER NINETEEN

$\mathcal{P}$oppy waved at Garrett from the corner. Concern radiated from her tight lips and the crinkle between her eyes. She made her way through the crush of people toward him.

"Is something wrong, Poppy?" Garrett searched the room for Rhys in case he needed to fetch his friend to his wife's aid.

"I cannot find Aurora. None of us have seen her in nearly an hour. It's not like her to disappear at a ball. She always stays close. Have you seen her?" Shades of panic threaded through Poppy's voice.

"I'm sure she's just gone to the lady's retiring room." Garrett scanned for Aurora's familiar blond hair but saw no sign of her.

Poppy shook her head and threw out her clenched fists. "I already checked there. Mercy searched too. Faith tried some of the private rooms. No one has seen her. I'm really becoming concerned."

The failure of so many in finding Aurora heightened Garrett's concern as well. "I will help with the search."

Her shoulders relaxed. "Thank you."

Checking closets and bedrooms meant that he caught several couples in compromising positions, and with each discovery, he felt profound relief that Aurora was not engaged in something untoward.

The gardens were dimly lit, as the lateness of the evening meant that several of the torches had guttered out. It wasn't particularly easy to make his way down unfamiliar paths, but having failed to find Aurora in the house, he decided to give the garden a look. It would only cause a scene to call out for her. The Wallflowers and their spouses would be discrete in their search. If word got around that the Countess of Radcliff had gone missing at a ball, the speculation would not be favorable for Aurora's reputation.

The shuffle of stones in the darkness halted his progress. A soft feminine hiccup came from the right. A knot formed in the pit of Garrett's stomach, but still he followed the sound.

In the moonlight, Aurora glowed in a heap of skirts like a fallen flower in the damp grass. She leaned against a perfectly good bench with her head resting on her arm and her arm resting on the stone bench. Another hiccup sounded and jerked her entire body.

Lord, she was more endearing than ever. He wished he could just admire her as she was rather than come to her rescue, but there was no choice. "Rora, what are you doing, my dearest."

She looked up, her head lulled to the other side, and with heavy lidded eyes, she gazed at him. "I exceeded my limit on punch."

Too adorable for words, Aurora with her hair mussed and her gown fluffed out around her without a care to smooth herself into perfection. "I can see that for myself, but why are you sitting out here on the ground? Your friends are worried about you."

Unfocused, she blinked in the direction of the house. "It wouldn't do to be seen in public in my state. I thought to wait for my head to clear. The bench was unsteady, so I sat here."

He had to hold back his laugh over her claim that the bench was unsteady rather than her head was spinning. "I see. Shall I take you home, Rora?"

"I should not like for people to see me as we saw Hexon when he drank too much in Cheshire." Her frown was nearly as adorable as her bewildered look when he'd found her.

Garrett knelt in the grass in front of her and took her hands. "Sweet, sweet girl, you could never be seen in such an ugly light. I'm not condoning your overindulgence, but your disposition is far afield from Hexon's. He hides a hateful nature, and that nature was revealed due to excessive drink. You hide no such duality."

Still unable to keep her gaze steady, she shrugged. "I hide a great many things, Garrett. I always have."

He kissed her forehead. "Not always."

Canting to one side, Aurora nearly collided with the bench. Garrett gripped her with one hand on her waist and the other on her shoulder. Easing her over, he shook his head. "Stay here, dearest. I shall tell our friends you are safe and then take you home.

Whatever she muttered was lost in her stupor.

Glad that distance from the house gave some privacy to the spot where Aurora had attempted to hide herself until the effects of alcohol had eased, Garrett still gazed about for intruders. He didn't want her found by anyone in his absence. With that in mind, he rushed back to the house and searched for a member of their small circle of friends.

Mary Yates spotted him before he could slip away. She rushed across the ballroom to intercept him. "Your Grace, I feared you'd left early."

Ever since Aurora's strange reaction to him dancing with Mary, he'd noticed how Mary's eyes narrowed whenever she spotted a Wallflower. Disdain in her eyes betrayed the forced smile on her lips. At some point, he would have to hear the full story, but at the moment, he had no time for Lady Mary. "I do have to leave. Perhaps I will see you at the theater on Wednesday." He took her hand and kissed it.

A warm smile lit her eyes, and then something else as her gaze drifted to something behind him.

He knew before turning that one of the Wallflowers was nearby. There, a few feet away, Mercy scanned the crowd. Yes, he would have to hear the story at some later date. "Good evening, Lady Mary."

Making a low curtsy, she said, "Your Grace."

Garrett left her and walked to Mercy. "I found her. She's a bit under the weather. I'll see her home."

Mercy's eyes widened. "Shall I come with you?"

"There's no time to alert more of our circle. Please inform the others. I shall see her safely home." Garrett knew sneaking one lady out the side garden would be difficult enough; he didn't want to worry about a second.

With a nod, Mercy left him to his duty.

Mary was still watching as he spoke to Mercy. He wondered if she'd follow him from the house. Something told him she might. That wouldn't do. He offered her a smile and walked to the front of the house and out the front door.

Once he'd alerted his driver to bring the carriage to the back gate, he rounded the house and entered the garden through an alley gate. When he returned to the bench in the grassy clearing where he'd left Aurora, he found only her slippers.

Heart pounding, he scanned the moonlit garden. Where could she have gone? He'd been sure she would remain until he returned. The notion that someone with nefarious intentions might have found her and taken her away caused panic to rush up from his gut.

"Ouch." Her voice was soft and came from the other side of a high shrub.

"Rora?" Scooping up her slippers as he passed, he then rounded the shrub. "What are you doing?"

Blinking up at him, she was the most adorable thing he'd ever seen. "I seem to have lost my shoes."

He lifted the soft leather dancing slippers into her view.

A wide smile split her face. "There they are."

Did she have to be so adorable? He steeled his desire to sweep her up and take her home with him and reminded himself that she was not his. He knelt with the shoes with intentions of helping her into them, but her left foot sat in a puddle of blood.

"What have you done, Rora?" In one motion, he stood and thrust the shoes into her arms then lifted her off her feet and carried her to the bench.

"Garrett?"

He lifted her foot. The stocking was torn, and the bottom of her foot was cut at the heel with several other deep scratches. "Oh, Rora."

She listed to one side, and Garrett steadied her. "Garrett, I don't feel myself." She pressed her palm to her cheek. "Do you think you might take me home now?"

With one quick tug, he untied his white cravat and pulled it from his neck. He made a bandage of the cloth that should hold off any further bleeding while he transported her home. "Yes, dearest. I will take you home now. You hold on to your shoes, and I shall hold on to you."

Cradling her in his arms, he lifted her again and made his way toward the garden gate. His carriage was already waiting, and with a quick glance to see they would not be spotted, Garrett put Aurora in the carriage then joined her. He had a thought to have his man take her home. Her servants would care for her. However, without a cravat, he couldn't return to the ball.

"West Lane, Reggie. Take your time. Her ladyship is feeling ill."

The driver called softly to the horses, and they bumped down the street.

Aurora leaned her head against the side of the carriage. Her voice was weepy and hardly a whisper. "I'm sorry, Garrett. I've been a terrible friend to you."

Brushing her mussed hair from her face, he imagined

other times when her hair had been out of place. There were few, but he'd had a part in mussing the golden tresses, and somehow that made him happy. "You are a great friend to me, Rora."

"No. I cannot give you what you want, and yet I have toyed with you for my own pleasure." She turned and pressed her head against his shoulder.

It was impossible to regret holding her, even in her drunken state. He traced the curve of her spine. "I had my fair share of pleasure as well, dearest. I never thought you playing at anything. You have been honest with me."

A long sigh pushed from her lips. "Perhaps Mary has changed her ways and will make you a proper wife. I suppose she is pretty, and she is assuredly rich."

"Can we not speak of Lady Mary? Tell me why you drank so much and why on earth you walked in sharp stones without your shoes."

"Did I?" She looked down at her feet where they peeked out from the edge of her skirt. "I've ruined my stockings."

"Can you answer my questions, Rora?" He eased her cheek around with the palm of his hand and met her glassy gaze.

As she found focus, she smiled. "I only went to have a taste of the punch. It was quite nice. Then Mary goaded me, and I took a second glass. I went to the garden, but somehow found myself back in the dining room with another glass. When my head got all fuzzy, I decided the garden was the proper place for me."

He might have scolded her if she wasn't so endearing. He might have kissed her if she hadn't been so inebriated. What was he to do with this woman who had stolen his heart? "And what of the shoes?"

Aurora stared at the soft leather footwear in her lap for a long moment. "I have no notion of why I took them off." She drew a long breath and pressed her cheek to his chest.

Garrett held her in his arms. While it was not the first time, he always felt as if each time might be the last. He cursed Radcliff for the hundredth time and kissed the crown of her head. The scent of roses and the grasses from the garden filled him. Holding on to these little moments might be the only joy he'd find in his life. He committed this small happiness to memory as the carriage drew to a stop in front of Aurora's West Lane home.

The door opened, and Reggie poked his head in. "Can I assist you, Your Grace?"

Aurora was fast asleep. Garrett handed Reggie her shoes. "If you would knock on the door and give those to the butler, I shall carry her ladyship. Once we are inside, take my carriage home. I don't want to start the tongues wagging when they see my crest sitting here."

"How will you get home, Your Grace?" Reggie looked at the sleeping form of Aurora then back at Garrett.

"It's not far. I'll walk or find a hack." Knowing full well, he'd never find transportation, he wished he'd worn more appropriate walking shoes. However, he was in dancing shoes and the journey would be uncomfortable.

Reggie held the door with one hand and as soon as Garrett and Aurora were out, he closed the door. "I'll come back with a horse within the hour, Your Grace." He glanced at Garrett's feet. "I'll have Bronson fetch some proper shoes as well."

It was hard to keep a serious expression in place. "You're a good man, Reggie."

With a nod, Reggie bounded up the steps and banged the knocker.

Tipton assessed the situation without remark or expression. He held open the door, took Aurora's shoes and made no comment as he rushed forward to open the parlor door for them.

"Thank you, Tipton. Her ladyship has injured her foot. Do you think some clean water and bandages might be brought?" Garrett placed her on the chaise at the far end.

Tipton glanced out the window as the Corwin carriage rolled away. Turning back, he raised a brow. "Shall I make preparations for Your Grace to stay the night?"

"My driver will return for me within the hour, Tipton. I'll just see to her ladyship and trouble you no more this night." Garrett was not used to being questioned by a servant, but the display of loyalty to Aurora from her butler overtook any slight.

"I shall gather what you need. Would you like me to call my lady's maid to tend her?"

Garrett shook his head. He wanted more time to cherish this woman. It was selfish, but he didn't care. "I will tend her injury myself then carry her up to her maid."

"As you wish, Your Grace." There was something in the stoic butler's voice that bordered on amusement as he left the room.

Garrett untied his cravat from her foot. The cut on her heel still oozed blood. It was wrong of him to wish she needed him all her days and not just when she was drunk and injured or needed him physically. He dabbed away the blood. Loving her independence, he also wished there was something he offered that she couldn't do without.

She pulled her foot back as he dabbed at the wound.

Unable to help himself, he leaned down and kissed her ankle. "I'm sorry, my love. I do not wish to hurt you."

With a sigh, she gazed at him through hooded lids. Her hands folded across her abdomen. "You never could. I wish you had—"

The door opened, stopping her wish mid-sentence. Tipton carried a bowl of water, a towel, and several rolled bandages on a tray. "I thought it best not to wake the entire house, Your Grace. Her ladyship's maid will be upstairs waiting when you are finished here."

"Thank you, Tipton." Garrett dipped a corner of a towel in the water and sponged away the dried blood.

He never heard the butler leave, but when he looked up again, he and Aurora were alone. Unwilling to worry about gossip and what the servants might think, Garrett pushed those notions aside. He ran his thumb across the heel of her foot and felt a sharp edge.

Damned pebble was still in her skin. He stood and went to the small desk in the corner.

"Are you leaving? There was a dreamy quality to her voice as she lay watching him.

Searching the desk, he located a small knife she likely used to open her correspondence. "No. You still have a small stone in your foot, dearest. I need something to pluck it out."

"Ah. Well, it serves me right for drinking too much. I never do, you know. I don't like to be out of control."

"I know." He wished she were sober now, so he could seduce her into being out of control with him. However, she was in no condition, and he was a gentleman and her friend.

Returning, he spread a second towel across his lap and lifted her foot to rest there. "This may sting, love. I shall try to be quick."

She closed her eyes. "I'm stronger than I look."

"I know how strong you are, but I hate to be the person causing you pain." The idea actually made him a bit ill. However, she suffered more from the stone, and he'd not let her get a blood infection because he was too weak to pull a tiny pebble from her flesh.

"You are the most gentle man I know. It is what I love best about you."

Had he misheard her? Had she said she loved him? No. His mind must be playing tricks on him. With his thumb he found the pebble again, lifted her foot to an angle where he could see the offending foreign matter, and before he could think too much about hurting her or her loving him, he used the small silver knife to pry loose the stone.

Her high-pitched cry was stifled the instant after it escaped.

"I'm sorry, sweetheart." He clutched her foot with a gentle hand and pressed a kiss to the top. The pebble lay on the towel in his lap and her foot trickled blood anew. Putting the knife aside, he washed the wound before wrapping it in a clean bandage.

He felt her gaze on him before he looked across the chaise to find those crystal blue orbs following his every move. "You are an extraordinary man, Garrett."

"I only did what anyone would do who found you injured." His heart pounded, sending blood rushing to his head.

Leaning back, she smiled and closed her eyes. "I think you overestimate what people do for each other. I have a very close circle of friends, and while over the years the circle has grown, we are very careful about who we allow inside. People are not nice. At least, not many are truly good."

Rubbing circles around the top of her bandaged foot, he couldn't bring himself to break the contact. "I hope you count me among your growing circle."

Then she was staring at him again. "You have been my most trusted friend even before there were Wallflowers."

"Thank you." He held his breath, though he couldn't think why. Shaking off the effects of being so close to her and listening to her voice, he stood. "I'll take you up to your maid. She will see to you."

In his arms again, she pressed her cheek to his shoulder. Her breath tickled the skin at his neck. He would give almost anything to stay with her, but not like this. Not when she would likely remember nothing in the morning.

Halfway up the steps, she said, "I do love you, Garrett, you know that."

Mid-climb, he stilled. Everything inside him froze, wishing there were truth in her words. "I think in the morning you will feel differently, dearest."

A low sigh blew from her lips. Her voice was dreamy and slow. "No. I won't, but I'll keep my feelings to myself when the punch wears off. I always keep my feelings to myself."

At the top of the stairs, he didn't know which way to go. His body was on fire and his heart shattered into a million pieces. Part of him wanted to run back down the steps and carry her away with him. However, the part of him that was the Duke of Corwin drew a long breath and looked down the hall both ways. To the right, a door stood open with light pouring out. He turned and carried her to the open door. Inside, a young maid waited to take over his duties.

With the briefest instructions about Aurora's foot, he left her, sitting on the edge of the bed with glassy eyes, and little hope she would remember anything she'd said or done.

CHAPTER TWENTY

Mercy, Faith, and Poppy all arrived just after eleven the next morning. Aurora's head still pounded despite several remedies sent up by Cook. She judged her poor health as punishment for bad behavior.

Every moment of the day before played over and over in her head. Why had she let Mary Yates turn her into a drunkard? Why did it have to be Garrett who'd found her and took her home?

Of course, the Wallflowers only came to make sure she was alright. They had been wary of Garrett being her chaperone, but there had been little choice short of alerting the entire ballroom to her state of inebriation.

They demanded full disclosure of the events after she left the ballroom. She could have said that she was too drunk to remember, but once she began the tale from Mary's badgering in the dining room, she couldn't stop herself.

"So, Garrett brought you home and tended your wound?" Poppy cocked her head and pointed to Aurora's bandaged foot.

"As I said, he got a stone out of my heel, washed and bandaged my foot before taking me up to Gillian." Inside, Aurora cringed at the memory of the things she'd said to him as he carted her to bed. Why on earth had she told him she loved him? It did no one any good and probably only hurt him in the long run.

"And you let him go?" Faith threw her hands up in the air and let them fall.

"What would you expect me to do?" Aurora had no idea what Faith was about, but she doubted she would like it.

Crossing her arms, Faith shook her head. "I fear what I might say would be unwelcome."

Poppy jumped up, crossed to the door, and bolted it. "Then I will say it. Have you lost your mind, Aurora? That man loves you to distraction. Why would you not give yourself a chance at happiness? I know for certain you wish to have children. He is your chance for both of those things. Why do you insist on pushing him away?"

"You know very well why." Aurora's hold on her emotions was slipping. "You saw me all those years when Radcliff controlled my life. You tended me and called for the surgeon when I was near death. How can I ever let my person fall into the control of another again?"

All three stared at her with wide eyes.

Mercy asked, "Do you believe there are similarities between Radcliff and Garrett?"

"No! What kind of similarities could there possibly be?" Aurora raged at the notion that anyone could make such a comparison.

"You tell us, Aurora." Mercy's voice was soft and steady.

"Radcliff was a monster. Garrett is the kindest man I know. He would never harm anyone." She would defend Garrett to the death if necessary. How dare anyone doubt his goodness. Her heart pounded and roared in her ears.

Faith raised her brows and leaned back in the chair. "Then Garrett is the type of man who would limit a woman's ability to make her own choices."

The notion was ridiculous. "You know perfectly well that Garrett is fond of independent women. He brought Helen to me. He respects that a woman may be a sensible and often resourceful person perfectly capable of knowing what is best."

Poppy took a biscuit from the tray and sat on the end of the chaise. "Then certainly Garrett would restrict the movements of any wife he might take. He certainly wouldn't wish his wife to have interest beyond keeping his house."

Standing, Aurora looked down at the three of them as if they'd lost their minds. "Garrett Winslow would be proud of his wife's accomplishments, and if she had a talent for something, he would support her fully. Any woman would be lucky to have his attentions."

They stared back at her.

All at once Aurora's heart crumbled into a million pieces. She sank to the settee and tears poured from her. Face in her hands, she tried to speak, but the sobs just kept coming.

She'd chased away the only man she would ever love. She sent him right back into the arms of someone like Mary Yates.

Poppy sat beside her and held her around the shoulders. "It's good to see you let this all out, Aurora. You've been holding in so much for too long."

After several moments of sobbing, it became clear what Aurora must do. "You're right, Poppy. I have always wanted a child. It's not too late for at least that. I shall find a man who is amenable to an arrangement where I live separately once an heir is born. Surely there are many men who need an heir but would prefer the company of their mistress."

Faith looked about to jump across the table. "What are you talking about, Aurora? I thought we were discussing Garrett."

Shaking her head, Aurora dismissed the notion. She dabbed at the corners of her eyes with a napkin from the tea service. "Garrett is my dear friend. He would never suit. He deserves a proper wife who will nurture their marriage. I only want children and nothing more. It would be unfair to drag him into such an arrangement knowing his feelings for me."

"Hera's curse." Poppy threw up her hands.

"It's official, you have lost your mind." Faith got up and pulled the cord for Tipton before unbolting the door. "I'll not sit here and listen to any more of this."

Tipton arrived a moment later.

"I require my gloves and pelisse, Tipton." Faith narrowed her gaze on Aurora. "I hope you regain your senses, Aurora."

With a nod and an even deeper frown, Faith exited the parlor presumably to wait for her things in the foyer.

Mercy sighed. "I know what you're attempting, Aurora, and I understand."

"It is doomed to fail." Poppy leaned back and put her hands over her stomach. "It's a great thing to want a child, but you do not have the right demeanor for a loveless marriage."

"Don't I?"

"No. You don't." Mercy agreed with Poppy. "You have endured more than anyone should have to with regard to a bad marriage, but to go into the commitment without any hope of love, or even contentment, seems far too cold."

Aurora shrugged off the assessment. "You had several offers of marriage, Mercy. You must have considered some of your offers from men such as Mr. Garrott or Mr. Baker."

The blush that pinkened Mercy's cheeks told the truth of it. "I had few options and was a burden on you and my aunt. However, despite my consideration of such men, I never agreed to marry anyone who I didn't feel I could have a loving marriage with."

"That's just my point. One can be content without love. I must find someone who will be just as happy to make such an arrangement and has no expectation of personal attachment." Aurora began to make a list in her head of eligible men of the ton.

"Hades' fire," Poppy said. "We can't have you searching for such a ridiculous thing on your own. Who do you plan to court?"

Rolling her eyes, Mercy gave a nod. "Do not think that I approve, Aurora. I'm as put off by this notion as Faith, but I agree with Poppy. We can't let you undertake such a process on your own. Once Faith has thought it through, she will likely agree and join the cause too."

A great weight lifted from Aurora's chest. She knew it would all turn out right with her friends behind her. "The gossips say Lord Belham is looking for a wife."

Poppy made a face. "He's quite a bore. Harmless though. If you don't plan to spend any time actually having to speak to him, I suppose he'd do."

They were less than enthusiastic assistants, but by the late afternoon, they had made a list of three eligible men for proper investigation.

"I'm certain Belham will be at the theater on Wednesday, if you wish to speak to him. I can invite him to the box with Rhys and me if you wish to join us and make out his character." Poppy sighed and toyed with a bit of torn fabric at the edge of her bodice. Perhaps Mercy can invite Lords West and Potsum to her dinner party next week."

A crease formed between Mercy's eyes. "I was planning to invite Garrett. Won't it be awkward if we invite an extra few men?"

The strangeness of the conversation wasn't lost of Aurora. It would be uncomfortable to be courting other men with Garrett present, regardless of the unevenness of the table by sex. Swallowing down her true thoughts, she said, "Garrett will have to learn to live with my decision at some point. It may as well be at your dinner party as far as I'm concerned."

"You'll have to invite a few extra women, Mercy." Poppy bit her lip. "I'm sure Geb will be invited, and you don't want to have three extra men. Is Aunt Phyllis in town?"

Mercy nodded. "I already had my aunt included. Your mother would be thrilled with the notion of you searching out a husband, Aurora. Shall I invite her?"

"Good Lord, no. After how she treated you before you

became a countess, I'd not think you'd ever want Mother in your home." Aurora's mother had always treated Mercy like a servant fit only to play her collection of expensive instruments and entertain the guests at her parties. Of course, once Mercy became a countess, that all stopped, and a sudden warmth of respect always fell from Mother's lips. However, the past still shone, and Aurora wouldn't wish for Mercy to do anything that would make her uncomfortable.

Mercy's shoulders relaxed. "I could invite Mary Yates to keep Garrett busy and entertained."

A knot formed in Aurora's gut.

"Would you want Mary in your home?" Poppy pulled a face as if she'd eaten bad meat.

"I could just marry Malcolm Renshaw and be done with it. He's not titled but comes from a lofty enough family." Aurora stared out the window thinking of other options.

"Malcolm!" Mercy gave an uncharacteristic shout. "Need I remind you that I had to stab him once, and you threatened him not a fortnight ago."

"He can be reasoned with, and he will eventually need a wife," Aurora shot back.

"No." Mercy crossed her arms over her chest and said, "Just because I have forgiven Malcolm for his transgressions, does not mean I want my dearest friend married to a man who will sneak and connive to gain what he wants. Even this business at Whickette Park was underhanded. He could have just come forward and asked about the missing treasure he seeks, but instead, he wove a lie about being in the neighborhood and implied he wished to court you. He is not the kind of man who will honor his vows."

Shrugging, Aurora tucked her feet under her skirts. "I

don't want a man to be faithful. I just want one to give me a child and then leave me alone. Malcolm might suit."

Poppy looked back and forth between the two, and with a heavy sigh, put stop to the debate. "We can put him on the list as a last resort. The other three are titled and have no bad habits we know about. We shall see if you trust one of them enough to venture further, Aurora."

"Prudence Mayweather is out of mourning. I will see if she'd like to join us. She could use a bit of company." Mercy's mention of their schoolmate who lost her husband in a carriage accident brought the conversation to a halt for several long seconds.

"She's Lady Harcourt now, is she not?" Aurora thought of the skinny girl with wide brown eyes and realized she'd not seen the baroness since they were all in Switzerland.

Mercy smiled. "Yes. She has a very nice home here in town and a cottage in the country. I called last week, and she seemed a bit bored."

"Who is bored?" Garrett asked from the parlor door.

Tipton stood beside him showing only the merest annoyance. "The Duke of Corwin to see you, my lady."

Despite her pulse rate tripling, Aurora couldn't help her amusement at Tipton's expense. "Thank you, Tipton. I can see him clearly enough."

"Shall I call for more tea, my lady?"

Her head still ached. "Yes, please, and maybe a few canapés Tipton. I could eat something."

"Of course." Tipton bowed out of the room.

Garrett bowed as the ladies stood to curtsy. "I'm sorry to interrupt, ladies. I wanted to check on you, Rora. How is your foot?"

"It's nothing," she said. "A bit sore, but nothing to signify."

She sat and tucked the bandaged foot under her skirts. "Will you sit?"

"I'm glad to hear it." He sat in the chair closest to her. "I worried I'd failed to clean the wound properly."

Mercy stood, as did Poppy, forcing Garrett up again. Smiling, Mercy said, "We must go. We've been here long enough, and now that you have more company, we'll not worry over you."

Narrowing her eyes on her friends, Aurora saw they were plotting to leave her alone with Garrett. Not that she worried overmuch. She would have to see him eventually, though she thought she'd have more time to conjure up what to say. "Thank you for checking on me. I shall see you at the theater."

Poppy did a poor job of hiding her amusement. She practically bounced with mirth. "Yes, of course."

They curtsied and quit the West Lane house.

Garrett stared after them a long moment. "That was strange."

"They are just amusing themselves. Thank you for checking on me, but I'm fine, Garrett."

He sat beside her. "I have no doubt, but as you were under the weather last night, and we are friends, I wanted to see for myself that you have recovered."

"Very kind." In the light streaming through the window, his light brown eyes shone with flecks of gold and amber.

"Who was Mercy saying was bored?" The tea arrived, and before Aurora could move, Garrett poured for them both and placed two treats of cucumber and salmon on her plate. He met her gaze directly.

Swallowing down the urge to kiss him, she took the offering. "Thank you. We were discussing who Mercy will invite to her dinner party. Lady Harcourt is out of mourning, and Mercy will ask her to join."

"I see. You are acquainted with the baroness?" He sipped his tea.

"She attended the Wormbattle School for Young Ladies while we were there. I've not seen her since, but she was a kind girl, and Mercy has kept in touch." Lord, if her heartbeat didn't slow, she would show signs of distress before long. She ate a canapé, made a deliberate effort to chew slowly so she wouldn't have to speak for a few moments, then took a sip of tea.

"I wonder if you remember the events of last night, Rora?" He watched her intently but there was no judgment, only calm inquiry.

Aurora swallowed down the lump in her throat. Lying was a perfectly sane option, but there had never been any lies between her and Garrett. The idea of starting falsehoods now made her stomach even queasier than her bad choices of the night before. "I remember." She couldn't meet his gaze and stared into her tea.

"Then you recall what you said to me on the steps?" He put his tea aside.

Placing her own cup and saucer on the table, she met his stare directly. "I can only put the incident down to too much punch. I apologize if you thought it more than that. I care for you very deeply as a friend, of course, but it will never be more than that."

Pain lanced through his eyes and struck her directly in the heart. It was bad enough to break her own heart, but to break his as well was too much to bear.

Garrett closed his eyes, put his palms on his thighs and

took several long breaths before he looked at her again. "I see. Then you are still determined to never remarry."

Again, a lie would be so easy. Aurora bit the inside of her cheek. "Actually, I've decided to find a suitable father for my children. I shall make an arrangement with a man of good standing for whom feelings will not interfere with an amicable marriage."

A look grew in Garrett's eyes that she'd never seen before. Fierce and dangerous, he was hardly recognizable. "And who are you considering for this lofty position?"

"There's no need to be rude, Garrett. You and I do not suit. I want you for my friend but cannot give you what you wish for." She folded her hands in her lap and forced herself to keep from fidgeting.

"Who, Rora?"

"The other Wallflowers and I have come up with three possibilities. Of course, they will need to be investigated for bad habits and such. I am currently thinking of the Earl of Belham, Viscount West, and the Marquess of Potsum."

Garrett blinked several times, took a deep breath, and let his gaze fall back on Aurora. "I am sure you will find a suitable arrangement with one of them." Standing, he crossed to the door before stopping and turning back.

"Was there something else, Garrett?" She wanted to kiss him, to feel his arms around her again, but what would be the point? He deserved a wife he could cherish and possess, and she would never be that wife.

"Only the irony." He grabbed his gloves and hat from the table near the door.

Aurora searched his face for some clue to what he meant. "I don't understand."

"For years, you Wallflowers have gone to great pains to keep away from the cold loveless marriages arranged by so many families of the ton. Now, it seems, it is all you could want. You will be a wonderful mother, Rora. Of that, I have no doubt, but what kind of example will you have set for your sons and daughters in your business arrangement of a marriage?"

"That life is not always fair. It is a good lesson to learn early on." It took all her energy to hold down the despair churning inside her.

Garrett's shoulders slumped. He shook his head. He met her gaze. "I fear you have learned that lesson far too well, dear friend. I wish you well on your quest."

And he left.

Aurora held down tears until her stomach ached with them.

CHAPTER TWENTY-ONE

$\mathcal{A}$ highly touted new soprano meant that the theater was filled to capacity. Garrett didn't generally mind a crowd, but he'd been in a foul mood since Aurora's declaration that she would marry, but she wouldn't marry him.

Mary Yates and her mother, the countess of Flitmore had been stalking him for a fortnight and it was becoming tiresome. Even as he attempted to make his way to his box, he spotted the two tenacious women parting the crowds to get to him.

"Your Grace," Mary called before he was far enough away to make a pretense of not hearing her.

It wasn't that he didn't find Mary attractive. She was lovely and exactly as a young lady should be. She was both accomplished and smart, but since the reaction he'd gotten from Aurora and the other Wallflowers, he'd paid attention to the small things. Mary could be cutting to those she thought beneath her, and Garrett found that distinctly unattractive.

Trapped, he plastered a warm smile on his face and turned. "Lady Flitmore, Lady Mary, how nice to see you again."

Lady Flitmore fanned her ample bosom with an elaborate fan. "These things are always so hot, Your Grace. We were to sit in Lady Decatur's box, but it is so full I thought I might perish from the heat."

"Are your friends with you this evening, Your Grace?" Mary batted her eyelashes. Her expression was perfectly balanced between adoration and coyness. It should have been alluring, but instead Garrett was repulsed.

Something about her was all wrong and it had nothing to do with her trying to catch him as a husband. Most young ladies of the ton would jump a moat to wed a duke. He was used to that. It was something more and Garrett couldn't quite put his finger on it. "No. I'm on my own tonight."

"Just you in that big box?" Lady Flitmore practically purred. She dipped forward so that her breasts were precariously close to tumbling out of her sapphire gown. One might think *she* was after capturing a duke in marriage rather than her daughter.

Mary frowned at her mother and slid to the side to block the embarrassing display.

Grateful for that, Garrett had to hold in a laugh. "Would you ladies like to join me? I'm sure it will be cooler than Lady Decatur's box."

"You are too kind." Mary didn't quite simper, but it was nearly that vulgar.

He escorted them up the steps and down the hall to where an usher waited to open the curtain and help them inside. Garrett saw that his guests were seated and said, "Ladies, I shall return in a moment. I see the Earl of Marsden and need a word. Make yourselves comfortable."

Practically running from his box, Garrett sprinted down the steps and found Rhys and Poppy near the main doors.

Rhys stepped back and Aurora was behind him. Dressed in a gown the color of wine with a low bodice and just a hint of lace, she was as elegant as she was breathtaking.

Beside her, the earl of Belham gaped at him and bowed. "Your Grace, good of you to condescend."

Oh Lord in heaven. "How do you do, Belham. Nice to see you, my ladies. Marsden, may I have a word?"

Wide eyed, Rhys stepped out into the lobby. "What on earth is wrong with you, Garrett? Since when do you call me by my title?"

"Belham is not within our circle. I wouldn't want to start rumors of any kind. Is Rora being courted by that buffoon?" Garrett's stomach literally heaved at the notion that Michael Perch, earl of Belham might lay a hand on Aurora."

"Is that why you pulled me out here?" Rhys looked back to make certain his wife and sister were safe.

"No. I just needed to get away from my own box. It seems Mary Yates is determined to invade my world."

Rhys had the nerve to laugh and not a polite chuckle, a full guffaw.

"I don't see what's so funny. She's pretty enough and has plenty of money. It might be a good match." Why Garrett was defending the idea, was a mystery to him.

"Other than the fact that it was Mary Yates who dubbed our friends and family 'wallflowers' and made their lives hell while away at school. Other than the fact that Mary Yates might be the only woman who all four Wallflowers agree is vile. I see nothing wrong with the match. However, far be it from me to tell you who to court." Rhys let another laugh spill out.

"Oh." Garrett looked back at Aurora. "Don't let her marry that dunderhead."

Rhys shrugged. "As you well know, Rora has a mind of her own. I have little control, but if it's any consequence, I believe she's already bored out of her head. He speaks of nothing but insects."

"Bugs is it." It made Garrett strangely happy, but maybe that was the kind of man Aurora wanted. They would have nothing in common and therefore nothing to keep them under the same roof.

"You had better get back to your guests, Your Grace." Rhys winked and returned to his wife's side.

Poppy gave Garrett a sympathetic smile and a helpless shrug that surely indicated she wished he were their companion rather than Belham. However, Aurora didn't look at him at all. She paid close attention to whatever Belham was pontificating over and had the blank look she'd perfected over the years. No emotions showed on the outside, and she looked perfectly content to anyone who didn't know her well.

With no options, Garrett returned to his box and wished he had a large glass of whisky to get him through the evening.

By the end of the second act, he thought he might poke his own eyes out. Mary had been perfectly charming, but her mother never let up about all of Mary's talents. It was a running dialog of why Mary would make an excellent wife.

When the music started again and both ladies were engrossed by the soprano, Garrett excused himself from the box and wandered down to the lobby.

The elaborate decor was awash with deep reds and golds. A chandelier filled the lobby with light.

A swish of wine-colored dress poked out from behind a curtain. Beyond was another row of boxes, which lay across from his. There might be any number of women wearing that color tonight. He might be about to make an ass of himself, but he couldn't stop as he crossed the carpet and eased the curtain back. "Rora?"

She gasped. The shimmering light of the candles and crystal caught in her sky-blue eyes and shimmered off the diamonds in her hair. "What are you doing?"

"The same as you. Hiding." He let the scent of roses and promise fill him up.

Pulling her shoulders back she pursed her lips. "I am not hiding. I just needed some air and some quiet."

"Why are you doing this to us?" The question was out before he could stop himself.

"Doing? I'm doing nothing to us. There is no us. You will see in time that I have the right of it." Her words came in a rush that was far too practiced even in the required whisper of the theater.

Taking her hand, he tugged her down the hall to a small alcove where a curtain would properly hide them from anyone getting a break from the music or the company. It was dark and the sounds were muted. He pulled her close so her body pressed to his. He could barely see her, but he felt her breath coming harder. "What I see is that you are dooming us both to a life of misery. I could live with that for myself, Rora. It's what I have always expected. But the idea of you living out your life in a loveless marriage breaks something raw and needy inside me. I'm begging you to reconsider."

Silence followed, but a tear fell on his hand where he still held her upper arms. He skimmed his hands up and down her skin. "You said you didn't mean the things you told me when you'd been drinking, but I say a drunken man's words are a sober man's thoughts. I'm sorry you're afraid to love, but do not lie to yourself, Rora. You are capable of great passion."

"Garrett, why must you make this so difficult." She blew out a breath. "You are angry and maybe jealous. I should not have given myself to you."

"You think this is about sex?" He kissed her forehead and breathed in her scent. "I love you, Rora. That will never change."

"That is exactly why we cannot be together. Don't you see. You will be irrevocably hurt should you marry a woman who will never return your affections." Her voice was a mask of cool reserve.

Garrett ran one hand along her jaw. His thumb caressed her lips.

They parted on a gasp and Garrett leaned in until his lips pressed to hers. She stilled as he drew her bottom lip between his. He treated her top lip the same.

Her hand curled around his neck and she toyed with the hair at his nape.

Under his gentle caress her mouth opened to him and their souls mingled in an exchange of breath. A sigh puffed from deep inside her and he was lost to the possibilities of a life with Aurora.

His body burned for all of her, but they were in the middle of a theater and he was still a gentleman. "May I come to West Lane tonight? I would like to speak of a possible future with you, Aurora."

She spread her hand across her chest and caught her breath. "There is no future. I'll not deny we have passion, but I cannot be what you need or deserve, Garrett. I know you think I'm being foolish. I know you disapprove, but I'm a grown woman and make my own decisions. I would appreciate it if you would respect them."

The pain in his chest bloomed until every part of him ached. "Of course. If that is what you want, I'll not bring up my wishes again."

"Those are my wishes." Her voice wavered, but she said nothing more.

"Then you had better go back to your seat. I will return to my box in a few minutes. We wouldn't want anyone to think we were together."

For a long moment she didn't move and part of him thought she might be having a change of heart, but then she whispered, "Good-night Garrett."

With his head leaning against the wall, he waited as she left him in the dark alcove without the slightest hope. He understood she feared giving her life over to a man but now he saw it was more than that. She must have expected to love Radcliff. She must have gone into her marriage with a girls dream of love and happiness, and had found only misery and pain. Her notion of marrying an unfeeling but mild man had its merits, but she could never be happy with such an arrangement.

One thing was certain, she was a grown woman and he had been thwarted by her for the last time. He vowed not to renew his affections and wishes and he would abide by his word.

Garrett pulled his shoulders back, left the niche and went back to his box.

Mary and her mother looked at him when he entered, but asked no questions. Perhaps they had seen Aurora return to her box a few minutes earlier and supposed where he was. It made no difference. Mary Yates was not likely to be his duchess, but someone would have to fill the role. It was time to put childish notions aside and do his duty.

Still, his gaze drifted to Rhys's box. Aurora listened intently to something Belham said then smiled. Even at that distance it was obvious Belham would never elicit any passion from Aurora. She went through motions as they were expected and evaluated him like one might a stock animal.

Garrett stood, looked at the wide-eyed ladies in his box and couldn't bear another moment. "Ladies, enjoy the rest of the performance. I must go."

He gave them no opportunity to argue, but rushed from the box, down to the lobby and outside. His carriage was buried behind several others. Giving Reggie, his driver a nod, he walked away from the theater.

The first threads of autumn's cooler air filled the late summer night. The streets were quiet with most people already out for the evening and not yet heading home. It was a good time to walk. He would be home in thirty minutes if he kept a good pace. Perhaps he'd even be in a better mood.

Aurora had made a list of men to investigate and pick from. A list he was excluded from because she had feelings for him. Perhaps she had the right of it. He would make his own list and find a suitable wife to be his duchess. It hardly left one awash with notions of romance, but without love, what was the point of searching for romance.

In the morning, he would contact Wesley and decline the dinner party invitation. He cursed. What would he say, he was too much of a coward to face Aurora for an evening so he wouldn't dine with any of his friends? Then would that be only the first of dozens of invitations he'd have to refuse to avoid her? No. He'd not abandon his friends, nor would he refute his word to be Aurora's friend no matter what.

It would be difficult for a time, but then they would get used to the sight of each other with their respective spouses.

The knot that had formed in Garrett's gut tightened, and he feared he must grow used to its presence.

CHAPTER TWENTY-TWO

Aurora arrived at the Earl and Countess of Castlewick's townhouse early to see if she could be of use to Mercy on the eve of her first dinner party.

Autumn had arrived and the weather was cool with the promise of an early winter. It would mean the bulk of society would be coming to town earlier than usual. The entire summer had been rather cooler than normal and Aurora wished less of the ton had been around. Another escape to Whickette Park and the Castlewick School might be in order. If for no other reason, to escape the mess she'd made.

She stood outside Mercy's music room and listened to the sound of the guitar.

"I can see you there, Aurora. Why don't you come inside?" Mercy never missed a note as she issued the invitation.

"I didn't want to interrupt. It's very beautiful whatever you're playing." It wasn't exactly a lie, but neither was it the truth. The music was beautiful, but Aurora had not stayed in the hall to avoid interruption.

"You were woolgathering. Tell me what you were thinking about?" Mercy put the guitar aside. "I have some time before our guests arrive, and the staff here barely allows me to do anything. They're so efficient, I only walk through and nod my approval."

"I was thinking that I dread seeing the Marquess of Potsum almost as much as I dread seeing Garrett, and I'm seriously thinking of running off to Cheshire to avoid the coming season." There, it was out. She'd said it and she didn't feel bad about it. Well, not much anyway.

"You asked me to invite Potsum, Aurora." Mercy leaned forward and took Aurora's hands.

"I know. And my reasoning is still sound." She wanted a baby and not to be bothered by the affections of a husband. It was a good plan.

A maid stepped inside.

"Lila, will you take my guitar up to my room. I'll not need it tonight and I'd hate for it to be ruined." Mercy crossed the room to hand the maid the instrument.

When they were alone again, Mercy looked back at Aurora. "I never thought the idea very sound to begin with. How can you be assured that a man like Potsum won't fall in love with you?"

"Love? He hardly seems the type."

Mercy shrugged. "Even a stuffy man can fall in love, Aurora. At least with a man like Garrett, you know he'll always put you before anything else in his life." She held up a hand to stop Aurora's excuses. "I know everything that's going on in that head of yours and we must agree to disagree. I will support whatever decisions you make."

"Even if I run away to a certain girls' school for a few months." Aurora raised her brows in an attempt at humor.

The knocker sounded in the front hall. Mercy had a wide-eyed look of horror for a moment before she steeled her features. "It's only friends."

Aurora rose and took her arm. "That's right. It's only friends. It will be a very fine night."

They stepped into the hall. Mercy squeezed her hand. "If you must retreat to the country, then you shall have my support in that as well. Only promise me you will find someone to escort you. You cannot go all that way by yourself. It's far too dangerous."

With a nod, Aurora's agreement was half-hearted, and they went to the parlor where Wesley was already greeting Poppy, Rhys, and Mercy's Aunt Phyllis.

Mercy played the pianoforte in the parlor while they waited for the rest of the guests to arrive. Her play was so riveting that Aurora could escape into it for a while. The strains of some piece she thought might be Handel nearly brought tears to her eyes. Of course, Mercy cried openly whenever she played, but Aurora couldn't allow herself to show that kind of emotion. In fact, she wouldn't allow such sentiment into her heart at all.

While seeing her friends was always a delight, her mission was to see if the Marquess of Potsum would suit as the father of her children. She shrugged off how merciless it sounded in her own head.

Aurora knew the moment Garrett arrived. Her skin seemed to warm, but that was not possible. She had decided irrevocably against any additional emotional or physical contact with Garrett and that was the end of it. The fact that the memory of his hands and mouth on her skin was the only joy in her life, made no difference. Actually, those realizations were even more reason to dismiss him as nothing more than a friend.

Refusing to turn and look at him, Aurora kept her attention fixed on Mercy at her pianoforte.

The warmth of Garrett reached her through his coat as he sat down next to her. "Good evening, Rora."

"Hello, Garrett. Did you bring Lady Mary with you?" Why had she said it? She didn't know why she couldn't bare the idea of Mary Yates becoming Garrett's duchess. It should mean nothing to her. Yet, Mary would play his heart out and he was too kind to take such a beating.

A low chuckle quashed any jealousy. "I noticed some of my favorite people do not care for Lady Mary. As I'm fond of spending my leisure time with the Wallflowers and their spouses, I thought it best to end any pursuit of that particular lady."

Mercy stopped her play and smiled as she rose and crossed to where the last of the evening's guest had joined the party. Paul Trout, the Marquess of Potsum and Lady Prudence Harcourt were the last to arrive.

Aurora met Garrett's kind gaze. "I would never presume to tell you whom you should or shouldn't court. Though, I'll admit to some relief that Mary will not be joining our circle."

"Would you care to tell me why this gives you such ease?" Garrett rose as she did to join the others.

With a shake of her head, Aurora bit her bottom lip. She could go on and on about everything that was wrong with Mary Yates, but that would be unkind. "To tell you my thoughts on the matter would make me no better than those I despise. It will have to be enough to say she and I do not get along well."

A curl of his hair fell forward on his forehead. It was all she could do to keep from brushing the lock aside. He ran his hand over his hair to adjust the curl, but only succeeded in making himself look rakishly handsome. "Perhaps I will ask Poppy for more information. She tends to be more loose-lipped."

Taking her cue from his devilish smile, Aurora covered her laugh with her gloved hand. "You might do better."

They reached the others and Lord Potsum immediately sought her out and Garrett slipped away from her side. The room seemed to cool at his departure, but Aurora brushed the foolishness aside and made a curtsy for the marquess. "Lord Potsum, it is good to see you."

Paul Trout had inherited his title from an uncle who'd had no sons. Aurora had been encouraged by the fact that he'd arranged a nice home for his aunt and her daughter rather than toss them out in the cold. "I was honored to be invited."

His bow was economical but gracious. His mouse-brown hair had begun to recede, and his blue eyes never quite remained on her face as if he were uncomfortable with any direct address. Several inches taller than her, he was still the shortest man in the room, and she noted he'd chosen to wear boots with a heavy heel to raise himself up.

Vanity was no crime and if it were, she would be as guilty as anyone, so she shrugged it away. "How is your family?"

"Well enough. My aunt has taken her daughter to buy clothes for the season." He sighed. "Mother is still in the country and will not arrive until the true season begins."

It was indeed early for gatherings among the ton. Most of society would not arrive in London for another month, but his tone was more snobbish than she would prefer. "I'm sure your cousin will enjoy her season. I hope she makes a good match."

Aurora knew her response was the expected one, and she privately hoped whomever his cousin chose would be kind and of her own choosing and not some sop foisted upon her. She kept those thoughts to herself.

Potsum sighed yet again. "Margery is a plain girl, but a good sort. I shall try to do my best by her as it is what my mother and uncle would wish."

"It is good of you to look after them." Aurora wondered at his sour expression.

He waved a hand and gave an eye roll. "Trying, but necessary I suppose."

Unsure of what to respond, Aurora just nodded and excused herself to join the others as dinner was announced.

It was probably just the shock of seeing Garrett escort Prudence into dinner as it couldn't be jealousy that made her gut tighten. She'd liked Prudence when they were in school. She was a nice girl and likely a fine woman. Aurora should be pleased that a nice man was looking after her at the dinner party. After all, they had widowhood in common as well as having attended the same school.

Potsum offered his arm and Aurora had no choice but to take it as they entered the dining room. She should be pleased that her plan to find a disinterested husband was working out. Potsum was attentive, but certainly not in any kind of romantic light. He seemed as if he were going through some assigned steps like one would during a dance. That should suit Aurora perfectly.

Garrett pulled out Prudence's chair and said something quietly into her ear that made her smile and joy lit up her wide brown eyes. He smiled too and the sight sent a jolt through Aurora. It took all her years of training to keep her expression reserved and calm. It wouldn't do to make a fool of herself in front of Potsum when she might want to marry him.

Mercy had seated Garrett next to Prudence and the two chatted quietly throughout dinner. Potsum sat beside Aurora, but it was torture to get him to speak at all.

"My lord, do you have any hobbies which you enjoy?" Aurora asked after an entire course of peahen had gone by without a word from him.

"I ride." He put his fork aside and dabbed his lips with his napkin. "I enjoy a good ride. Do you ride, Lady Radcliff?"

Now she was getting somewhere. "I do. I'm sure not so well as you, but I've had training."

"Women rarely ride really well." He turned to speak to Wesley as if his statement should have been sufficient conversation.

It was not his attitudes or dinner chat she was after. It shouldn't matter if she even liked the man as long as he was kind and preferably absent, which his treatment of his relations indicated he was.

Rhys leaned in from her other side. "What do you think, Rora? Is he for you?"

"He could use a bit of polish," she admitted.

"Then you will make a project out of him?" Rhys might be her brother and tended toward protection, but he also had a way of putting things into perspective.

"I don't believe so. Though I'm running out of options."

The look of sympathy on her brother's face was worse than if he'd teased her about her plans. "You shall work it out. You are a brilliant woman and will certainly find the right person to spend your life with. Now that mother isn't badgering you, it will be easier."

There was some pleasure in knowing the incident in Cheshire had cured her mother of her terrible matchmaking habit. "I'm thinking of going back to the Castlewick School for a few weeks. I probably should have just stayed there and seen to the new students as they arrived."

Wesley leaned in. "I had a letter from Malcom yesterday. My cousin is quite taken with the place. He's still on his treasure hunt, of course."

Aurora grinned. "Helen wrote me last week to say he's been a big help to them and has an astounding knowledge of geometry and engineering. He's been teaching the girls."

A strangled noise drew everyone's attention to Poppy, who listened from across the table. She swallowed down a mouthful. "I would have thought it beneath him to teach girls such manly pursuits."

"Evidently not." Mercy smiled at the footman who filled her wineglass. "He quite enjoyed the teaching and seems not to care about the sex of his students."

Aurora liked it when they all talked across the table like family. Of course, it was not proper, but she loved it just the same. "Helen said he barely spends two hours a day on his hunt for treasure. He arrives at first light from the village, breaks his fast with them and then if any of the girls are interested teaches them something of building or how much weight might a stool hold depending on the width, height, and bracing."

A scoff from her right and Potsum said, "What would any girl need to know this for? It's totally impractical. Better she learn to balance the household accounts and play the harp for catching a husband."

The table was silent for longer than was comfortable.

Faith looked ready to jump across the space and poke out Potsum's eyes with her fork.

Prudence cleared her throat. "It might be nice to know more than how to decorate a pillow and add a column of numbers. I for one find the notion intriguing. Do you have room for me at your school, Lady Radcliff?"

A twitter of laughter vanquished the unease at the table.

Aurora could tell she would still like Prudence. "For you, Lady Harcourt, we shall always make room."

Prudence had a small yet charming gap between her front teeth. She grinned and blushed perhaps from the attention of the full table. She'd been shy in school and it seemed some of that had continued into her adulthood. "I think it an admirable pursuit to wish to educate women. We did not have much kindness in our schooling."

Faith sighed. "Agatha Wormbattle could be very harsh and had little nice to say, that is true. However, we did get an education and we had the other girls to support us."

"You four certainly were lucky to have each other." Prudence's voice was kind but also sad.

Had she had any close friends? Aurora couldn't remember her with any particular group of girls. She'd been friendly with them and others, but had she been genuinely close to anyone?

"We were." Poppy said with a smile.

Garrett asked, "Did you get into as much mischief as these four, Lady Harcourt? When Rhys and I visited Switzerland, they were always taking advantage of our good nature and getting into trouble."

"I had my fair share of fun and even wandered around Lucerne with these ladies a few times. I helped Lady Castlewick find a music teacher for some strange instrument from Spain. That was quite an adventure." Her eyes looked far away, and she was as innocent as that young girl for a moment.

Mercy clapped. "You did! It took an entire day. I had heard from a violin player in town that there was a Spaniard musician on the east end. It seemed impossible, but we found him."

Potsum bristled. "Two young girls wandering the streets of a big city like that going to men's establishments. What kind of school was this?"

"We were a bit wild," Aurora admitted. "But we survived quite nicely and even learned a few bits about living in English society."

"I should not like to think of a daughter of mine running wild in a foreign country without a proper chaperone." Potsum's face had twisted like he'd bit into a lemon.

"Nor I, my lord." Prudence's sad admission quieted the fury floating around the table.

Aunt Phyllis rescued the dinner. "The happy ending is, that Mercy did learn to play the guitar and it's the most magical sound imaginable."

Mr. Arafa who had silently watched the byplay throughout dinner, grinned. "That is a certainty. Our hostess plays each and every instrument with such skill. If she wished to be at court entertaining kings and queens, she would be famous."

Mercy cringed. "I think I shall be satisfied with playing for friends, Mr. Arafa, but I thank you for the compliment."

After dinner, Aurora escaped up the stairs to a small parlor that Mercy kept for when her close friends called. It was meant to be the lady's bedroom, but since she and Wesley shared a bedroom, she'd converted the space into a warm oasis of calm and femininity.

The place where a bed should have been held two chairs and a long, overstuffed sofa. A long table separated the seating and a fire burned low in the hearth.

It was unladylike, but Aurora sat leaning against the arm of the sofa and closed her eyes. Potsum was out. She couldn't possibly spend any time with a man that shortsighted and fussy. Not that she had any intentions of sending her daughters away to school as punishment. But, if she were gifted, tenacious and wanted to study, Aurora wanted her father to support her endeavors. Potsum was not that man.

The door opened.

Aurora didn't open her eyes. Faith had probably come to check on her. "I'm fine, Faith."

"It's not Faith, I'm afraid." Garrett's warm soft voice whispered from near the door.

She sat up as if a fire had been lit under her. "You shouldn't be in here."

He inched closer. "I was worried when you didn't return."

Had she been gone so long? "You will have to stop worrying over me. When you marry a nice lady like Prudence, she'll not be pleased to have you seeking out another woman no matter your innocent intentions."

"Lady Harcourt is lovely. I'm sure she would understand.

However, as I'm not currently married to anyone, I see no harm in checking on an old friend." He sat across from her in one of the wine-colored chairs.

"People will talk, Garrett." Her heart hammered so hard her chest hurt.

He cocked his head. "Most of the people in this house tonight are our closest friends and besides, the other men are smoking while the ladies take cake. I have never cared for cigars. No one else will even notice I've slipped out for a few minutes."

Of course, he was probably right, but she'd been determined not to repeat their intimacies and being alone with him fleshed out those memories and made her delightfully uncomfortable. "I'm fine. I just needed a moment to think."

"About Potsum?" His frown caused deep lines around his beautiful mouth.

She nodded with a sigh. "He's not very enlightened, but he's handsome enough and needs an heir."

The fury in his eyes made her think he would give her the fight she'd fished for, but he remained silent a long minute. His jaw ticked and his fists relaxed. "I'm glad you are well, Rora. I will return to our party. Don't remain up here too long or the Wallflowers will come looking for you."

He got up and crossed to her. For a moment, she thought he would lean down and kiss her, but a breath later, he left the room and closed the door behind him.

CHAPTER TWENTY-THREE

Garrett hadn't lied. Prudence Harcourt was lovely. She was also smart and constant. A widow, so there should be little hysterics. Garrett even liked her.

He drank down his brandy and stared into the fire blazing in the large hearth at White's Gentleman's Club.

A hand waved in front of his face. Rhys stared wide eyed. "Where were you just then?"

"Sorry, did you ask something?" Garrett couldn't remember what they'd been saying but it had something to do with Lady Harcourt.

"You said you called on Lady Harcourt and I asked if you like her." Rhys said slowly as if he were speaking to an imbecile.

Garrett laughed at his friend. "I do like her. She's a nice woman with a good head on her shoulders."

"Will you offer for her?"

Shrugging, Garrett said, "She's barely out of mourning for a husband she loved very much. I don't think the timing is quite right."

"You may be correct, but she has a good income and other men will go sniffing around, so if she's the one you want, you shouldn't tarry long." Rhys finished his brandy and called for a footman to bring them both another.

"I will keep that in mind." He told the lie with ease. Lying about his marital intentions had become second nature to him. Since he had no idea what he was going to do beyond finding a wife he could tolerate that wasn't Aurora, all he could do was fib until the situation sorted itself out.

"Speaking of callers." Rhys took his brandy and set it on the table beside him. He sank back into the leather chair and steeped his fingers under his chin. "Aurora seems to have embraced the idea of remarrying."

Garrett's gut pressed up into his gullet and he had to swallow hard to keep his brandy from returning. "Has she?"

"My mother told me that Lord West has joined the fray of men bidding for her hand and Potsum is a daily caller at West Lane."

"You might want to look into Potsum's finances before you give your sister any advice on the matter." Garrett tried and failed to keep his disgust from his voice.

Leaning forward, Rhys frowned. "Have you already done so?"

With a shrug, Garrett couldn't quite meet his friend's eyes. "That would be inappropriate as I have nothing at stake. I'm just making a suggestion to a friend."

Deep creases around Rhys's mouth spoke of his rising anger. "Bollocks to that, Garrett. What do you know?"

Several men turned and stared as Rhys's voice rose.

Suddenly his brandy didn't appeal. "It would be unwise to speak of it here."

Rhys rose immediately. "Fine. Then you will accompany me back to your home where you will divulge anything and everything that might pertain to this subject, or you and I shall have a problem."

It was understandable that Rhys wished to protect his sister, but Garrett had no idea of the passion that hid inside his oldest friend on the subject. It was clear it would never do to keep withholding the information. He had planned to wait until it was certain Aurora would accept an offer. "Very well."

Rising they left the club under the watchful gaze of many members. Rhys had made a scene and it would lead to speculation.

The carriages pulled forward and Rhys huffed out a long breath. "Tell me this, Garrett. The information you now conceal, would you have ever divulged it if I hadn't just made a scene in public?"

"Of course. If Potsum offered for Aurora, I would have gone to her with the information." A sudden realization that Aurora might not have believed him at that late date gnawed at him.

Still, the admission caused Rhys's expression to ease. He instructed his driver to follow to Garrett's townhouse and climbed into Garrett's carriage.

"Shall I tell you now or do we wait until we're at my home?" He'd started investigating Potsum the morning after the dinner party. Something about the man didn't sit right.

Rhys's eyes flashed in the carriage's lamplight. "Tell me everything and tell me now. If you think for one moment I will allow my sister to enter into another disastrous marriage, you don't know me at all."

Shame washed over Garrett. Of course, his friend suffered over what had happened to Aurora. He'd been a fool not to see it. "At the Castlewick dinner party I overheard Potsum lamenting his need to keep his aunt and cousin housed and fed. He even mentioned paying for his cousin's clothes for the season so she might find a husband. It seemed odd to me that a Marquess should worry over what was not only his duty, but a very small expense."

Sitting back, Rhys scowled. "I heard him talking about it too. After dinner when the men joined the ladies for cake, he was telling Mercy's aunt how he hoped his cousin would marry and take one more responsibility off his plate."

"I doubt there was a person at the event that didn't hear some story about his troubles." Garrett attempted calm but was sure a sneer donned his lips.

"Honestly, I didn't give the matter much thought. He's such a dullard, I didn't think Aurora would actually allow any type of courtship."

The carriage rounded a corner and Garrett noted they were getting close to his home. "Perhaps the rest can wait for a warm fire and good wine."

One could practically see the wheels turning inside Rhys's head as he considered a man who looks for sympathy, when taking care of his family is his duty; if not by law, then by honor.

The carriage stopped and neither waited for the driver to pull down the step. They jumped down and climbed the stairs where Casper, Garrett's aging butler opened the door. "Your Grace, you are home early."

Garrett handed over his hat. "Casper, can you pull a bottle of the 1790 Madeira for us? Lord Marsden and I have some business to discuss in my study."

Taking all the outerwear, Casper gave a nod. "Of course, Your Grace."

Once inside the warm study with a good fire burning and wall to wall books of every kind, Garrett felt more himself. This was his place. He'd taken over this townhouse long before his father passed as his parents rarely came to town. The tall shelves were packed with books he shipped from all over the world, and he relished the memories he'd made finding each and every one.

Rhys scanned the shelves. "Quite a collection."

"It's a bit of a hobby I picked up on my journey around the continent. I think the staff was happy to have me home just so they wouldn't have to sort through any more shipments of books." Garrett lit a taper from the fire and, with it set several other candles aflame in the candelabra on the table. On either side of the table two high backed, royal-blue chairs sat near the hearth. He sat and offered Rhys the other chair.

"Before you tell me about Potsum, will you tell me something else?" Rhys shifted in the chair as if the topic had gone from maddening to uncomfortable.

"I will try." It was the best he could offer before hearing what the question was. He'd not betray Aurora. Not even to her brother, and Rhys's discomfort gave Garrett a foreboding feeling. Could her brother know he'd been intimate with Aurora?

Rhys looked everywhere but at Garrett for over a minute. Then he met Garrett's gaze. "I know it's a secret you keep, and I know I'm not supposed to say anything, but you've been in love with Rora most of our lives, man. Why don't you offer for her?"

Relief and panic in equal doses washed over Garrett. Had he been so obvious? He supposed so. He swallowed several times before he was able to speak, and even then, he wished Casper would arrive with the damned Madeira. "I did. She was not receptive to the idea."

"Damn." Rhys's shoulders slumped and he hung his head. "I'm sorry, Garrett. I know she feels for you."

Casper opened the door and brought a decanter of deep red wine with him. He placed the wine on the table between them, went to the cart near the window and procured two cut-crystal glasses and brought them to the table.

"I shall pour, Casper. Thank you." Garret's voice was sterner than he'd intended.

Casper raised one gray brow. "As you wish. If you have no further need of me." He bowed and left the study.

Taking up the crystal, Garrett poured two glasses. His heart broke every time he thought of Aurora's refusal to marry him. Lifting his glass, he sipped the rich wine. He certainly didn't want to relive the experience with Rhys. "After the dinner party, I looked into the status of the dowager Marchioness of Potsum and her daughter. I also looked into the activities and mother of the current marquess."

Rhys held his glass but didn't drink. "What did you find?"

"It's very good wine, Rhys. Don't let it go to waste." He

was stalling. Gossip was not something he often indulged in, but he thought Aurora would more likely listen to her brother on this subject then she would him. And she should not accept any offer from Potsum.

"I'll drink, you talk." Rhys sipped the wine.

"His aunt and cousin are living in squalor in a small cottage near Plymouth. His uncle gave provisions for them, but Potsum has contrived a way to keep that money to himself. In the year since he's been marquess, he's spent a great deal on schemes that have not gone well. He's used his cousin's dowry, leaving her with nothing but her charms to offer. He is paying for one season of clothes. I have that from the modiste, but she is yet to be paid. His mother has not been seen in over a year, and I have sent out a letter to the country estate in the lake district to find out if she's even still alive. I'll give him credit for keeping all this quiet while pretending to be the savior of all. He's deeply in debt and needs to marry someone with available cash." Garrett hesitated to tell the rest.

"And…" Rhys prompted. His friend knew him too well.

Garrett sighed. "And I went to his club and listened to some talk where it was implied that he had every intention of, and I quote, "selling the ridiculous school of hers as his first act as her lord and master."

"He didn't actually say lord and master?" Rhys's eyes were wide, and his mouth pulled in a tight line.

"Those were the words I heard just last night. I've been vacillating on what to tell Rora, but this will be better. She needs to know, but will accept the information better coming from you." A weight lifted from Garrett. It didn't ease his pain, but perhaps his worry.

"He plays at being so mild and at ease. I would never

think him acting a part the entire time." Rhys set aside his half-empty glass.

Garrett filled it. "He does a good job, and according to the modiste has threatened his cousin and aunt with homelessness if they so much as say one word about his financial state."

"They told the modiste?" Rhys stated the obvious.

Garrett grinned. "Madam Bouchard is a good listener and a very sympathetic ear."

"I see. She wheedled it out of them."

"It would seem so," Garrett confirmed.

Rhys stood and paced. "So, he needs Rora's money. How far will he go to get it? Do we have another Hexon on our hands?"

A knot formed deep in Garrett's gut. "Somehow, I think Potsum might be worse. We could see on the surface what Hexon was; a drunk, a man of low regard for women, a bigot to be sure. Potsum strikes me as more dangerous. He is very adept at hiding what he is. He fooled us at the dinner party, and he certainly fooled Aurora into believing in his altruism toward his family. After his bad behavior at dinner, that can be the only reason she's still considering him."

"I will speak to her." Rhys sat and drank his wine.

Awash with relief, Garrett refilled his own glass.

G arrett had considered not going to the Dunworth Ball. Lady Dunworth was the sister of Nicholas Ellsworth, and Garrett felt compelled to attend. Part of him couldn't resist a night where he would see and perhaps speak to Aurora. It was foolish self-torture, but he couldn't resist.

His internal debate had lasted long enough that he was now quite late in arriving at the elegant townhouse of the Earl and Countess of Dunworth. It was just as well, as sneaking in late allowed him to avoid the curious gazes of the ton.

Aurora was like a beacon in a deep blue gown that spoke of the sea and sky. The flowing material clung to her curves as she spoke animatedly to her friends. Her golden hair was woven with pearls and sapphires allowing him a delicious view of her neck with just a few curls laying along her shoulders.

Swallowing his desire, he plastered on the disinterested expression of a duke and crossed the ballroom. Before he reached the object of his desire, Prudence Harcourt waved shyly from the edge of the dance floor where she stood alone.

Garrett smiled. "How do you do, my lady?"

"I am well, Your Grace. This is quite a crush." She referred to the crowded ballroom.

"Elaine Trent rarely comes to town let alone does she throw a ball. Society is clamoring to get in." Garrett noted Prudence's pale blue gown woven with silver thread. It suited the shy widow and her slight figure.

"I suppose that is true."

Garrett offered his arm. "I was just going over to speak

with our mutual friends, if you'd care to join me, Lady Harcourt."

She took his arm. "I would like that very much. I admit to being a bit out of place in such a large crowd. My mother is in the music room with a group of dowagers. I know I'd be welcome, but I feel even more awkward with them. It seemed easier to get lost in the crowd."

Patting her hand, he sympathized with Prudence. "You look very lovely this evening and should be confident to roam about the ball."

A warm blush flushed up her pretty face making her even prettier. Several men looked on as they journeyed across the room. There was nothing more attractive to the shallow men of the ton than a woman who was sought after by a duke.

Ridiculous.

"Garrett! We thought you'd decided not to come," Poppy said.

"I was late in dressing this evening." It was the truth at least in part.

Aurora's cheeks paled. "Lady Harcourt, you look beautiful. How good to see you again."

Prudence leaned in and whispered. "I think I shall have to beg the duke to walk with me more often. I would swear I had more attention just now crossing the room than I did during the entire two seasons before I married."

The group laughed at her jest and Garrett couldn't help being impressed that she'd not only noticed the attention, but the cause. Not that she wasn't very attractive, but it took more than a pretty face to impress society.

To that point, Decklan Garrott arrived as the first strains of music began. "Lady Harcourt, if you are not otherwise engaged, may I have the honor of this dance?"

Prudence smiled and wagged her brows at the group before she turned her attention to Decklan. "I would be delighted, sir."

"She could do better," Poppy mused.

Mercy shrugged. "He's a good sort and has a decent living now. She could do worse."

Wesley laughed. "It's only a dance, ladies. Let's not marry the poor woman off just yet."

Garrett had promised himself he'd keep his distance, but the waltz was playing as he'd missed the first set with his tardiness. Garrett leaned in and breathed her fresh, warm scent. "Rora, will you dance with me?"

Without looking at him, she nodded and took his arm.

He took her hand in his, framed her back with his other arm, waited a beat and joined them in the swirl of dancers. "I hope you don't mind my asking."

Looking up, her gaze was watery before she lowered her chin and wouldn't meet his stare. "No. Never that. I thought perhaps you would ask Prudence, but I suppose Decklan was faster."

"Look at me, Rora." His heart tore in half when she complied. So much emotion raged in her, but he had little reference to sort it out. It was so rare to see any emotion displayed by Aurora. "If I'd wanted to dance with Lady Harcourt, I would have asked her when I escorted her across the room. I hadn't planned to dance at all, but then you were there. I find it hard to resist an opportunity to hold you in my arms."

"You shouldn't say such things." She drew a ragged breath.

He shrugged. "It is the truth."

"I'm going to Cheshire." She blurted it out much louder than was necessary.

Inadvertently, he gripped her tighter. Perhaps his body wanted to keep her close and stop her from running away from him or whatever she needed to escape. "When?"

"In a few days. I have a few things to go over with Helen." Her throat bobbed with several swallows.

Mesmerized by her neck and desperate to kiss his way along the hallow of her throat, he gave himself an inward shake to remind of where he was. "Who is taking you?"

She pulled her shoulders back. "No one. I'm a grown woman and can travel between my own properties. I shall bring two extra footmen for safety, but cannot tolerate waiting on a man to carry me here and there."

"I see." He held back his desire to chuckle as she would likely take it for condescension. It wasn't that at all. She was brave and strong and so damned adorable he longed to pull her tight and kiss her until they were both breathless.

Fire flared in her eyes. "Are you laughing at me?"

God she was incredible. "Not at all. You are a grown woman of means and certainly can make your own decisions. I assume your footmen are reliable and your maid will be with you."

"Of course. And my driver, John has been with me for years." She missed a step and he righted them. "I will be fine."

"You'll send word and let someone know when you arrive safely?" When she stiffened again, he softened his tone. "You cannot fault me for worrying over you, Rora. It's not as if I can help it. You are my friend, my dearest and most precious friend. I only want to know that you are safe and happy."

A soft smile pulled at her full lips. Lips he would die for. Lips that drew him in like the proverbial moth to a flame.

Then those lips were moving and he had to snap out of his daydream.

"I do not like it when we quarrel or disagree, Garrett. You told me once that we would always be friends no matter what happened in our lives apart. I had begun to think you were mistaken in that assertion."

"No, Rora. I shall love you all the days of my life regardless of where our lives take us." He took a modicum of satisfaction from her gaping mouth and flushed cheeks.

They whirled around the room in a flurry of colors, but only looked into each other's eyes. Garrett wanted to beg her to reconsider or at least ask her if he could accompany her to Cheshire. He did neither as those were not the things she wanted from him, and he had said he would not renew his desire to marry her. If she changed her mind, she would have to come to him. He prayed every waking hour that she would do just that. Chest and stomach in knots, he steadied his breath and reveled in the moments of the dance where nothing else existed beyond Aurora and him.

Garrett bowed as the music ended, regretting the need to let her go.

Potsum stumbled as he ran across the room toward them. "Lady Radcliff, this is my dance, I believe."

Her lips twitched between amusement and annoyance as she curtsied to Garrett. "Thank you for the dance, Your Grace."

"The pleasure was mine."

Grabbing her elbow, Potsum gave Garrett a curt nod and tugged her deeper onto the dance floor.

CHAPTER TWENTY-FOUR

Aurora had been set upon by Lord Potsum as soon as she arrived at the ball and couldn't think of a good reason to refuse him a dance. At least, not one she wished to say publicly.

The things her brother, Rhys had told her about him, made her skin crawl. She had to admit he was a fine actor, but also a man of no integrity. He held her elbow too tightly and might leave a mark with his thumb. She tugged it away. "My lord, you needn't bully me. I said I will dance with you and here we are awaiting the music."

A slight twitch of his thin lips might have indicated amusement. "Here we are indeed, my lady. And I could not be happier. You have been on my mind a great deal lately."

The music started and he was forced to stop whatever nonsense he was about to say and join a foursome for the quadrille. She prayed it would be a short version.

When they came together, he attempted a grin that looked as if he were just baring his teeth. Aurora hoped she hadn't flinched, but she feared she had as the man's expression was horrifying.

She supposed she was being overly dramatic, but knowing what she did, she found Potsum even more unappealing than she had at the dinner party. Thankful each time the dance pulled them apart, she prayed the last strains would soon free her from his company.

It began to occur to her that she attracted the most despicable men, but she brushed the notion aside. After all, she'd never met Radcliff before they were engaged. Her father had forced him on her. Wesley had wished to marry her and he was a good and honorable man. He was just the wrong man. Hexon, well, she put him in the same category as Potsum. Malcolm Renshaw had not really wanted her. He just wanted his treasure hunt.

Then there was Garrett. Even now, she felt his gaze on her, watching, making sure she was safe. Her entire body sighed, though she'd never let the whole of society see such a display. Heaven forbid Potsum think she was lamenting his attentions.

When the music ended, she practically ran from the ballroom, but Potsum followed calling her name.

Unable to bear a scene, Aurora stopped at the doors to

the veranda and faced him. "Did you wish to say something, my lord?"

"I would request a private conversation with you, Lady Radcliff." He bowed.

Aurora scanned behind him for some friend who might rescue her, but found the room readying for another dance. "As we are attending a rather crowded ball at the moment, sir, it seems poor timing for a private talk."

He gazed into the distance head cocked, before meeting her stare. "Be that as it may, I require your time, Lady Radcliff."

Short of making a bigger scene, she nodded her assent and walked outside. The cooler weather and the lively dance kept most of the ton indoors.

Potsum took her elbow again and moved her to one side of the veranda. There was no one else so far from the doors. As soon as they arrived near the low wall that served as a rail for the enclosure, Aurora pulled her arm free. "If you please, my lord."

As if he'd not manhandled her twice, he widened his eyes in confusion. He recovered promptly, and his expression returned to bland indifference. "I wish for you to be my wife."

Aurora waited for more, but it seemed that was the entirety of what he would say. "I see."

"What is your answer?"

Temper bloomed in Aurora's chest as a fiery heat she had to tamp down lest she make a public display of herself. "As you have not asked a question, my lord, I suppose I am to infer from your wishes that there is some proposal afoot."

"I wish to marry you."

It was almost impossible to keep from rolling her eyes,

but Aurora had learned long ago to keep her feelings tightly locked away, and this imbecile would not make her lose her composure. "I heard you the first time, my lord. As you apparently deem those wishes enough to win my response, I shall reply in similar fashion. I do not wish to marry you, Lord Potsum."

Stepping back, he said, "I am a Marquess. I have power in this land. Women want to marry men with power."

She softened, feeling slightly bad for him. "I suppose that is true of many, my lord. However, while I am flattered by your offer, I must decline."

His pasty cheeks turned bright red, as did his ears. If he'd been a cook-pot he'd have blown his lid off. "I will not be treated thus." He reached for her arm.

Aurora stepped back. How had she come to this? *What a fool she was.* "Do not touch me, sir. You have no rights here. I am not some girl forced to marry by a bullying father, and I shall not be bullied by you. You made your request, and I have declined your offer. If you are a gentleman, which you purport to be, you will incline your head, indicate your regret, and leave me in peace."

Lowering his hand, Potsum looked like his eyes would burst from their sockets. He inclined his head. "I understand, Lady Radcliff. You require more time. I shall call in a few days, and we shall discuss my offer in private."

Before she could tell him not to bother, he spun and strode back to the house.

Leaning back, she let her hips meet the stone wall. How on earth had she not seen before what a fool she was to think a man like Potsum could be what she needed. Was it so hard to find a man to give her a child? All she wanted was to be safe and love a baby with all her heart. It didn't seem that much to ask.

"Rora, are you alright?" Garrett stood a few feet away.

Dinner must be served, as the rest of the veranda was empty, and the music had stopped inside. There he was, beautiful with the moonlight gleaming in his hair.

"Have I been missing so long you needed to make sure I wasn't drunk in the garden again?" She straightened and brushed out her skirt.

He chuckled and closed the distance between them. "I saw you leave with Potsum, and it may be ungentlemanly of me, but I watched from the window to make certain you were safe."

Always her hero. Always reliable. Garrett never disappointed her. "You are a very good friend, Garrett."

Sorrow touched his eyes despite his smile. "May I escort you in for dinner?"

The idea of returning to a crush of people who may already know of the scene with Potsum turned her stomach. "I think I shall take my leave. I have a touch of a headache."

He offered his arm. "I will see you home then?"

Warning bells went off in her head. She shouldn't be alone with Garrett, yet her body must disagree because her hand landed on his arm as if of its own accord. Her skin tingled where she touched him, and heat emanated through the contact, making her breasts ache and her insides clench with need.

"Do you have a wrap I should collect for you?" There was a hitch in his voice. *Could he feel the same heat?*

She nodded. "It would be unseemly for you to gather my things. I shall just go and collect it and meet you at the front."

Inside, the heat stifled her. Panic fringed her sight as she ran through the house to the foyer and asked for her shawl. The minutes it took for the footman to retrieve the lace and satin cloth gave her too much time to think about what she was doing. Leaving a ball with a man and for what possible reason?

Longing. Need. Desire. Escape.

Grabbing her shawl, she muttered her thanks and rushed into the cool night. Having already called for both carriages, Garrett stood at the bottom of the steps. Her driver, John, stood with the door open for her.

It was time to stop being a fool. "John, please take the carriage to West Lane. His Grace is going to see to my saftey."

John closed the door and bowed. "Of course, my lady."

As he stared at her, hints of the gold in Garrett's eyes flashed in the light from the house. "I don't understand, Rora."

Garrett's driver opened the carriage door, and Aurora stepped inside. Whatever she was doing couldn't be spoken of in the street. Not that she was certain what she was about.

A moment later, Garrett sat opposite her, watching her while the carriage rolled down the street. "We're going to my house?" The lilt in his voice was warm, and the shock of her announcement on the street must have ebbed, as his mouth tipped up at the corners. Though he didn't gloat, he looked pleased.

Aurora leaned forward and took his hand from his knee. She held it in both of hers. "I wanted to thank you for the information you gave Rhys regarding Potsum. As he has just proposed, in a manner, it was good to know his true character."

Silence thick between them, he took her hand and turned

the palm up. His thumb traced the lightest circle on her wrist, just above her white glove, and heat flooded her.

He lifted her hand and pressed his lips to her pulse. "I'm glad the information was useful and sorry to have been ungentlemanly in my gathering of it. It was not my place."

One finger at a time, he tugged the glove free and pressed another kiss to her palm.

It would have been no surprise if she burst into flames immediately. His gentle caress and the softness of his lips shot fire through her landing directly between her legs. "Garrett," she breathed.

"What is it you want of me, Rora? I should redirect this carriage and drop you at West Lane, but I have no willpower where you are concerned. If you bade me make love to you right here in the carriage, I shall do as you ask." Sadness and hope tangled in what he said.

Was that what she wanted? "I hardly know how to answer, but I don't want you to set me on the curb in front of my house and leave me tonight. Tonight, I want you, Garrett. I don't want to crawl into my cold bed alone and wish for things I cannot have because of a man long dead and not missed by anyone."

He gently pulled her forward and into his lap. Tucking her head under his chin he held her. As his fingers caressed up and down her back and warmed her even through her corset, she yearned for more of his touch to warm her and make her whole. "Radcliff has not condemned you, Rora. You have done that to yourself. What troubles me is the why of it. Why have you decided so vehemently against love?"

With her cheek pressed against his chest and his heart pounding in her ear, she was safe from the Radcliffs and Potsums of the world. His question struck her so deep, old pains emerged from the wound. "I was a foolish girl. When my father informed me that I would be married after I returned to England, I was happy. In the weeks we traveled from Lucerne to home, I imagined my life as the Countess of Radcliff and it was a grand life. My fiancé wrote to me and sent a miniature of himself. He was handsome, and his smile looked so full of charm. The girls and I giggled all the way back to London about the love I would share with my husband. By the time we arrived, I was in love with the idea of him."

Garrett drew her tighter against him and kissed the top of her head. "But the reality was not anything like the idea."

"No. I knew on my wedding night, and my heart broke." Tears welled up from the cauldron she'd kept covered for so many years. "It shattered so irrevocably that I swore never to give my love to anyone again. I promised to keep my emotions hard and firmly inside."

"And a fine job of it you've done, Rora." He wiped her tears with his knuckles. "But what has it left you with?"

She opened her mouth to tell him how sorry she was, but he cut her off.

"Don't answer. Please, Rora." He swallowed several times, his Adam's apple bobbing against her forehead.

She tipped her head back and kissed his neck. "Will you make love to me, Garrett? I need you so very badly."

The carriage pulled to a stop in front of Garrett's townhouse, but the driver didn't dismount. Probably, the poor man didn't know what to do with the current situation.

After easing her to the bench, Garrett jumped down before lifting her to the ground. "Come. I already told you I have no willpower to tell you no."

The butler opened the door, and Garrett led her up the

steps without a word. Of course, servants would talk, but if her reputation was ruined, so be it. Worst case, she'd ruminate in Cheshire until the gossips found another target.

Her pulse pounded in her ears as she allowed him to lead her down a hall to his bedroom. The large bed was draped in green velvet, and a fire had been lit. Several books stacked on the table beside a chair near the hearth spoke of a man who used his mind and not just his hands or title to change his surroundings.

Curious to see what such a man read in the privacy of his bedchamber, Aurora broke away from his handhold and went to the books. Wordsworth, Shakespeare, and a book about farming. She smiled. "A poet and practical. You are a rare breed."

When he didn't respond, she turned and found him standing halfway between the closed door and her. His watchful eyes never wandering from her face. "I love poetry." He shrugged. "I'm no poet though."

"I like the Coleridge poem in this one, *The Rime of the Ancient Mariner*. I must have read it a hundred times." She caressed the spine of the book. "Of course, my copy is not so fine as this."

He shrugged and stepped closer. "A hobby of mine."

"Have you other hobbies?" She cringed, remembering asking Potsum a similar question and despairing at his lack of interests.

Step by slow step, he drew closer to her. "Besides reading and collecting interesting books, I love a good game of pall-mall, I like to swim in the lake at my country home. I enjoy horses and racing. I have a great many interests. Do you have any hobbies, Rora?"

How marvelous to have been asked. Men never asked

women about things they liked, as it was assumed that once they married, they would give up all for their husband's likes. "I don't know if I would call them hobbies, but I have several very fine tea sets and I really love finding and procuring them for my Tuesday tea with the Wallflowers. I play the pianoforte, though not in the way Mercy does. When she is not at West Lane, I play for my own pleasure. I too love to read, but maybe not about farming."

He took her hand from where it trailed along the back of his chair and pressed his warm lips to her knuckles. His smile pierced her soul, as if he were a conquering angel sent down from heaven to heal her. "I didn't know about the teapots. That is a charming hobby."

"I don't generally talk about myself. I don't suppose I ever have been much for chatting on about me. Women are taught to be interested in what men want. Having goals, like my school, is not ladylike. Of course, you already know that." She rounded the chair and stood with her hand in his, arms wrapped together like two snakes entwined, their bodies nearly touching with just their arms between them. Looking up into his eyes, she thought she could be happy if this moment never ended.

"We can sit up all night, and you can speak of nothing but you, Rora." Those beautiful eyes looked into hers as if he really meant what he said. "I would love to hear all about what you think and feel behind those staid expressions."

"Does that mean you don't want to make love?" Her gaze flicked to the bed.

With his free hand, he gripped her chin and turned her attention back to him. "I want you happy. I want you. I want you in every way including in my bed. But that is not all I want, Rora. If it will satisfy you to sit by the fire, drink wine, and talk all night, I will feel like the richest man in the world to have your company."

Her body vibrated with desire, need, and more, something she couldn't name. When she spoke, her voice was breathy and soft. "While that sounds like a wonderful way to spend an evening, Garrett, I burn for you so hot, I may turn to ash if you don't kiss me very soon."

In the span of a breath, his mouth was on hers. He didn't ask permission, but pressed inside consuming her. His tongue danced with hers like a frantic waltz while her heart pounded and her limbs went weak.

As he gentled the kiss, she nipped his bottom lip then sucked it into her mouth. "Garrett, why is it like this with us?" Her skin tingled with sensitivity, and she clutched him like a buoy in a raging sea.

Reaching around and up, he slid her hat pin from the coif of her hair and placed it atop the stack of books. He proceeded to remove every pin holding her hair and ran his fingers through the loose tresses that spilled down her back. "You don't want me to answer that question, Rora. Though, I long to tell you over and over again."

She curled her fingers into his soft hair at the back of his neck and breathed in the safe, spicy scent of him. "You really believe this is more than desire made real?"

He swept her into his arms.

Gasping, she held tight around his neck. "You believe feelings have something to do with the way I desire you? Men desire women they do not care about all the time. They bed them and they walk away without a care. What makes this different?"

At the bed, he placed her on the mattress and followed her down until his body trapped her with the most delightful pressure. "I didn't come to you a virgin, Rora. I know the difference between lust and love. While I'll admit they are not mutually exclusive, the addition of caring and deep affection with desire results in what we have between us, and I have not experienced it with another woman."

The pounding of her heart stopped. She wasn't even sure she breathed. His declaration stole her ability to do anything more than stare up at him in wonder.

"I've terrified you." He brushed her hair from her forehead and laughed. "I know you would prefer if I kept my feelings to myself."

"No." The word flew out like a plea before she could think to stop it.

"No?" He pressed a kiss to her cheek and then the other. "You wouldn't prefer my silence on the subject of love?"

"You said something tonight that I can't seem to let go of." She took a deep breath, as he rolled to his side and studied her. "You said I had done this to myself."

The accusation pummeled her mind. All she sacrificed in the process of punishing herself for things that were not her fault, Garrett had whittled down to that one sentence. What had she gained? Safety? If so, it was a false security at best.

She sighed and ran her hand along his arm.

CHAPTER TWENTY-FIVE

Garrett *had* said those words in the carriage, and he'd meant them, but the possibility that he'd hurt her with them shot an ache to his heart. "I only want you to let go of the past, Rora. I did not mean to upset you."

Lightly she traced a path from his temple down his cheek to his jaw. "I was already upset, and you were right. Radcliff was a monster, of that there is no doubt. But denying myself happiness was all my own doing."

"Was?" His heart might explode. He was half hope, half

agony hearing her use the past tense with regard to what she had kept at bay.

Looking up at him, she was a goddess in the fire and candlelight. Her eyes shone a deeper blue, and her skin was flushed and warm. He could lay there staring at her for a lifetime.

Aurora tugged on his cravat, and when it came loose, she tossed it aside and skimmed her fingertips along the vee in his linen blouse. "I never before told anyone about my heartbreak. The Wallflowers know that Bertram broke my body and my spirit, but only you know about what my heart suffered. I thought if I spoke it aloud, it would give his actions more validity."

He wanted, no needed to hear the rest. Refusing to let her stop before it was all out, he prompted, "And?"

Wonder lit her face. She lifted her chin and met his gaze. "Saying it was freeing. I'm not sure I had ever let myself know how devastated I was by his betrayal. My father was no treat, but he protected my mother from harm. I thought there was something wrong with me that made Bertram want to hurt and even kill me."

Unable to keep his hands to himself, he let one fall to her hip and pulled her close. "You are perfect, Rora."

"I'm not, but I'm not what Bertram made me into either. I deserve happiness!" She paused and shifted her gaze to the space between them, suddenly shy. "And maybe even love."

The hand of God may have taken hold of his heart, because Garrett couldn't breathe from the weight expanding and tightening around his chest. The world narrowed to a pinpoint before expanding to the bed and Rora. "What are you saying?"

Her breath shuddered as she drew it in, but she kept her

gaze locked with his. "I think I began my foolish decision to find a disinterested husband like Potsum or Lord West to avoid the possibility that I could love you. If I loved you, then you would have the power to destroy me. With those other men, there was no risk of heartbreak."

If she kept talking, he didn't hear much after her confirmation of loving him. He shook his head to clear it, and indeed, she was still rattling on.

"You see, if I married someone benign, I could be safe and perhaps have a child. I—'

"Stop." He pressed a finger to her lips. The contact was almost too much to take, but he couldn't listen to more until he knew if he'd heard her correctly. "Did you infer that there is a possibility you could love me?"

A fresh warm blush pinkened her cheeks. "Of course, I love you, Garrett. How could I not love you? You are the best man I know. No one treats me as equally as you. No one looks at me as you do. No one makes me feel as safe and important as you do."

He swallowed and closed his eyes, lest he embarrass himself on a sob of pure joy. It took several more gulps of air before he looked at her and found the ability to speak. "You are not now going to tell me you love me like a brother, are you?"

A devilish smile pulled at her exquisite lips. Slipping her hand inside his shirt, she grazed his nipple.

He drew a sharp breath as the sensation shot straight to his shaft, which was now fully alert.

"I love you in every way there is to love another person. I thought loving someone would make me weak, but there is power in love, is there not?" She edged closer until her hips pressed to his.

Garrett lifted her at the knee and wrapped her leg around his thigh, bringing them even tighter and making sure she knew the power she held over him. "There is, and so much more that we have yet to discover, sweet, sweet Rora."

Pushing away, she turned her back to him. "Will you help me out of my gown and stays?"

It was all too much. He'd nearly resigned himself to some loveless life where he fathered sons and kept his own council about all other things. If he were lucky, he would find a wife who was a friend, and they would do well together. The life he imagined and this dream in front of him were so dissimilar, he shook with the rocking of the sudden change.

Holding in the wave of emotions that assailed him, Garrett closed his eyes. Sitting on the edge of the bed, he took several long breaths before he reached for the ties at the back of her gown. "You're not going to vanish like all my other dreams, are you?"

With a voice as out of breath as his own, she whispered, "You shall have a hard time getting rid of me."

Hands at her waist, he drew her back until his forehead leaned against her curved back. "I shall never wish to be parted from you, Rora, my love."

Relaxing a fraction, she leaned into him.

It might have been a second or an hour they remained locked in that moment of perfect declaration. Standing, he brought her with him. He slid his hand to the ties again and unlaced them. The regal fabric fell to the floor, leaving her in her corset and shift. The boned contraption had left deep red marks at her shoulder blades, and as he let it fall, he kissed the marks then trailed more kisses to her nape, the curve of her neck and shoulder, then back up to her ear.

He was more drunk on Aurora than any wine or spirits

had ever made him. Lightheaded with the thrill of her, he pulled the ties of her shift and let the thin fabric fall to the floor before lifting her from the mountain of fabric and lowering her to the bed.

With quick efficiency, he tore out of his clothes and leaped onto the mattress beside her.

Aurora laughed, full and round, like she had when they were children. "I'm glad you're enthusiastic. I thought I would have to encourage you."

Nothing would ever match the joy rocketing through him. "Tell me again that you love me."

She cupped his cheek with her hand. "I love you, Garrett. I think in my most secret place, I have always loved you."

Possessing her lips, he branded the feel of them into his soul and plunged his tongue into her sweet mouth. She was sweetness and fire, and he would never have enough of this magnificent woman.

She moaned against his mouth and arched into him, entrusting her exquisite body to his care.

Garrett wanted to worship her for hours, but his body rang with need so encompassing that waiting was impossible. "You shall have to forgive me, but I cannot wait."

A slow smile spread, filling her eyes with both wickedness and delight. "I don't know when I've heard anything so romantic."

Lord, but she was amazing. Pulling her against him, he rolled until she straddled his hips. With his shaft trapped and pressed at the apex of her, he was at once in heaven and hell. Perhaps it was purgatory, but he couldn't bear the pleasure much longer.

She rocked forward, her wet folds sliding along his rod. Her breath caught, and she repeated the motion again and again with her head thrown back and soft cries falling from her lips.

No amount of experience could prepare a man for such perfect eroticism. Reaching up, he cupped one perfect breast and rolled the tight nipple between his fingers.

She quickened her pace.

Garrett lifted her hips enough to maneuver his shaft to her center. "Look at me, Rora."

Her passion and the flickering light turned her eyes to the same dark blue of the gown lying on the floor. She met his stare as she pressed onto him, crying his name until she was fully impaled, and he was near to bursting.

Holding perfectly still, he wanted to give her time to adjust, but then she moved. Riding his shaft in beautiful fluidity.

Garrett sat up and suckled one nipple and then the other. Her slow canter and impassioned gasps were too much. He rolled her to her back and pressed harder and faster, meeting each of her cries with one of his own. His body tight with pleasure, he slid his hand between them and found her bud slick and hot.

At his touch, she exploded with pleasure. Her sheath pulsed around him, taking him over the edge.

Rolling them to their sides, he held her through the shudders and pulsations. Still linked intimately together, each vibration rocked him with ecstasy. "Are you alright?"

"Mmm." She nuzzled her head against his chest and under his chin like a cat settling in. "I'm better than that." As if to prove it, she eased her hips forward taking his exhausted shaft deeper.

"You may have to wait a few minutes for whatever you're

thinking, my love." Though the minute the notion was broached, he grew hard inside her.

Again, she slid over him, and even at half arousal, it was exquisite to possess her and be possessed by her. Like an insatiable teen, he was hard and wanting in moments. "You're not sore, Rora?"

"I can't get enough of you, and I don't want you to leave or tell me I must go home." Panic laced her words, even as delight spread from her body to his.

Shushing her gently, he reached down and lifted her leg over both of his so he could fill her completely. Slower this time, he kissed her, and their tongues slid together, teeth gnashed and they breathed as one until they shattered in each other's arms and lay replete and satisfied.

They must have dozed, as when Garrett next opened his eyes, the sun was coloring the sky in pinks and oranges, and Aurora was nestled against his chest. He kissed her forehead, her cheek, and her nose.

She arched her back but didn't pull away. "Did we fall asleep?"

"I'm afraid so." He kissed her chin and down her throat before going lower and letting his hand cup her breast as he licked circles around her rosy peak. "I will take you home."

Tracing delicate lines down his chest until she held his shaft and made love to it with her hands, she said, "When?"

"Soon." As he made the halfhearted promise, his heart was near bursting, and his body shook with need. Kissing his way lower, he longed to taste her. The night before he'd been too desperate, but now he needed to put his mouth on her and give her pleasure.

She groaned a complaint when he moved too far for her to touch his shaft, but pleasure cried out of those same lips as he lapped at her folds, dipped his tongue inside her and teased her sensitive bud. Cupping her bottom, he slid his thumb inside her while lapping up the sweetest honey.

The most beautiful sight was Aurora coming apart with her hips bouncing off the bed and her pleasure spilling out in waves and cries. Garrett rose and pulled her to him, muffling her cries with his kisses. The servants would be rising, and the morning was going to be awkward enough. Still, he couldn't rush them out of the house. Not when he still yearned for more and she was so full of emotion and need. "I like seeing you like this."

She straddled his lap. "Wanton?"

"Alive and lively."

Impaling herself on him, she threw her head back and rode him like the goddess she was.

It was after nine when they finally rose from the bed, washed, and dressed. Garrett laced up her gown, as there was no proper lady's maid for such a morning. "I'm sure I've made a mess of this." He looked down at the laces.

"Don't trouble yourself," she said in a stoic voice.

Fear shot through Garrett, and his pulse raced. He spun her around to face him. "What is it? What's wrong?"

At first her mask of indifference was firmly in place, but then it cracked, and she relaxed her shoulders. "I think I should still go to Cheshire. There will be gossip, and if I'm not here, it will be less."

"You know I want to marry you. You can't possibly think I only wanted this." He pointed to the rumpled bed.

Blinking her glassy eyes, she shrugged. "I know you love me, and that was enough for this." She too gestured to the evidence of their lovemaking.

Garrett dropped to his knees in front of her and took her hands. "Aurora, my only love, make me the happiest man in the world and marry me. Do not marry me because we made love or because you think you must. Not even because you want a child. Marry me because you love me, and I love you, and we can be happy together."

A tear rolled down her pale cheek, and she bit her bottom lip. "I still worry my past will ruin any future we could have."

He had to force his gaze away from that lip and all the wonderful things he wanted to do with her in the rumpled bed, and other rooms of the house. and other houses. "Nothing can harm a future where you are mine and I am yours, Rora."

A second teardrop glided to her chin where Garrett captured it on his thumb and kissed the salty morsel away.

"You will tell me if I am not a good wife?"

Shaking his head, he said, "Impossible. But if you will tell me when I am not a good husband, I shall agree."

She gave him a solemn nod.

"What is your answer, Rora." His heart had firmly lodged in his throat, and there was no sign he would ever draw breath again.

"I once said I would never marry again, not even for a duke. It seems I was wrong. I will marry you, Garrett."

Rising, he lifted her in the air and spun her around the

room until they were both dizzy and collapsed on the chair by the fire.

A knock at the door forced them both to stand and brush out their clothes. "Come in."

His valet, Bronson, stepped inside and closed the door. He bowed his dark head. "I have called for the carriage. I assumed her ladyship would wish to leave before the streets become busy this morning."

Garrett liked Bronson. The man showed no signs of judgment or distaste. He stated facts and did so kindly and politely.

"I do need to be getting home. Thank you." As if she were exiting a parlor at an appropriate hour rather than a man's townhouse after a night of passion, Aurora lifted her chin and descended the stairs to the front door.

Garrett followed her, and Bronson trailed behind. "Bronson, Lady Radcliff and I will be going to her home, but I will return later to arrange a few things. I shall need to dress for a visit to the Archbishop of Canterbury this afternoon."

"I will see to it, Your Grace." Bronson paused. "May I be so bold as to congratulate you both and wish you joy."

"Thank you, Bronson."

The closer the carriage got to West Lane, the more Aurora twisted her gloves in her hand and chewed that delicious bottom lip.

"Are you expecting someone to be at your house?" It was difficult to be overjoyed and see her so worried.

"We left the ball without a word. Faith, Poppy, and Mercy will call this morning." Aurora frowned.

Garrett wrapped an arm around her. "They will be happy for us, or do you know something I don't?"

"No. I just feel foolish having sworn to never marry. Now I must tell them I will marry after all the trouble I put them through."

Unable to control his grin, he didn't bother to try, but kissed her head and held her for the rest of the short ride to West Lane.

It was early for callers, but not only were the carriages of her friends indeed present, but others were as well. Most notably, the Dowager Countess of Marsden. Even Garrett's joy dimmed at the idea of facing her mother. "This should be interesting."

Tipton opened the door as soon as the carriage pulled to a stop. He stood perfectly stoic and silent until they reached the top step. "The ladies, her ladyship, and the Marquess of Potsum are waiting for you in the great parlor, my lady. I tried to get them to come back later, but they insisted on waiting."

"Thank you, Tipton." Aurora drew a deep breath and lifted her chin like a soldier going to battle. "Garrett, you may leave if you wish. You are not required to face the firing squad."

"Where you go, I go, my love." He offered his arm.

Tipton's lips actually twitched in what might have been a smile before he returned to his standard repose.

They went to the double doors leading to the large parlor. Garrett opened the doors and they walked in together.

Poppy jumped up and clasped her hands together, her smile bright, though she managed to say nothing.

Faith and Mercy remained seated, but both smiled, and Mercy raised a brow.

"What is the meaning of this?" Aurora's mother narrowed

her eyes and slapped a folded fan against the arm of the overstuffed chair facing the large fireplace.

"Good morning, Mother, your lordship." She smiled at her friends. "This is an unexpected pleasure at such an early hour. What brings you to West Lane?"

Potsum sputtered, stood, and pointed his shaking finger at Aurora. "I gathered your mother at first light and told her of your rude dismissal of my marriage offer. We have come to show you the error of your ways. What on earth is he doing here? And why are you still in your gown from last evening?"

Both of Aurora's brows rose, and she cocked her head at her mother. The answer to his questions seemed obvious to everyone in the room but Potsum. "I shall spell it out for you if you wish, my lord."

Jemima stood and held up a hand. "That will be neither necessary nor appropriate, Aurora. I hardly know what to say, but I do wish to know if you plan to marry."

"Yes, Mother. I shall marry." Aurora sauntered over to the table and took a biscuit from the tray. The staff probably didn't know what to do with callers that early, so they served tea. Aurora ate it down in two bites and closed her eyes with delight. "I had no idea how hungry I was. Tipton, do you think Cook might put a small breakfast together?"

"For how many, my lady?"

Mercy covered a giggle, but Poppy and Faith made no attempt to hide their mirth.

Garrett struggled to keep his own laugh from escaping. He could see why Aurora was so attached to the butler.

Gazing around the room, Aurora made a show of counting. "Mother, Lord Potsum, will you be staying?"

Something that might have been a smile pulled

disturbingly at Potsum's mouth. "Since you have decided to use good sense and marry me, I shall be delighted to breakfast with you."

Even Jemima had to hide her amusement at the density of Potsum. She walked to the window and pretended disinterest.

"I'm afraid you've misunderstood, my lord. You see, I would not marry you if my life depended on it." She looked at the ceiling as if in thought. "Perhaps if one of my friends' lives were at stake." She shook herself out of the notion. "But that seems an unlikely scenario at this point, since I happily agreed to marry the Duke of Corwin less than an hour ago. He goes this afternoon to the Archbishop of Canterbury for a special license."

Potsum's mouth opened and closed like a fish out of water. Wide-eyed, he stomped his foot. "I asked first. This is very disturbing." He stormed to the door, took his hat from the table, and left, muttering about unfair and unheard of.

As soon as the front door closed, the Wallflowers rushed over and surrounded Aurora.

Garrett didn't know if he'd ever been prouder of anyone in his life. Even nervous and afraid, she'd pulled her shoulders back, lifted her chin and told the room what she wanted. Lord help him, but it was him.

The ladies were standing and chatting, but Garrett was awash with so much emotion he sank into a chair near the door and held his head while leaning his arm on a gilded table against the wall.

Maybe he hadn't truly believed she would marry him until the moment she'd made it public. Part of him expected her to falter or deny her feelings. Yet, here she was bubbling with excitement over marrying him.

Silence followed the chirping of happy women.

Aurora knelt in front of him. "Are you well, Garrett?" She cupped his cheek, and her soft cool hand was a balm for all his worry and doubt. Her eyes filled with trepidation, and a small crease formed between her brows.

"Forgive me, my love, but when all of one's dreams finally come true, it's a bit overwhelming."

Skirts rustled behind Aurora. Garrett glanced up and found the other ladies exiting toward the breakfast room.

Aurora rested her head on his lap. "I thought for a moment you were regretting proposing."

Rising with her in his embrace, Garrett kissed one cheek then the other before taking her lips and devouring her. Suddenly unsure if he deserved her, he knew he would spend a lifetime being the man who made her happy. Breathless, he broke the kiss. "Never. I have loved you for as long as I can remember, Rora. I shall go on loving you until they put me in my grave."

Her stomach made a perfectly timed grumble. She turned bright red and covered a laugh. "I think we have some years before that, at least if I don't starve to death this very morning."

Kissing her hair, he breathed in the scent of spring flowers and Aurora. She was everything. "We can't have that. I have plans for the rest of the day with my fiancée."

If the sun had not been shining already, it would have come out just to rival her bright smile. "Just today?"

He offered his arm to take her in for breakfast. She never looked away as she joined with him. A safety and permanence surrounded them, and his constant need to wander the world seemed distant and reckless. This woman was his world and all he would ever need. "And every day thereafter for as long as we both shall live."

EPILOGUE

One Year Later
The Castlewick School

urora surveyed the rolling hills where eight girls played, running between and around the ancient standing stones. Their laughter rippled on the breeze as they played a game of tag. Running a hand down her rounded belly, she closed her eyes and let the early autumn sun warm her face.

"They look happy." Poppy bounced her son on her lap while the little man gripped his mother's finger.

Faith, very close to going into her confinement, took Nick's offered hand and accepted his help to rise. "You've created something quite fine here, Aurora. You should be very proud."

Shifting closer, Garrett wrapped a hand around her and eased her back against him. "We spend more time here than we'd ever imagined. There's something about this school and the young ladies that is full of joy."

"I was surprised to find my cousin in residence yet again." Wesley pointed to the road where Malcolm walked with Miss Stein and seemed to be engaged in a heated debate. "I think he enjoys the challenge of a brilliant woman who won't back down if she thinks she's right."

"Who can blame him?" Garrett whispered in Aurora's ear.

There was no word yet invented to describe the power of her joy.

Mercy stood and stretched her lithe form. "I'm going for a walk. Faith, would you care to join me?"

"For a walk?" Faith pulled a face. "No. Wesley will walk with you, and I will go back to the house for a long nap."

Nick took Faith's hand and kissed it. "Then I shall return with you."

His sultry tone had Faith blushing even in her delicate condition.

Some of Aurora's favorite times were those spent with these people. All married now, but still and always the Wallflowers of West Lane. The thought made her cringe. There was no sense putting off the inevitable. "Before you go, I have news I must share, though I worry you will not like what I have to say."

Mercy faced her. "That doesn't seem likely. What is it, Aurora?"

She took a deep breath. "I am selling the West Lane house."

Even the laughter of the girls playing nearby silenced as all eyes stared at her. "It makes no sense to keep it, as we no longer use it," she rushed to add.

Poppy leaned forward and took Aurora's hand. "I think it's past time to let it go."

Heart pounding, Aurora must have misheard. "You do?"

Mercy sank back to the picnic blanket, her long legs folded underneath her. "Of course, we do. We didn't expect you to hold on to a house that you no longer need and still holds difficult memories."

"Some very good ones as well." Aurora thought of all the Tuesday teas the Wallflowers had shared in that house, and a knot tightened in her belly. Perhaps it was the baby giving her a shove.

"We will have tea in one of four very fine houses, Aurora." Faith rested her hands across her protruding stomach. "It was never the house. It was always the four of us being together, and that will never change."

"What of Tipton and the other servants?" Worry laced Poppy's voice.

Garrett said, "My London butler, Casper, has long wished to retire and has only remained at his post this long because of loyalty to my family. I have pensioned him, and Tipton has graciously agreed to take the post. As that house was not heavily staffed, we have placed those who wished it in our other homes."

"We could have helped with that," Faith scolded. "You needn't have taken on the full burden."

"I was quite timid about telling you." It was not an admission she was proud of, and heat crept up her neck and cheeks.

Rhys shook his head. "Brave enough to face some of the worst tyrants in London, but afraid of her closest friends. That's my sister. It's good to know you can still be silly, Rora."

"It's not silly." She pulled her shoulders back and glared at her brother.

"It is a bit." Mercy's gentle correction came with a warm smile. "We love you, Aurora. No decision you make would ever or could ever change that."

Nothing had changed, yet everything had. Somehow all her fears that their friendship depended on the house at West Lane seemed foolish and ill-conceived. "I'm relieved you're not upset with my decision, and now I too need a nap."

Garrett helped her to her feet, and they returned to the house. In the large bed draped with heavy brocade, Garrett curled in behind her. His warm body fitted hers to perfection. "Do you feel better?"

"Infinitely. I really thought they'd be sad to see the house we spent so much time in sold to someone else."

"Your friends are more concerned with your happiness than any piece of property."

He was right, and she closed her eyes and snuggled back until she felt the evidence of his arousal against her bottom.

Cupping one of her breasts, he kissed the back of her neck. "You are very naughty for a woman in your condition."

"And I plan to continue being so for many years to come." She loved the way their hushed voices hummed in the large room. They talked for hours in the dim light of evening. Garrett often told her about the places he'd visited and how he longed to show her some of them. Never had she dreamed she could find such passion and contentment with a man after Radcliff.

His caress stilled. "What are you thinking about?"

"I was wondering if we could have been this happy had not my past been so unhappy."

"A question that shall never be answered and makes no difference, my love. The past was what it was, and we are happy in the present. Is that not enough?" His lips grazed the shell of her ear.

Desire shot through her with such speed she moaned with both passion and a happiness never before imagined. "It is more than enough, my duke, my love, my dearest friend."

And it was.

I hope you enjoyed *Not Even For A Duke*. I admit to longing to
give Aurora her much deserved Happily Ever After.
She suffered so much and is such a good and worthy woman.

If you started with this book, you may want to go back to
read the stories of Poppy, Mercy and Faith in the other
Wallflowers of West Lane books.

WALLFLOWERS OF WEST LANE SERIES

The Earl Not Taken

Misleading A Duke

Capturing the Earl

Not Even For A Duke

ALSO BY A.S. FENICHEL

FANTASY ROMANCE

Reign of the Witch Queen Series

Light and Shadow

Wind and Water

Fire and Ice

Stars and Sea (Prequel Novella)

Blood and Duty (Novella)

* * *

HISTORICAL PARANORMAL ROMANCE

Witches of Windsor Series

Magic Touch

Magic Word

Pure Magic

The Demon Hunters Series

Ascension

Deception

Betrayal

Defiance

Vengeance

* * *

HISTORICAL ROMANCE

The Wallflowers of West Lane Series

The Earl Not Taken

Misleading A Duke

Capturing the Earl

Not Even For A Duke

The Everton Domestic Society Series

A Lady's Honor

A Lady's Escape

A Lady's Virtue

A Lady's Doubt

A Lady's Past

A Lady's Christmas

A Lady's Curves

The Forever Brides Series

Tainted Bride

Foolish Bride

Desperate Bride

Single Title Books

Wishing Game

Christmas Bliss

An Honorable Arrangement

* * *

CONTEMPORARY PARANORMAL EROTIC ROMANCE

The Psychic Mates Series

Kane's Bounty

Joshua's Mistake

Training Rain

The End of Days Series

Mayan Afterglow

Mayan Craving

Mayan Inferno

End of Days Trilogy

* * *

CONTEMPORARY EROTIC ROMANCE

Single Title Books

Alaskan Exposure

Revving Up the Holidays

* * *

WRITING AS ANDIE FENICHEL

Dad Bod Handyman (Lane Family)

Carnival Lane (Lane Family)

Lane to Fame (Lane Family)

Changing Lanes (Lane Family)

Heavy Petting (Lane Family)

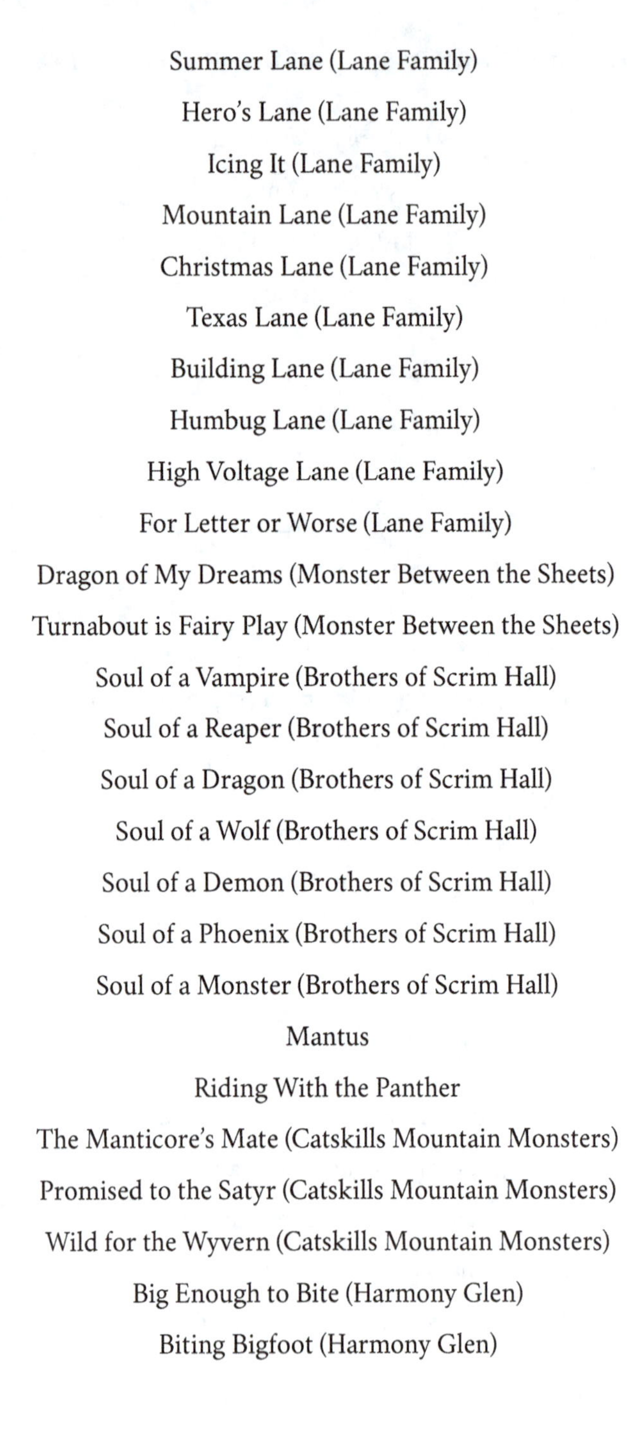

Summer Lane (Lane Family)

Hero's Lane (Lane Family)

Icing It (Lane Family)

Mountain Lane (Lane Family)

Christmas Lane (Lane Family)

Texas Lane (Lane Family)

Building Lane (Lane Family)

Humbug Lane (Lane Family)

High Voltage Lane (Lane Family)

For Letter or Worse (Lane Family)

Dragon of My Dreams (Monster Between the Sheets)

Turnabout is Fairy Play (Monster Between the Sheets)

Soul of a Vampire (Brothers of Scrim Hall)

Soul of a Reaper (Brothers of Scrim Hall)

Soul of a Dragon (Brothers of Scrim Hall)

Soul of a Wolf (Brothers of Scrim Hall)

Soul of a Demon (Brothers of Scrim Hall)

Soul of a Phoenix (Brothers of Scrim Hall)

Soul of a Monster (Brothers of Scrim Hall)

Mantus

Riding With the Panther

The Manticore's Mate (Catskills Mountain Monsters)

Promised to the Satyr (Catskills Mountain Monsters)

Wild for the Wyvern (Catskills Mountain Monsters)

Big Enough to Bite (Harmony Glen)

Biting Bigfoot (Harmony Glen)

Visit A.S. Fenichel's website

for a complete and up-to-date list of all her books.

www.asfenichel.com

ABOUT THE AUTHOR

 A.S. (Andie) Fenichel gave up a successful career in New York City to follow her husband to Texas and pursue her lifelong dream of being a professional writer. She's never looked back.

Andie adores writing stories filled with love, passion, desire, magic and maybe a little mayhem tossed in for good measure. Books have always been her perfect escape and she still relishes diving into one and staying up all night to finish a good story.

With over 55 published books, Andie Fenichel/A.S. Fenichel is multi-published in historical romance, paranormal romance, contemporary romance, and some interesting mixed genre romances too. Andie is the author of the several series, including Forever Brides, Everton Domestic Society, Witches of Windsor and more. Strong, empowered heroines from Regency London to modern-day New York are what you'll find in all her books.

A Jersey Girl at heart, she now makes her home in Southern Missouri with her real-life hero, her wonderful husband.

When not reading or writing, she enjoys cooking, travel, history, puttering in her garden and spoiling her fussy cat.

Connect with Andie Fenichel
www.andiefenichel.com

Email: asfenichel@hotmail.com

facebook.com/a.s.fenichel

x.com/asfenichel

instagram.com/asfenichel

bookbub.com/authors/andie-fenichel

pinterest.com/asfenichel

tiktok.com/@asfenichel

NOT EVEN FOR A DUKE by A.S. Fenichel

All rights reserved.

Copyright © 2021 by A.S. Fenichel

No part of this book may be reproduced in any form or by any electronic or mechanical means, including information storage and retrieval systems, without written permission from the author, except for the use of brief quotations in a book review.

This book is a work of fiction and any resemblance to persons, living or dead, is purely coincidental. The characters are productions of the author's imagination. Locales are fictitious, and/or, are used fictitiously.

AI RESTRICTION: The author expressly prohibits any entity from using any part of this publication, including text and graphics, for purposes of training artificial intelligence (AI) technologies to generate text or graphics, including without limitation, technologies that are capable of generating works in the same style or genre as this publication.

The author reserves all rights to license uses of this work for generative AI training and development of machine learning language models.

Edited by Penny Barber

Cover design by LoveTheCover.com